That Missed Call

That Missed Call

Kris Francoeur

**Other Books by Kris Francoeur available from
Willow River Press**

Tomorrow & Yesterday
Letting Go for Love

Coming Summer and Fall 2022

More Than I Can Say
That One Small Omission
Stained-Glass Window

For Sam, who listened to Yanni while I wrote – thanks
for always believing in me.
For Paul, thanks for being my true love.

Prologue

Luke opened the door. "Alex! Come on in."

Alex grinned as he handed his friend a bottle of wine. "Hey, Luke. Peter has you serving as doorman, huh?"

"I wasn't supposed to be, but-" He gestured down the hallway. "Hear the music? They're dancing in the living room."

"Who?"

"Peter and his sister."

Alex's expression was blank, so Luke continued. "His little sister Kat. You've met her, right?"

Alex shook his head. "No, I don't think so."

"Pete invited her to fill out the dinner table after you said Diana couldn't make it."

Alex tried to hide his confusion. Why on earth would Peter invite a *kid* to a dinner party?

Luke was clearly amused. "Anyway, when I left them, they were dancing a polka in there. You gotta check this out."

Alex followed Luke down the hall, still bemused. All he could see when he walked into the living room was

Peter's back. Then, Alex swallowed hard as a woman came into view. This was no *baby* sister. This was a gorgeous young woman wearing a simple dark green sweater with a cowl neckline and a flowing black skirt that swirled around her ankles as she moved. Momentarily at a loss for words, Alex just stared.

Noticing the stranger, the woman abruptly stopped dancing, her face darkening with a heated blush. She quickly silenced the music by pushing the power button off.

Looking around in surprise, Peter laughed and casually draped an arm over her shoulders. "Alex," he exclaimed, "glad you made it." Kissing the top of his sister's head, Peter continued, "Alex, this is my baby sister Kat. Kat, this is Alex. I can't believe the two of you haven't crossed paths yet."

Kat put out her hand, trying not to gawk at the stunningly attractive man standing in front of her. "Nice to meet you. Sorry for the polka…"

Alex extended his hand and felt the warmth of her small one sliding into his. "I'm Alex."

She grinned. "I gathered that."

"Huh?" What was she talking about?

Her tone was teasing. "Peter just said so. He just introduced us, remember?"

Alex pulled himself together and grinned back at her. "Nice to meet you too, Kat. Love the polka."

Just then, the doorbell rang again. Luke turned some soft piano music on while the rest of the group moved toward the brightly lit kitchen and dining area. Moving ahead of Alex, Kat tried to forget how much she liked feeling her hand in his.

Seated at the table, Alex was pleased to find himself across from Kat. As the boisterous group settled in, he realized Kat knew the other two members of the band well, and even knew one of their dates. He passed a plate of antipasto to her. "How is it that you know Will and Dana, and even Maggie, but not me?"

She smiled, trying to fight the surge of warmth she felt in response to his gaze. He was *so* gorgeous. Had she ever seen a man this attractive in real life? His dark brown eyes met hers directly, and his chestnut waves of hair nearly reached his shoulders. His skin was tanned, unusual in New York in the winter. Had he been traveling, or did he live elsewhere? She abruptly realized she had not responded. "Will and Pete have been friends for years. I met Dana last year when I was home for Christmas. And Maggie's mom is friends with ours."

"So, why haven't we met?"

"With college and traveling, I haven't been around much. We must have just missed each other."

Peter gave a piercing whistle from the other end of the table. "Kat, Alex! Hello, join the rest of us."

The two laughed and the conversation shifted back to the whole group chatting together.

Over the next few hours, the eight of them ate, laughed, and all but Kat drank numerous glasses of wine. As the evening continued, Alex felt a growing frustration that the group dynamic was thwarting his efforts to have a one-on-one conversation with Kat.

At the end of the evening, Alex extended his hand to shake Kat's one more time. "It was great to meet you."

He noticed her cheeks turn pink. Had she enjoyed meeting as much as he did? "Likewise," she said. Her voice was husky.

"Maybe we'll see each other again," Alex offered.

"I'd like that."

After the guests left, Kat said goodnight and slipped into the guest room. Normally, when she was home on college break, she stayed with her parents, but her dad needed to go out of town on business and her mom had gone along. Kat would have been fine at home alone but staying at Peter's felt like a true vacation.

Sliding under the covers, she lay in the darkened room, the only light coming from the city lights beyond her window. Who *was* Alex? And who was his girlfriend? Was it serious? After all, she had not accompanied him tonight.

Kat replayed every second of the evening. Alex had seemed interested and had spent more time talking with her than anyone else, but maybe that was just her impression.

Was he interested or just being polite? Their age gap was obvious but was six years really a problem? She wondered what dating an older man was like.

But this was silly, Alex had a girlfriend. Nothing else mattered. She certainly found him fascinating and attractive beyond words, but he was taken. She needed to keep that in mind and not act like such an idiot.

Yeah, right… No matter how much she wanted to pretend otherwise, she was going to fall asleep remembering every word he had spoken and every smile that had lit up his face. His gorgeous face. This was going to be a long, sleepless night.

The next morning, Peter handed his sister a cup of coffee. "You enjoyed last night?"

"Yeah, it was fun." Kat gazed into her mug, feeling foolish as she thought about the hours she had spent fantasizing.

"Want to do it again?"

His question confused her. "You're having another dinner party?"

"Remember how I said I'm going to *Don Giovanni* tonight? Alex's girlfriend bailed on him again, so we have an extra ticket. Want to go?"

The word *girlfriend* sucked some of the excitement out of her daydream, but even if she was remotely in the picture, she sure did not seem to be around much. Kat's eyes sparkled when she thought of the potential the evening held. "I would love to," she said.

Alex felt jittery when he pushed the doorbell that evening. Luke answered once again, and the two of them walked into the kitchen, laughing about déjà vu.

Just a few minutes later, Kat entered the room as Alex turned around.

He swallowed hard. As he had been talking to Peter and Luke, he told himself last night's reaction to her probably came out of a *lot* of good red wine. She was

Peter's baby sister, but no matter how hard he tried to convince himself otherwise, what he saw now was a gorgeous, interesting woman wearing a simple but sexy black dress, her strawberry blonde hair pulled up into a modest twist.

He tried not to stare, but his eyes followed her elegantly plunging neckline as it dove just deep enough to show an observant man that she was braless. The shimmering fabric skimmed curves that would keep most men awake at night. Black stilettos showcased her legs. At a loss for words, Alex tried to think of something intelligent to say.

Kat felt unexpectedly shy. "Hi, Alex."

"Hi, Kat."

Peter looked up from the sink where he was washing his hands. "Hey, isn't that the dress Jess gave you for Christmas?"

She nodded, uncomfortably aware that she had become the center of attention. "Yeah."

Luke grinned. "Well, you look fabulous in it. Jess has good taste."

Kat walked around the center island to hug him. "I'm so glad to see you tonight, Luke. I didn't think I would see you again before I left. And thanks for the compliment," she said with a wink.

"It wasn't a compliment; I was just stating the obvious. Besides, I had to come over—you know how much I love the opera."

Kat wrinkled her nose. "And Peter."

He kissed her cheek. "And *you.*" He grinned at Peter. "He's pretty okay too, I guess."

Alex smiled as he realized he was assigned the seat next to Kat at Lincoln Center. He watched in fascination as she gave the performance her entire concentration. She turned toward him at intermission. "I had forgotten how much I love the opera," she said.

"It shows." Alex looked at the glow on her cheeks. "How long since you've been?"

Her eyes narrowed as she thought back. "Probably four years. My dad and I used to go pretty regularly, but it's hard now with my schedule." She sighed happily. "But the last time we came, it was *La Boheme,* which is my all-time favorite."

As they chatted, Alex was intrigued by the depth of her knowledge of opera, something many people knew little about.

After the last bow, Alex held Kat's coat for her and tried to hide his pleasure as he realized she was blushing just a bit when she thanked him.

Peter took her arm. "Okay, brat, how about some dinner now?"

As the group approached their table at the restaurant, Kat hesitated. Where should she sit? Rationally, she knew Alex was too old for her. Never mind that he was supposed to be with a date. But on the other hand …

Before she could make up her mind, Peter and Luke sat together on one side of the table, leaving an empty chair next to Alex. After a nervous hesitation, Kat sat down.

The waiter quickly appeared, ready to take drink orders. The men ordered beers, while Kat asked for a seltzer. Alex looked at her quizzically. "You don't want anything stronger?"

"Want has nothing to do with it," she said. "I can't."

Alex did not understand. "What do you mean?"

She was clearly embarrassed by the question. "I won't be twenty-one until next fall."

Alex tried to hide his surprise. Holy shit! He had been thinking how much he would like to spend more time with her, and now he realized she truly was just a kid.

The waiter reappeared with their drinks, and they all ordered dinner. Over the meal, the four of them laughed and joked, and Alex began to forget about the six-year age difference as he enjoyed himself more than he had in months.

Coffee had just been delivered to the table when two well-dressed men walked by the table holding hands. One of them did a double-take. "Peter! Luke!"

Within moments, introductions were made and the two men pulled up a set of chairs. After finishing their coffees, the newcomers broached the idea of going dancing. Peter and Luke were both obviously tempted but hesitated as they looked at Kat.

She rolled her eyes. "Guys, just go. I'm tired anyway, so I'm happy to head back to the apartment and get a few hours of sleep."

Peter patted her hand. "No, we'll go home too."

She shook her head. "No, you won't. Go have fun, I'll be fine."

As the two started to argue, Alex held up his hand in a gesture of peace. "I'll walk Kat home. You guys go out. We'll be fine."

Kat bristled. "I don't need anyone to walk me home. You can go too," she said.

He tried to hide the excitement he felt at the idea of spending some time alone with her. Age difference be damned, he wanted to get to know her better. "Kat, I'll walk you home and then head home myself."

When they left the restaurant some time later, Kat had not decided whether she felt annoyed or pleased.

She did not say anything for almost a block, so finally Alex spoke. "Did I do something wrong?"

"No," she said, sharper than she intended.

He grinned. "Then why are you giving me the silent treatment?"

Kat drew a breath and said, "I don't need an escort, you know."

He put his hand on her arm. "I never said you did."

She shook off his hand, reminding herself of the word *girlfriend*. Trying to push desire away, she decided to focus on her earlier anger. "Yes, you did. You made it sound like I needed a babysitter."

"No, I didn't. You just *heard* it that way. I offered to walk you home so Peter and Luke could go out without worrying about you." He grinned, trying to break the tension. "Besides, it was the perfect excuse for me too."

"Meaning?"

"I was included in the dancing invitation, remember? No offense to anyone, but dancing at a gay bar wasn't really what I was in the mood for this evening."

Kat looked at him and laughed. "You're right. The way you look *and* going solo? You'd be mobbed in minutes."

Alex smiled at the unexpected compliment. "So, can you forgive me and let me walk you home?"

Cheerful again, Kat slipped her hand through the crook of his elbow. "Deal. It would probably sound stupid for me to say that I really *wanted* to walk through the city alone at this hour anyway."

"Especially looking the way *you* do," he quipped.

The two of them chatted easily as they walked through the chilly streets. When they reached Peter's apartment building, Kat stopped and turned to him. "Do you want to come up?"

Alex looked down at her, her eyes sparkling in the streetlight. "I'd love to. Just for a few minutes though. I know you want to get some sleep."

Kat made tea and the two of them sat on the couch, warming their hands on the mugs. Hours passed as they talked, laughing until their sides hurt.

Alex rose as the mantle clock chimed for the third time since their arrival. "Okay," he said, "I need to go. You need sleep." At the door, he touched her cheek. "Thank you."

"For what?"

"For going to the opera tonight, and for letting me walk you home. I had a great time." His voice was warm. "I don't remember the last time I laughed so much."

Kat rose on her tiptoes and kissed his cheek. "You're welcome," she said. "Thank you for keeping me company, it was a lot of fun."

"My pleasure." He paused with his hand on her arm, now suddenly nervous. "Kat, would you go out with me sometime? I mean, just us?"

For a moment, she fought the urge to jump up and down and shout *yes*. Then cold reality forced its way through. Her voice trembled a bit. "Alex, I'd love to, but…"

"But, what?"

"As much as I don't want to bring this up, don't you have a… umm…"

"A what?"

"A girlfriend. You have a girlfriend, right?"

Alex felt relief rush through him. She was not turning him down out of lack of interest. "I don't have a girlfriend."

"Since when?" She sounded suspicious as she narrowed her eyes. "She was supposed to be here last night, and tonight…"

Alex took her hand. "I broke up with her last night."

Her brow furrowed. "Oh?"

He smiled. "It just didn't feel right once I realized I would rather work up the nerve to ask you out."

A smile spread slowly across her face. "Really?"

"Really."

She squeezed his hand. "Okay, so ask me again," she enthused.

"Kat, would you like to go out with me sometime?"

"Yes." Her eyes clouded. "But I'm going back to college tomorrow, so I won't be back in the city for quite a while. At least a couple months."

Disappointment flooded him as he understood the reality. "Oh, right. So, I guess when we're both in the city, we'll go on a date? In the meantime, how about you call me sometime?" His voice deepened, quickly adding, "But I do remember how stressful the last semester of college is, so no pressure. I'll leave it in your hands, okay?"

"Okay. So, I should call you?"

"Please."

She paused, knowing how often she would think about him until then. "This week will be insane with going back, figuring out classes, books, and all that crap. It probably won't be until later this week."

"Works for me," he said, taking a deep breath. "The ball is in your court, so to speak."

A notepad sat on a nearby table, and Alex bent over it and scrawled something. "Here's my number. Use it anytime."

Kat took it, trying to hide her delight. "I will."

"If I don't answer, feel free to leave a message. I'll get back to you."

She grinned. "Promise?"

Smiling like a little kid, he started to laugh. "Cross my heart."

For the second night in a row, Kat slipped under the covers thinking only of Alex. He had asked her out. He wanted to go out with her. Shit, he had even dumped his girlfriend on the off chance that she would go out with him. Kat hugged herself. That amazing man wanted to go out with *her*. Holy shit!

Kat wiggled happily. Alex wanted to go out with her.

Chapter One

Five years later

The phone would not stop ringing, no matter how much Kat willed it to. It just kept buzzing. She reluctantly reached for it while she checked the clock. She pushed her hair away from her face and gave the answer button an annoyed stab. "What?" she groused in Spanish.

"Nice manners." The voice was firm but calm.

"Fuck off," said Kat. "I need sleep. What do you want? Jesus, we just saw each other a couple hours ago."

"Yeah, yeah."

"Seriously, what do you want?"

"I need you. Now. Paco broke his arm."

"What the hell are you talking about?"

"He was playing on the stairs this morning and he took a header. Looks like a bad break; they're going to pin his arm together in about an hour."

"What do you need?"

"I have an interview this morning, and it has to be today. I need you to cover for me."

There was no question that she would do it. "Of course," she said. "Where and when?"

Kat grabbed a notepad and scribbled down the basic information. After hanging up, she showered and pulled a lightweight sweater over her head. She slid snug black jeans up over her hips and completed the outfit with a pair of black Keds. All in all, it was her normal uniform for interviews like this one.

As she walked out the door with her bag slung over her shoulder, she hooked a pair of gold hoops into her ears.

Kat strode quickly through the quiet streets, grateful that her apartment on Madrid's Plaza Mayor was only eight blocks from the hotel where she would do the interview. The April sun was beginning to glint off the windows of the buildings and a light breeze swirled through empty streets.

It was going to be a gorgeous day. Kat began to plan. If the interview went well, she would be home and typing it up within a couple hours, and then she could spend the rest of the day on the final chapter of her latest novel. Spending much of the day by herself while she wrote in her own space was her idea of a perfect day. When the draft was done, she would stroll down to the square, grab a drink and some tapas, then get some sleep.

At the Hotel Emperador, Kat pushed through the revolving door, approached the front desk, and smiled at the flock of housekeepers dusting every possible surface. Kat found it oddly reassuring that all good Spanish hotels did things in almost the same way, at almost the same time of day, every day.

She strode up to the front desk. "I'm looking for a Mr. Tamaro," she said in Spanish. "I'm here to interview him."

The concierge smiled at the beautiful woman in front of him. "Good morning, miss. He is in the restaurant, by the windows. He is the young American."

It always amused Kat that Spaniards never realized she was an American too. Her years of living in Madrid had made her one of their own.

Kat looked around the restaurant, spotting a dark-haired man at a corner table by the window, just as the concierge had described. That had to be him.

The man looked up as she approached. His eyes widened as he immediately recognized her. His voice clearly expressed his surprise. "Kat?"

For a moment, Kat thought she might faint. Holy shit, she thought she would never see him again.

The man stood and they hugged each other awkwardly. Kat tried to accept the realization that the same Alex she had been thinking of for the past five years was now standing in front of her. "Alex?" she blurted, "what the hell are you doing here?"

"I could ask you the same thing." He swallowed, struggling to wrap his mind around the fact that she was standing in front of him. "I'm waiting to be interviewed. Some guy named … Hell, I don't remember his name … That doesn't even matter now," he laughed, still staring at her.

Kat's eyes widened as she understood the meaning of his words. "Oh, gosh… I'm the guy."

He shook his head in confusion. "What? No, they specifically told me to look for a *big guy*."

Kat motioned for him to sit. "Have a seat and I'll explain."

He sat, still clearly stunned, as she explained. "My friend Secu was supposed to interview you today, but he had a family emergency, so I'm covering for him." She shifted uncomfortably. "I hope that's okay."

What could he do but agree? "Of course." Alex narrowed his eyes. "Did you know you would be interviewing *me*?"

Kat shook her head more vigorously than strictly necessary, her face flaming with embarrassment. She felt uncomfortable realizing he could view the situation as a tactical maneuver. "No," she said, "I never even knew your last name until now. I mean, even when I listen to the band's CDs, I don't read the liner notes. When Secu gave me a quick rundown this morning, he must not have made the connection. Honestly, I was still half asleep when he called."

Alex swallowed the brief hope he had had, thinking perhaps she had agreed to take the interview in order to see him again. Surprisingly disappointed, he fought the urge to ask why she had never called. "Okay. Well, then…"

Kat answered his hint with her most practiced professional smile. "Let's order breakfast and get to work."

Over eggs and toast, Kat peppered Alex with standard questions using her phone to record their conversation. Alex watched her in fascination, surprised at how different she was in a professional role than the mercurial young woman he remembered.

Kat turned the phone off. "That's it. Thanks, Alex. I'll work up a draft today, and if you want, I can give you an English copy to review before I send it to the magazine."

"Don't bother. I trust you." Hoping to see her relax now that their business was done, Alex gave her his most charming smile as he poured more coffee into her cup. "Okay, so now tell me about *your* life. Last I heard, you were headed back to college, and now I find you here in Madrid."

Not quite meeting his eyes, Kat chose her words carefully. "I went back to college, and after I finished, I moved here."

He chuckled in disbelief. "That's it? I just gave you all the gory details of my life, and you wrap five years up in…" he paused to count "twelve words? You moved here to do what? I mean, I gather you're a reporter."

She nodded. "I am. A writer, a reporter. I do some work for papers and magazines, and I also write fiction."

"And you live here full time? What about the house in New York? Peter told me you own it jointly now."

"We do, but really, I live here."

"How often do you get home? Knowing how close you and Peter are, I imagine it's pretty often."

Kat squirmed, knowing how strange this would sound. "My career is here. I go occasionally."

"Only occasionally? Your brother is there."

"We get together fairly regularly—here, there, or other places. Anyway, my life is here now."

He thought she sounded almost melancholy. "And you're happy like this?"

The corners of her mouth quirked in what could pass for a smile. "It's the way I want it."

To Alex, this conversation felt like pulling teeth. Who was this Kat? So different from the one who had captivated him at the opera. He was asking questions that should have elicited more than one-sentence responses, and she was giving the absolute minimum in response.

They continued to talk for a while—or rather, Alex talked and Kat listened. Finally, he looked at his watch. "I have to run over to the theater to make sure we're ready." He hesitated. "Would you like to come to the concert tonight? Then after, maybe we could have a drink."

Kat's expression was serious. She frowned slightly, then slowly nodded. "I'd like that. I'd love to go to the concert."

Alex stood. "Okay, I'll have a ticket for you at the box office." He paused. "I'd be happy to leave two tickets, if you like."

She shook her head. "One will be perfect."

Alex tried not to grin. "It'll be there under your name. The concert starts at eight."

Kat nervously entered the theater twenty minutes before showtime. Why was she here? She could have easily begged off, and now she was here all dressed up, and she would have to hang around until after Alex was done, like some sort of friggin' groupie. Like the loser she had been that night years before, sitting around waiting for the damn phone to ring.

The concert was flawless. Despite her uncertain mood, Kat found herself mesmerized by the music and Alex's performance. No matter how much time had passed or how her life had changed, he was still so attractive she could hardly think straight in his presence. How was she going to get through drinks while keeping her walls up?

After the concert, Kat wandered out to the lobby with the rest of the crowd. Feeling increasingly uncomfortable, she slid out of the crowd to stand along the wall covered in tapestries, believing this to be the best place to wait.

When a hand touched her arm, she jumped, immediately defensive. A slight man dressed in the theater uniform stood next to her. "I'm sorry, miss, I didn't mean to startle you. Are you Katherine Weston?"

"Yes," she answered uncertainly.

"Mr. Tamaro asked me to escort you backstage."

Kat bristled over Alex's presumption that she would *want* to go backstage, but silently followed the man.

In the dressing room, Alex was shrugging into a leather jacket, chatting happily with the small group in the room. He grinned when he saw her. "Kat, you made it."

Despite her earlier irritation, she felt strangely pleased by his obvious pleasure at seeing her. She was glad she had put thought into her outfit. "Hi, Alex."

Always gracious, Alex quickly shook hands with the other visitors while subtly moving them toward the door. When the last person had left, he turned back to her. "I'm so glad you came."

"It was a great concert," she said. "You should be proud. You wowed the Spaniards, and they love nothing better than to find fault with an American."

He was more pleased by her praise than he had expected and was inordinately glad she had dressed carefully tonight. The black dress kissed her curves and left her elegant shoulders bare. "Thank you, I'm really glad you enjoyed it."

"I did. It was great to hear your solo music. I have to admit, I've never heard you perform anything other than your stuff with the band."

"Yeah, quite different, isn't it? Now, how about that drink? Where do you want to go?"

She thought for a moment. "There's a small bar near your hotel. It's usually pretty quiet."

"Sounds great. Do you want to walk or take a taxi?"

"Let's walk."

As they walked through the soft glow of the streetlights, Kat described the histories of the places they were passing.

They had walked several blocks when she slowed a bit. "Alex, do you mind if we stop quickly at my apartment? I forgot my phone."

"No problem. You said you live on Plaza Mayor, right? I'd love to see it."

They walked into the plaza, streetlights reflecting off the windows and the statue in the center of the square. All around the square were small cafes, their outside tables mobbed with chatting people. Kat guided Alex down a narrow alleyway he would never have noticed without her.

As she stopped in front of an ornate wrought-iron gate, a small gray-haired woman came running to open the gate before Kat could pull the key from her purse. The woman grinned happily and warmly kissed Alex's cheeks as Kat made introductions. In her apartment, Alex chuckled. "That is the sweetest woman ever."

Kat nodded, throwing her purse onto a small chair in the entryway. "Isn't she? If I don't see Marta for a day or two, she leaves a note in my mailbox to let me know she's worried." She thought back. "I got really sick last year; she made soup and kept me company one night when I had a fever that wouldn't break."

"Really?"

"Yeah. She was so worried I was alone. All I remember is I needed a drink of water really badly, and there she was."

Alex fought a surge of sadness at the thought of Kat being sick and alone. Why the hell was she living here? There had to be more to the story. "That was really kind of her."

Kat motioned at the rest of the apartment. "I just need a minute to grab the phone and use the bathroom."

She rolled her eyes, "You probably didn't need to know that, right?"

He grinned, seeing a blush stain her cheeks. "No problem."

"Anyway, before I started telling you about my bodily needs, I was going to say feel free to look around."

While Kat was in the other room, Alex wandered through the small kitchen, dining room, and living room before calling out, "It's a great apartment. How did you manage to get it? It must be nearly impossible in this neighborhood."

"The same family has owned it for generations," she called out from the next room. "I dated one of their sons for a bit in college. He's married now and lives in Sevilla, so they lease it to me."

The rooms were warm and comfortable. A few knickknacks were scattered around, along with several photos- a few of Peter and Luke, a framed portrait of a woman who resembled Kat (likely her older sister), another of the same woman with two small children, and a picture of Kat's parents. Alex's eyes clouded as he recalled the shock he had felt upon hearing of their deaths in a car accident four years ago.

He was still looking around when Kat appeared in an open doorway, a neatly made bed visible behind her. She tucked her phone into her purse as she walked into the living room. "Are you ready?"

"I am."

They walked the few blocks to the bar in almost complete silence. They chose a corner table lit by a small candle. Kat looked at Alex quizzically. "Red wine?"

"That would be great."

Once the bottle arrived and had been poured, Alex raised his glass. "To coincidences. We meet again."

"To coincidences." Kat sat quietly, relishing the rich, smooth warmth of the wine. As they sipped, Alex attempted to get a conversation started but was again frustrated by her abbreviated answers and lack of laughter.

It might have been the wine or late hour, or the candlelight making her hair shimmer, but he could not resist any longer. "Kat, what happened?"

"What do you mean?" she said, sounding guarded.

He fumbled for the right words. "I mean, the world was your oyster just five years ago. You loved life, you loved to talk about *anything*, and you laughed. I have spent hours with you today, and while you are happy to ask me questions, you barely respond to anything I ask you."

His words stung, but Kat maintained her demeanor. "I don't think I've changed."

He shook his head, now convinced more than ever that he was right. "No, you have. I looked around your apartment. Aside from a few family photos, it's about as personal as a hotel room. And it's clear you don't want to talk about your life; you deflect every question I pose." He felt his frustration building. "What the hell happened?"

Kat took a last sip of wine and straightened in her chair. Her stomach churned. "Nothing happened. I'm just me," she shrugged. "As for my apartment, that's how I like it."

"And you are clearly next to alone here."

"You have no way of knowing that," she said, icily.

Alex would later regret his next words, but at that moment he needed to make her see his perspective. "No, you're right; I don't have any way of knowing that, except I do know you didn't have a date on a Friday night. I know I was in your apartment and saw no sign of a romantic relationship. So, I don't think it's illogical to conclude that you're alone."

Kat worked to keep her tone even as she responded, "Alex, you're making a lot of assumptions. But if you must know, I'm not dating anyone. Is it a crime to be single? You're here in Madrid and have no one with you, does that mean you live like a priest?"

"I was here to do a concert, the last of a series," he asserted. "As I said this morning, I have been on tour for months now, and more to the point, we're not talking about my life, we're talking about yours. We've talked about nothing but me all day. Every time I try to get you to open up, you give me a polite non-answer. So, I'll say it again: It's obvious to me that something happened to you in the last few years. What was it?"

Kat felt pressure building in her lungs as she fought back tears. There was no way she could let him see how much damage his words were doing to her, and she had to get out of there before she lost her composure.

Taking a deep breath to steady herself, she responded as calmly as she could manage. "Alex, nothing has changed since we last saw each other. Maybe we just remember those nights differently. They were great, and they will always stay that way in my mind. But it was a long time ago, and a lot of things have happened to us both since then, and we've probably sealed those evenings in our memories, perhaps making them more than they really were." She rose and dropped several folded bills on the table. "I have to go," she said softly. "Have a safe trip home."

Alex stood hurriedly, nearly knocking the table over. "Wait, don't go," he said. "Please, I'm sorry if I was out of line. Stay."

Swamped with a crushing fatigue, Kat shook her head. "You're not sorry. You meant it, and I'm sure with the best of intentions, but it's none of your business. So, if you'll excuse me, I'm going home. Goodbye, Alex."

Kat spun on her heel and walked out of the square without another look back.

Back at her apartment, Kat carefully locked the door behind her, then turned her phone off. She changed into a faded tee that had belonged to her brother, then climbed into bed. She curled up, wrapped her arms around her knees protectively, and cried.

Nearly a month later, Alex was back in California sifting through the mail when a small ivory envelope slid through his fingers. Recognizing the Spanish royalty on the stamps, he immediately tore it open. The handwritten note was brief.

Dear Alex,
Please forgive my behavior when you were in Madrid. I loved your concert, and it was nice to see you.
Katherine Weston

Alex opened the smaller enclosed envelope to find two tickets for the San Francisco Opera. A smile crossed his face; he had spent the last few weeks thinking about Kat. Maybe she had been thinking of him too.

The phone rang shrilly, interrupting his reverie. "Hello?"

"Hey, Alex, it's Peter. How's the west coast treating you?"

Alex grinned. "Hey, Pete. Life's pretty good. Always full of surprises." He looked again at the tickets. "I was just thinking about you."

"You were? That's weird."

Alex focused on the conversation, "Yeah. Anyway, what's up?"

"I'm calling about the wedding. You're coming, right?"

Having momentarily forgotten about Will's wedding, only two weeks away, Alex rubbed his forehead. "Of course, I'm coming."

"Cool. You can plan on staying here."

"What?" Alex was confused.

"Stay with us, we have the room. Come as early as you want and stay as long as you can. We can do the wedding shit and then have some time to plan for the fall, hang out, and relax a bit."

Alex paused, then made up his mind. "That would be great."

"Okay then, it's settled. Just let us know your flight number the day before, and we'll pick you up at the airport."

"Great." As he looked again at the tickets, Alex wondered if his words could have motivated Kat to do more than just apologize; maybe she would return to the states sometime soon. "Hey, Pete… Did Kat mention she interviewed me in Madrid?"

"Oh, yeah, she did. She said it was great to see you. And I don't know what happened when you were there, but-"

"But, what?"

"Well, she mentioned coming home to visit sometime soon, which she hasn't done in ages."

"Really?"

"Yeah, I mean, when I brought up the idea of Thanksgiving, she didn't immediately shoot me down, which is huge."

"Really?" Alex had a thought. "And what about the wedding? Is she coming home for that?"

"No, and Mariah is *really* hurt. You know it was Kat who introduced the two of them, right?"

"Yeah."

"So, she was invited, but said she couldn't make it."

"Oh," said Alex, disappointment washing over him.

"Anyway, just to plant the thought, you're welcome to join us for Thanksgiving."

The day was suddenly growing interesting. "I would love to," he said, trying to sound casual. "Hey, you know… Kat sent me a note, and I want to call her and thank her. Do you have her number right there?"

Ten minutes later, Alex sat staring at Kat's number. Taking a deep breath, he punched in the number. After all this time, here he was the one calling her.

Alex counted five rings as he mentally rehearsed his message. The phone screeched just before a voice came on the line. "*Diga.* Hello?"

"Kat? It's Alex."

There was another screech. "Alex, hold on, I'm just getting off the metro. Give me just a second."

Alex waited, hearing the now recognizable sounds of a subway station. Kat's voice came back on. "Hi, sorry about that."

"No problem." He tried to sound relaxed. "I just got your note, and I wanted to call and thank you. You really didn't need to apologize."

"Yes, I did. I was a bitch." She laughed. "Anyway, I was a jerk, and you didn't deserve that."

"Well, I disagree, but I still really appreciate the thought, and I love opera, as you know."

"Good. If you didn't notice, they're open-ended tickets, good for any show that still has seats. I figured that way, you could pick the performance."

"That was really sweet of you. Anyway, I owe you an apology for the things I said. I was out of line."

"No, you weren't. Besides, it's over. Let it go."

That made him smile. "Deal," he said. "How are things?"

Kat sighed. "They're really busy. I'm doing a series of pieces for a magazine, so I've spent a lot of time on trains lately. The good part is that I've visited a couple towns I've never been to before."

Alex suddenly realized this was more information than she had given him the whole time they had been together in Madrid. Maybe what he had said *had* made a difference.

Fifteen minutes later, Kat said, "Alex, this call is costing you a fortune. I should let you go."

Alex started to argue but decided not to end another conversation by pressing any issue. "Okay, but how about you shoot me an occasional email?"

He could hear paper rustling. "I can do that," she said. "What's your address?"

Not more than twenty minutes later, Alex's email buzzed. The new message was short, but enough to make him smile. *Hey, Alex. Thanks for calling. Send me an email when you get bored — Kat*

Chapter Two

A week later, the bleating of a garbage truck woke Alex. He lay in bed until he finally had to admit he just was not going to get any more sleep.

Casting a resentful glare at the clock, he dragged himself out of bed and into his clothes, determined to start the coffee and commence caffeine infusions as soon as possible.

When he stepped out to retrieve the newspaper from the front steps, he noticed a dark haze hanging over the morning half-light. Truck exhaust mixed with the sweetish tang of garbage briefly dominated the odiferous New York City mélange.

Back in the kitchen, Alex had not progressed beyond scanning the headlines when Peter stumbled in, yawning. "Damn, I really appreciate the city sending out its mobile alarm clocks on the day I actually have the *option* of sleeping in. Good thing nothing smells better than coffee."

Alex turned the page. "It should be ready." He sent Peter a mocking look. "I hate to remind you, but we could've had more sleep if we'd left the club earlier," he playfully chided.

"And miss the final set?" Peter poured himself a cup of coffee and reached for an orange.

"Good morning," Luke said from the doorway. He walked over to Peter, and the two men exchanged a tender kiss.

Peter tugged on the lapel of Luke's charcoal gray suit. "Nice. How come you always look better than me?"

"Because I go out and buy clothes. *You* root around in the rag box for t-shirts that haven't been turned into dust cloths yet." Luke's smile took any bite out of his words.

Peter held up his hands in mock surrender. "Okay – I give. Buy me clothes this weekend, please."

Luke claimed a section of his orange. "I will try to, either this weekend or next. Too bad I can't wait for Kat to come home and go with me."

"*If* she comes home." Peter tried to keep the wistfulness out of his voice.

Alex was confused. "I thought you said she would be here for Thanksgiving."

Luke nodded. "Yeah, she said she *might* come, but every time we try to pin her down, she changes the subject."

Peter inhaled deeply. "I just wish she'd move home for good." He gestured around the kitchen with one hand. "We own the house together, but other than paying her share of the insurance and taxes, she hasn't actually stepped foot in it for over a year." He realized that Alex was looking at him strangely. "How'd you sleep, Alex?"

Alex wanted to ask a hundred questions about Kat, but Peter was clearly done with the subject. "Like a rock." He grinned. "It must be the clean air and quiet streets of New York City."

With a brief smile, Peter powered up his phone. "I forgot to turn it on after I charged it last night, but I suppose it doesn't matter since three a.m. isn't a great time to return messages."

Peter looked at his phone in shock. "Holy fucking shit."

Before the other two could ask him about his reaction, the front door buzzer sounded. Peter looked up from his phone. "Who could that be? And, oh, my god, Kat's coming home!"

Luke rolled his eyes, "I'll get the door. And then you can tell me what the fuck you are talking about."

As Luke left the kitchen, Peter glanced at his phone one more time, then looked at Alex in wonder. "Kat's really coming home."

Alex was completely confused. "What?"

Peter's eyes grew wide. "She's finally coming home, and I didn't have my phone last night, so I missed her text."

"What did it say?"

"That she was getting on a flight yesterday, from Madrid to Bogotá, and Bogotá to here." Peter's face paled as he looked at the next message. "Oh shit, she says if I get the message in time, to text her and meet her at the airport. If not, she'll get a cab."

Just then, their big black mutt skidded out of the kitchen and made for the front door, barking madly. Luke appeared in the doorway with a big smile on his face. "Hey, Pete, I think we should have checked your phone last night…"

A feminine voice rose from behind Luke. "Max, get down. Damn it, Max, get out of the way."

Peter lunged for the hallway as Kat and the dog came into view. He snagged the wiggling dog by the collar. "Max, knock it off. Kat, welcome home!"

"Hey, at least *Max* is happy to see me." Simply dressed in a white blouse, and black slacks, Kat had restrained her strawberry blonde hair in a neat knot. She had several black travel bags slung over her shoulders. Dropping them unceremoniously on the floor, she crouched down to hug the big dog. Smiling, she stood up and sent a stern look at her sheepish brother. "Hi, Pete. Remember me? Your darling baby sister? The one you keep begging to come home and then leave stranded at the goddamn airport?"

Peter lifted her off the floor in an enthusiastic hug. "Welcome home! And why the hell didn't you call from the airport?"

Still held in Peter's arms, Kat whacked the side of his head with enough force to make him wince. "Duh. I texted you, no response, so I just got a cab." She grinned. "You ass."

"Okay, okay. I apologize, and I'll keep apologizing for the next few days. I'll make it up to you, I promise."

She grinned. "You bet you will."

Kat suddenly caught a glimpse of Alex at the kitchen table and could only stare at him in shock. His dark brown hair, waving to midway down his neck, was a bit longer than it had been in Madrid. She noted a few more sun streaks, which seemed to emphasize the hazel in his eyes and his golden skin. Realizing she had been silent too long; she blushed and fumbled a greeting. "Hey, Alex."

He stood quickly and offered an awkward hug. As his arms wrapped around her, Kat desperately wished she had known he would be there; she would have freshened up at the airport. For just a moment, she gave in to temptation and leaned against him, enjoying the sensation of her body against his. Flinching slightly as she realized what she was doing, she stepped back, forcing herself not to look away.

Gazing down into her bright green eyes, Alex felt as if everything in the world had paused, and he did not care if it ever started again. "Hi, Kat. Welcome home."

Abruptly aware that she was still staring, Kat spoke a little too quickly. "Thanks. I didn't know you'd be here. You didn't say anything in your emails."

Peter and Luke exchanged a quick glance. Since when were they emailing each other?

Alex answered cautiously, trying to gauge whether she was happy to see him. "Yeah. I'm here for the wedding."

"Oh." Another silence, and then Kat noticed Peter and Luke watching them like the latest reality show. She narrowed her eyes at them in warning before turning back to Alex. "I mean, that's great."

Luke thought it was time to get everyone to relax. Standing up, he pulled Kat's favorite mug out of the cabinet. "You want some coffee?"

Thank God! "That would be great."

He handed the steaming mug to her, and continued, "How was your trip? And how long are you staying?"

Kat started pulling pins out of her hair. "My trip was good but long as hell." She tried to smile. "I don't know how long I'm here for. I should head back early next week. Anyway, the last few days have been insane since I was north up until just two days ago."

Peter tipped his head. "I didn't know you were in the north."

Her face lit up. "I needed more info for an article on the anniversary of Ibárruri's death, but while I was there, I met a fabulous woman in the village. I spent hours with her—she worked with the Basque miners during their uprising. Needless to say, I have enough notes to carry me for a while once I'm done with my current draft. And I hit the apple harvest perfectly." As the last pin came out, her curls tumbled to caress her neck and shoulders. She grinned at Peter and Luke in self-satisfaction. "A case of *cidra* will arrive later today."

"Great!" Peter looked at Luke with a gleam in his eyes. "What made you change your mind about coming?"

She rolled her eyes. "I had no intention of going to the wedding, but when Mariah kept calling and calling, I finally caved."

"I had just gotten back to Madrid. I mean, I haven't even done laundry. I just threw a few clean things into a bag. Then I called the airlines and ended up going out to Barajas to get on standby. Finally, I got on the Avianca list for a flight. You know your options are bad when you feel lucky to be going to JFK via Colombia. But even after I made the final list for the flight, we got delayed because there was a threat."

She shook her head in disgust. "I sat on my bags and waited. They didn't even check our luggage through for an hour until they had about a million troops at the airport to inspect them. So, I played thirty-seven hands of Crazy Eights with some kid named Nicodemus. Why the hell would you name a kid Nicodemus? Talk about setting him up—with that name, *everyone* is going to beat the shit out of him." As she spoke, she flipped her head upside down, briskly rubbing her fingers over her scalp. When she straightened up, the waves were in wild disarray. "It was a really long day or night, whatever it was."

Peter reached over and tugged on a curl. "Since when do you travel with your hair on top of your head instead of in a braid?"

She yawned. "A few hours into sitting around the airport, I decided I had to get my hair *completely* out of my way or rip it out of my head. It kept sliding out of the braid and it was driving me crazy."

She rolled her shoulders and circled her head, deciding it was time to get herself out of the spotlight. "Anything new with you guys?"

Peter shrugged. "Nothing much. We've been busy as hell, but I can't say anything exciting has happened. Oh yeah, Josh called a couple of days ago."

"He did?"

"Yeah, he's coming to the city either tonight or tomorrow, and he'll be at the wedding."

"Great! Is he staying here?" She sounded so happy, that for a moment, Alex felt a stab of jealousy.

"No," said Peter, "he's dating someone named Kim. He's staying with her while he's here from Boston and he's bringing her to the wedding." Peter scowled as he tried to remember the conversation. "He originally said something about stopping here to see you, expecting you'd come for the wedding. He was bent out of shape when I said you *weren't* coming."

"That was my plan, but when 'Riah started to cry, I couldn't take it." She shrugged. "Besides, I sort of missed you guys." Kat stood up and stretched her arms over her head. "What are you up to today?"

Luke brushed crumbs off his jacket and looked at his watch. "I have to be at the gallery at nine-ish."

"Well, shit." Peter tipped back in his chair. "Since we didn't think you'd be here, we haven't been filling you in about anything. You probably have no clue about all the plans for this week." Kat shook her head and waited for him to continue. "Alex and I are heading out to the grocery store this morning while Luke is working. We planned on staying in tonight."

Kat nodded. "Okay, then what?"

Peter ate another bite of orange. "We're heading to the shore tomorrow. We invited Sasha and Beth, and Josh and his date will come up to stay with us. They'll come the day *after* tomorrow. Then on Friday, we have the pre-wedding final fitting crap. We have the rehearsal and rehearsal dinner that evening, which you don't have to go to. Then the wedding is on Saturday, and there's a brunch on Sunday." He shook his head in amazement. "It's like a whole marathon wedding thing."

"And then? How long are people staying with you?"

"With us," he automatically corrected. She rolled her eyes at him. "Everybody will be heading out either Sunday afternoon or Monday morning. Will that work for you?"

Kat thought for a moment. "That makes sense. Sure, the shore would be great."

Luke noticed the shadows under her eyes. "What are you going to do today? No offense, but you look like you should get some sleep."

"I will. You know me, I can't sleep on a stupid plane. I thought I'd grab a shower, then take a nap." She looked at all three men. "Who's making dinner?"

"You are," Luke and Peter yelled in unison.

Kat laughed and swatted her brother with a dishtowel. "I'm the damn guest, and I have to cook?"

"You're not a guest," Peter scoffed. "This is your house too. Besides, you cook better than we do."

"No, I don't. You're just hoping I'll make one of your favorites." She sighed, accepting her fate. "Okay, what do you want? You'll probably need to get the groceries for me."

Luke answered before Peter could. "Lasagna. Please, Kat, lasagna."

"Fine." Kat turned to look at Alex. "Alex, can you join us for dinner?"

"If it isn't a problem, I'd love you." Horrified, Alex realized his slip. "I mean I'd love to." *I would cancel dinner plans with God to spend the evening with this woman,* he thought.

Kat chuckled. "I didn't realize I was so appealing when I haven't showered in days."

Peter snorted. "Don't let it go to your head, Kat—you look disgusting. Alex, please join us."

"I'd love to." He smiled at Kat. "Thanks for the invite."

"You're welcome." Kat stood up to make her way to the walk-in pantry. Looking around quickly, she jotted some things down on the back of an envelope she had pulled from the recycling bin. She opened the fridge, poked around for a moment, and sighed. "You two really don't cook too often, do you?"

Luke shook his head. "No. I mean we cook sometimes, but we usually wind up calling for take-out if we don't go out. Your cooking is one of the reasons we want you to move home."

"Of course it is." She squeezed Luke's hand. "And helping you put up with my brother. Anyway, here's what I need for tonight."

Peter looked at the list. "Fine. We'll get it all."

"Great." Kat leaned over and kissed the top of her brother's head. "Pete, will you bring some of this shit up for me?"

Peter nodded as he finished his coffee. Wrinkling her nose at Luke and Alex, Kat grabbed the smaller bag and a package wrapped in brown paper. "See you later, boys."

"Definitely," Alex said before he could stop himself.

Kat grumbled as she climbed the stairs. "Jesus. At this point, these weigh a ton."

"You have the small ones," Peter exclaimed, slightly out of breath.

"Yeah, but I'm delicate."

Peter's snort was audible. "Delicate, my ass. Why is your room on the top floor anyway?"

"Because you claimed the bottom one. And as I recall, we all agreed that several floors between us would give the illusion of privacy."

"Who needs privacy? You're never here!"

Kat took a deep breath. "Let it go, Pete, before I feel so badgered, I head back to the airport."

"Fine, I'll stop." Once the siblings had reached the top floor, Peter dropped the bags on the couch and hugged Kat quickly. "Glad you're back, brat. I missed you."

"I missed you too." She leaned against him for a moment. "Thanks for bringing this stuff up for me. I'll see you tonight, if not sooner?"

"Bet on it."

Chapter Three

Around midday, Peter and Alex walked into the house, their arms overflowing with grocery bags. Peter cast his eyes toward the ceiling. "The house is really quiet. Kat must have fallen asleep."

Alex nodded. "Good, she looked like she needed it. Why doesn't she sleep on planes?"

"Kat hates to fly. No, on second thought, it's not the flying she hates so much, she *hates* the noise of a plane—says it gets inside her skull. She freaks out every time the sound changes, and if she tries to sleep and it changes? She wakes in pure panic. I mean, a full-blown, hands-sweating, dry-mouth, verging-on-hyperventilating panic. So, she reads or writes with AirPods in her ears when she flies."

Alex tried to imagine it. "Really? I just can't see Kat afraid of much."

"Actually, it's pretty amusing to watch." Peter grinned. "She'll sit, ready to stuff those buds into her ears the *second* they say it's okay... And on a day like today, when she has lousy flights and long layovers, she'll go for *days* without sleep, so as soon as she gets where she's going, she crashes hard. But then, when any of the rest of us would still need more sleep, she bounces up like the Energizer Bunny. You just wait, when she gets up, she'll be irritatingly energetic."

"Why doesn't she take something to take the edge off?"

Peter laughed. "Oh, we tried for years to convince her to do that, but she's afraid if she does take something, and something goes wrong, she won't be able to respond." He shook his head. "She is the only person I know who reads the entire safety brochure every single time she gets on a plane."

Alex tried again to picture Kat being such a Nervous Nelly. "Seriously?"

"Yeah. It's so tiring to fly with her that *we* take something for *her* anxiety."

Once the groceries were sorted and put away, Peter and Alex took Max for a long walk. On the way back, Peter's phone rang. After a quick conversation, Peter hung up and said, "Hey, Alex, Luke has a new painting at the gallery he really wants me to see. Do you mind taking Max back to the house?"

Alex took the leash. "Not at all."

A surprising wave of exhilaration hit Alex as he opened the front door. He unhooked Max and hung the leash in the foyer. Kat was standing at the island when he entered the kitchen. She was dressed in black jeans and a dark green fitted tee with her hair pulled back with a black scrunchie. He was amused to hear Twiddle on the stereo, thinking living abroad would have kept her from learning about the new indie band. She hummed as she kneaded bread dough, her arm muscles straining. He could not help but think their clean lines seemed to beg for his touch. The smell of yeast filling the room welcomed him, and for a moment, he pictured himself coming home to her like this every night.

When Alex moved closer, Kat jumped and a flash of fear crossed her face. He instinctively laid his hand on her arm to reassure her, the warmth of her skin sending a tingle of awareness up his arm. "I'm sorry, I didn't mean to scare you. I thought you would have heard the front door."

Her eyes still showed her nerves as she reached over to turn the stereo down. "Don't worry about it." She lowered the volume some more. "It was too loud for me to hear anything." She looked around nervously. "Where's Peter?"

"He went to the gallery to see some new painting. He thought they'd be back pretty soon." He looked around the kitchen. "Do you need help?"

"Not now. Once the dough's rising for the second time, there's a break." Inwardly, she groaned. Did she always have to sound curt with this guy? She tried to soften her tone. "I could use some help later though."

The idea of spending time with her sent a powerful surge of joy through him. "Great, then I'll go grab a quick shower."

After his shower, Alex walked into the sunroom to find Kat on the couch with the dog.

At the sound of his footsteps, Kat's chin rose. Her eyes wandered up his long legs encased in softly faded denim. She eyed his light gray t-shirt and lingered on the auburn highlights glinting in his damp hair. With a start, Kat realized he was watching her just as carefully, causing her to blush.

He sat on the couch across from her. "Am I interrupting?"

Her cheeks were red. "No. Max and I were just catching up. I really miss having a dog, so I tend to spend a lot of time talking to him."

"And does he answer you?" Alex teased.

"No, but he's a great listener. If I pet him, he'll listen for hours."

Max wasn't the only one, Alex thought. He tried to cover his grin. "A good listener is hard to find, especially one who keeps his mouth shut."

"Exactly. Give me a dog over a human any day."

Behind Kat, Peter and Luke quietly entered the room with a tall, handsome man with curly black hair. Kat was so focused on Alex that she did not hear the newcomer sneaking up behind her. Just as Alex was about to warn her, the stranger winked at him and bent down to kiss her neck.

A surprised squeak came rushing out before she jumped and turned to be wrapped in his arms. Her voice was joyful as she recognized him. "Josh!"

The man chuckled as he held her tight. "Hi, Ducky, how are you?"

"Oh, I'm so glad to see you."

After Peter made introductions, Josh sat down next to Kat on the couch, their fingers entwining in a motion that was clearly familiar to them both. Alex tamped down a flare of jealousy. Who the hell was this guy?

Josh spoke gently. "So, you *finally* came home."

Luke quickly tried to change the subject. "So, Josh, how was your trip?"

Josh grinned. "Nice try, Luke. Always the peacekeeper." He turned back to Kat. "So, is this a visit or are you here for good?"

Kat sat straighter, moving away from her friend with a cold look on her face. "A visit. Enough."

Keeping his voice neutral, Josh tried to pull her toward him again. "Oh, come on, Ducky. Are we pretending you live in Madrid just for work?"

Kat stood up and moved to the window, wrapping her arms around herself as if to ward off a chill. "My move to Madrid was personal and professional. And my decision to stay is as well." She turned; her face was tight with tension. "Alex, I'm ready to work on dinner now—Are you?" She turned back to Josh. "Are you eating with us?"

Josh's face showed his anger, but his tone was civil. "No, Kat. I promised Kim I'd be there in time for dinner. I just wanted to stop by here first. So, you're going to the wedding after all?"

She nodded. "Yeah, I finally caved, after a bunch of drunken calls from 'Riah."

Josh smiled. "Alcohol always did bring that out in her. Remember when we had to disconnect her phone?"

He paused before moving toward his friend. "Kat, I'm sorry if I pissed you off. Truce?"

Kat's eyes stayed wary. "Truce. But we're done talking about it."

Josh's eyes narrowed. "We're done talking for tonight maybe."

They could all see the angry glitter in Kat's eyes as she motioned toward the kitchen. "Can I see you privately?"

Kat closed the French doors between the kitchen and the sunroom, deliberately bringing them together gently, rather than slamming them as she was tempted to do. Taking a deep breath, she worked hard to keep her voice calm. "Damn it, Josh, thanks a lot for doing this in front of Alex, and to top it off, you call me Ducky too."

"I always call you Ducky, just like Mariah does." Josh thought for a moment. "Okay, so I should have waited until we were alone. Point taken."

"Thank you."

"But, damn it, Kat, you need to talk about it – to get it out of your system. And you hang up when I try to say anything over the phone. At least when we're face to face, you can't hang up on me." He reached out to touch her face, but she jumped back. "You need to get over it, Kat. Or at least deal with it openly."

"Why do I need to talk about it? It's not going to change anything. All it does is open old wounds." She suddenly sounded young and confused, and painfully sad.

"Those damn wounds never closed."

Sadness was instantly transformed into rage. "I don't get to get it out of my system. It *is* my system. It is my fucking reality, twenty-four seven." She shook her head, so agitated she did not care who heard her. "What the fuck do you want me to say, that it still hurts? Shit, yes!" She slammed her fist on the counter. "I don't ever get to walk away from that, ever. What the holy fuck do you want me to say, Josh, what? Tell me what I can say that will make you happy."

Shocked by her reaction, Josh shoved his fingers through his black curls. "Yes—no. I don't care what you say, just that you talk; to me, to Peter or Luke or 'Riah, or a therapist, or someone sitting on a goddamn park bench. I don't care who you talk to or what you say. It's been destroying you for years, and yet you say you're frickin' fine."

"You son-of-a-bitch, you sit and judge me?" She jabbed her finger into his chest so hard he winced. "How dare you condemn me for wanting to try to keep it together the best I can. Thanks a fucking lot, Josh." Her bitingly sarcasm carried into the other room.

With his hands on his hips, Josh yelled. "Damn it, Kat, listen to me!" Startled by his own volume, he took a breath and deliberately softened his tone. "I understand you've driven this so deep inside that we're losing you. I'm fucking terrified that we've lost you for good. I'm afraid I'll never see you love again or laugh so hard you cry, and milk shoots out your nose. You always kept things to yourself, I was used to that, but you were still connected to the rest of the world. But ever since it all happened, you've shut down."

He stood for a second, trying to find the right words, knowing he had only seconds before she would bolt. "Kat, it all had to impact you, and yet, no one ever even saw you cry. You didn't cry when it happened. You didn't cry at the funeral. And you didn't even cry when your parents died. You just plain shut down and shut us all out. And you keep saying you're fucking fine. But one thing you're not, is *fine*."

He stepped closer and touched her face. She jumped as if his hand had scalded her. "You're my best friend and I love you more than you know. All I want is for you to let it go and start to heal. And no matter how much you don't want to hear me say it, you're not going to heal in Madrid. You can hide there, but you can't *heal* there. The demons are here. You need to face them and move forward. We will all support you, do whatever it takes, but you can't heal there, and deep down, you know it."

Josh opened the French doors and left Kat staring woodenly ahead. He walked over to Peter and Luke. "I'm not sure if I made things worse or better."

Only bits and pieces had been audible in the living room, but Peter met Josh's eyes calmly. "It needed to be said. Hopefully, you helped, but it certainly can't hurt." He shook his head. "But, you know, you could wait a whole five minutes into your visit before pissing her off."

"Why wait when pissing her off is so much fun?" Josh laughed. "We all know exactly why she lives thousands of miles away." He stuck out his hand toward Alex. "Alex, it was nice meeting you." He grinned wickedly. "Don't give up on her."

Alex looked confused. "What?"

"When we walked in, you were looking at her like, as my mom would say, she's the cat's meow. Don't give up on her—she's worth it."

The silence after Josh left was almost deafening, and then Peter said, "Is he right?"

Alex shifted uncomfortably. "What do you mean?"

"Do you think she's the cat's meow?"

Alex rubbed his temple. "Damn, guys, I ..."

Peter chuckled. "I'm just giving you shit, man. I'm not serious."

Peter and Luke stood up, and Luke smiled warmly. "We're going to run downstairs and get cleaned up. We'll be back up in a few minutes."

Feeling like he was entering the lion's den, Alex walked into the kitchen.

Kat was rummaging through cabinets and occasionally slamming something on the counter. Alex could not hear exactly what she was saying, only words and phrases. "Damn him... *Madre de dios... Pendejo...* How dare he ... Who does he think... Stupid ass..."

Alerted by Alex's footsteps, she paused. "Can you cook?"

Alex tried to suppress a grin. If only she knew of the countless hours he had spent in kitchens. "I can manage," he said.

Relieved as she was that she would not have to guide him, Kat's stomach still twisted. "Could you make a salad?"

Alex headed for the wine rack next to the fridge. "Sure," he said, "I'm going to pour a glass of wine first. Would you like one?"

Kat sent him a searching look. "Do you like champagne?"

Alex thought a celebration was a bit odd, given the circumstances. "Yes."

She gestured toward the refrigerator. "There are several dark green bottles in the back- an apple champagne from Spain. I should probably just call it sparkling apple wine. Anyway, if you want some, glasses are to the right of the fridge."

Alex looked at her carefully. "Why do you bring apple champagne all this way?"

Happy for a neutral topic, Kat tried to calm her nerves. "Apple orchards are everywhere in northern Spain, and they all make *cidra*. Everyone drinks it non-stop during the apple harvest while it's still fresh, then they bottle it for the rest of the year. When I'm there, I get the more refined type that can keep in the fridge or in the wine cellar."

Careful not to bump into him, Kat went to the refrigerator herself and extracted a bottle, gracefully holding it over her head. "Traditionally, you pour the fresh stuff from over your head into a glass held around your knee, and then you drink it like a shot, dumping the dregs on the floor or ground when you're done. But we serve it in wine glasses."

Alex opened the bottle she handed to him and poured them each a glass. "To friendship."

She smiled sadly. "To friendship."

Taking roasted garlic from the oven, she took a deep breath. "I owe you another apology. You must think all I do is get pissed off, since once again, I put you in an awkward position of being around while I go off."

Alex's voice echoed his patience as he pulled salad ingredients from the fridge. "You never owed me the first apology and you don't owe me one now."

His response irritated her. "Bullshit. You must think I'm a real whack-job, screaming at everyone who crosses my path."

Alex could not understand how she could think such a thing. Couldn't she see the desire in his eyes? Even Josh had noticed his interest in her. "I don't think you're a whack-job, as you put it. It just seems I've managed to hit times when you've had a bad day or something."

She snorted. "How diplomatic. Anyway, I'm sorry."

"Stop being sorry. If you feel that badly, explain it to me. Tell me why he calls you Ducky. Then tell me why you *really* live in Spain."

Kat chewed on her lip for a moment, thrown off by his direct approach and unsure how to respond.

With a sigh, she decided she owed him *something*. She took a deep breath and steeled herself. "Mariah and Josh call me Ducky because, in college, I used to answer the question 'How are you?' with 'Ducky.' It just stuck somehow."

"And Spain?"

"About four or five years ago, I decided I needed to get away for a while. I went to Spain because I love it there." She leaned back against the counter. "It was never supposed to be forever, but somehow, I've just stayed. I know Peter and Luke want me to come back, but they don't push me. Josh has been my best friend almost forever, and he has never worried about whether I want to talk about something."

"Do you miss being here?"

Kat stared ahead stoically. "Yes." She shook her head. "No." She shrugged. "I don't know. I love being with Peter and Luke, I love being around some of my friends, like Mariah, and usually Josh, but I don't like how I feel otherwise when I'm here. It makes me feel like I don't fit in my own skin." She looked at Alex with stricken eyes. "I really can't explain it. I'm sorry."

"Stop being sorry. You didn't have to explain anything to me, really."

She shook her head forcefully. "Shit. Yes. I owed you an explanation."

Her posture was painfully rigid. Alex balled his hands into fists as he fought the urge to wrap her in his arms and soothe her. "Kat. Stop." He moved closer, watching her carefully for signs of fear or discomfort as he put his hands on her upper arms. "Look at me."

He was shocked to see her eyes filling with tears as she finally raised them. His voice softened. "Let's make a deal, okay? I want you to stop apologizing to me. I was an ass and too pushy in Madrid. You apologized when you didn't need to, and I loved the opera tickets, but you've done nothing here tonight that you need to apologize for." He chose his words carefully. "And deep down, I know you know Josh was only being a true friend."

Kat looked at him thoughtfully. She swallowed and sniffed quickly before taking in a deep breath. "Okay."

Peter and Luke entered the kitchen, breaking the moment. Alex and Kat moved quickly to finish the dinner preparations, and soon all four of them were eating and chatting companionably.

When the plates were empty, Peter cleared his throat. "Okay, brat. Since the two of you cooked, we'll clean."

She snorted. "You bet your ass you will. We'll sit here and watch."

While the other two rinsed dishes and cleaned the counters, Kat and Alex sat at the table. With a start, Alex realized that Kat had barely spoken. He touched her hand. "You okay? You're awfully quiet."

Kat shook herself. "I'm fine. It's just kind of nice to listen to other people talking. I'm having fun listening." She stood. "I'll be right back."

After she left the room, Alex looked at the other men. "Did I say something wrong?"

Peter shook his head. "No. Kat's like that sometimes. She gets really quiet while other people talk around her, and then she needs a few moments to herself. She'll be back."

Ten minutes later, the kitchen gleamed. Peter and Luke sat quietly on one of the couches in the sunroom as Max wrestled with a pillow in front of them. Kat walked back into the room and sat on the other couch with Alex.

Peter stretched. "Hey, you… There's some dessert in the kitchen if you want it."

Kat's eyes lit up. "Ben and Jerry's?"

"In the freezer. We got a bunch of different flavors, so bring them all out. We can just eat from the cartons and save dishes."

Alex followed her into the kitchen. "I'll get spoons."

Kat juggled eight pints of ice cream back into the sunroom. Dumping them on the coffee table, she kissed both Peter and Luke on the cheek. "Thank you," she said, "you got my favorite."

Peter tugged her ponytail. "We had them hand-pack a pint for you."

"You are *so* good to me."

Peter rolled his eyes at Alex, who was clearly amused by Kat's enthusiasm. "She really likes ice cream, and *really* likes White Russian."

"Wow, I guess so." He raised an eyebrow at Kat. "Remind me never to sneak a spoonful; you look like you'd hurt me." Taking a pint of New York Super Fudge Chunk, Alex sat on the other couch next to Kat, who was impatiently rolling the pint between her hands, trying to warm it enough to prevent a bent spoon.

Peter looked at Kat. "Hey, Jess called earlier today, while you were sleeping."

Kat immediately sat up, visibly interested. "She did? Why?" She looked stricken. "Shit, I should have called to tell her I was back. Was she mad?"

"No, she just called because she's coming to the shore on Monday after everyone leaves. She's bringing the kids down, and we're going to watch them for a couple days so they can have a little time alone. We figured we'd stay at the shore with them."

Kat's face lit up. "Oh, my god, I've missed the kids so much; I can't wait to see them. I can stay for a day or two for that."

Peter nodded, happy with her reaction. "Originally, Luke and I had planned on staying there for the rest of the week as a mini-vacation." He turned toward Alex. "Alex, how long can you stay? Do you want to stay at the shore for a couple days after the wedding? If you prefer, you can come back here. The house will be empty."

Alex checked his ice cream, which was still rock hard. "The shore sounds great."

Peter grinned. "Cool."

Happily eating her ice cream, Kat suddenly sat forward. "Luke, I almost forgot. I brought you a present."

This obviously caught Luke off guard. "You did?" His eyes widened. "Please tell me it's what I think it is."

"We'll see. It's on my bed, let me go get it."

Kat returned within minutes with a paper-wrapped package. "Here it is, and yes, it's what you wanted. You have to pretend to share it with Pete, but really the *cidra* is for him and this is for you."

Luke looked like a little kid as he pulled the paper off to uncover a small painting in a wooden frame. Clearly touched, he admired the delicate watercolor portrait of Kat sitting on a rock, writing. He held it reverently. "I love it. He captured that lost-in-space look you get when you're writing." He looked up. "And, oh, my god, his skill is growing by leaps and bounds. This will be priceless at some point. And it is so fucking cool that it's a portrait of you. I mean, collectors have Tixi's work, but how many people have a portrait he did of a family member?" He held it so both Alex and Peter could see it. "Alex, Kat is good friends with Tixi Gonzalez, one of the hottest painters in Europe right now."

Peter looked it over appraisingly. "It's gorgeous, Kat. The earlier ones we have are good, but Luke's right, this is going to a new level." He paused. "You'll help us write him a thank you note? Maybe we can send him a gift?"

"Sure, Pete. We can do that this weekend."

Luke looked again at the painting. "He has a new show coming up, doesn't he?"

Kat nodded. "Yeah, next month in Barcelona."

"Are you going?"

"Of course. I was going to ask if you wanted to come over and go with me."

Luke's eyes lit up. "I'd love to. Has the catalog come out yet?"

"No. I think he said it'll be out next week."

"Great, I'll order one right away."

Kat looked at her brother for a moment and then pressed her lips together. "Pete, I need to tell you something, and you have to promise not to flip out."

Peter turned his full attention to his sister. "Why would I flip out?"

"Because..." She cleared her throat and swallowed before continuing. "Because when Luke gets the catalog, and you look at it, you're going to see that several of the pictures in the Barcelona show are of me."

"So?"

Luke started to grin, knowing far more about the artist's work than Peter did. "Tell me you aren't part of his new emphasis."

Kat blushed and could not look Luke in the eye. "I am."

Peter was confused. "What does that mean?"

The sentence came out in a rush. "It means I might be naked in several of the paintings."

Peter's eyes widened. "You're what?"

"I'm naked. I mean, it's not like it was porn or anything. He painted me a couple times from the back, and one partially frontal, and I'm not wearing any clothes."

Peter's voice was dangerously high. "There are going to be naked paintings of you in Barcelona?"

Kat put up a hand to cut him off. "See? I knew you would flip out. Besides, this is art, nothing more."

"Bullshit. You're my baby sister, and men will be gawking at pictures of you without clothes."

"Hey, maybe some women will gawk too," she said, trying to add some levity.

Luke reached over to squeeze Peter's hand. "Calm down."

Peter tried to smile. "Are you guys still, I mean… Is Tixi still married?"

"No, we're not *still*… Of course, he's still married. I told you I was staying with Tixi and Monce last week."

"How does she feel about this?"

Kat rolled her eyes. "Tixi and I want nothing to do with each other that way, and Monce knows that."

Alex sat and listened as Peter narrowed his eyes. "His wife is okay with him painting naked pictures of a woman he dated for a long time?"

Kat's eyes began to glitter in irritation. "Pete, Monce has been my friend for as long as I've known Tixi. What happened in the past has passed. She knew he was painting me, he painted her too, and he's now beginning to play around with self-portraits. Anyway, I just wanted you to know."

Luke tried to lighten the mood. "Well, this will make the trip even more interesting. What does one wear to an opening when you are naked in the paintings?"

Kat snickered, appreciating his effort. "I was thinking of wearing nothing at all, so they will recognize me."

Alex smiled slowly. "Then, if that's the case, I'm going to the show too."

Peter took a deep breath, still agitated but trying to be reasonable. "Okay, I'm glad you told me. I know I'm supposed to be enlightened and all that, but I admit I'm not thrilled."

"Thank you." Kat started to laugh. "Okay, Alex, you have to admit this is a unique evening."

Alex grinned at her, finally seeing a glimpse of the girl from five years ago. "I can honestly say I've never had an evening like this before."

Chapter Four

Alex woke the next morning to find Kat already sipping coffee in the kitchen as she looked through the newspaper. Her smile was rested and genuine. "Good morning. God, you must have had the house to yourself in the mornings."

He chuckled. "Yeah, Peter and Luke haven't exactly been early risers, except yesterday, and that was only because the sweet sounds of garbage day roused them."

She shook her head ruefully. "Well, don't take it personally, they've always been that way."

"And you don't sleep late?"

"Don't I wish. I'm a complete insomniac." She looked guilty. "Shit, sorry about my manners. Would you like some coffee?"

He placed his hand on her arm. "Kat, don't worry about it. I'm perfectly comfortable here. So much so that I think the guest treatment went by the wayside long ago," he laughed. "But yes, I'd love a cup."

As she handed him a mug, he smiled. "Are you ready for the shore?"

"I am." She took a sip.

Peter walked into the kitchen, clearly struggling to wake up. Kat automatically poured him a cup of coffee and handed it to him.

Peter pulled her ponytail. "Good morning, brat. Thanks."

She swatted him. "You're welcome. And stop calling me brat."

Peter grimaced. "Sorry, kid." He poked his sister in the ribs. "We're leaving at two, remember?"

"I know," she said, "I'm ready to go. Frankly, I just kept everything in my bags yesterday, so I can dump them into the car this afternoon. I'm about to get dressed and then run over to Leo's. But I'll be back in plenty of time."

Peter looked confused. "Why are you seeing Leo?"

She sipped her coffee. "He called while I was at the airport. He really wanted to talk; I hate talking to him with distractions. I finally said I'd see him today."

Alex was interested. "Who's Leo?"

Kat rolled her eyes. "My agent. Since I'm rarely in the states, we do most of our business over the phone or email, so a meeting like this is unusual." She turned toward Peter. "It's just us tonight, right? Everyone else comes tomorrow?"

Peter nodded as he took a bite of a muffin. "Yeah, they're coming up late tomorrow."

"Good. That means we can get settled before things get crazy." She took a sip. "What are you doing this morning?"

"Luke is running to the gallery; I'm making sure we're ready here, and Alex has a quick meeting this morning too." He poked his sister. "Hey, how are you getting to Leo's?"

"I'll take a cab or Uber."

Peter motioned toward Alex. "Alex is headed in the same direction. Why don't you two share a ride?"

Kat flushed. "Alex, is that okay with you?"

"Sounds great. I need to leave in about twenty minutes."

"Great," she said, rinsing her mug, "I just need to change. I'll be right back."

Alex went to change as well, taking more care than normal. Fifteen minutes later, he walked into the kitchen and stopped short to stare. Kat had changed into a simple linen sundress, and she was breathtaking in it. Trying to control his growing desire, he took a deep breath. "Wow."

Kat blushed. "Thanks, Alex."

Alex tried to make his voice sound light. "You dress like this for your agent?"

Kat looked uncomfortable. "I wanted to make sure I looked like an adult. You don't think it's too much, do you?"

"Are you kidding," he said. "You're stunning."

Even Peter picked up on the note of desire in Alex's voice. Kat's blood began to surge as she looked at him, despite her attempt to deny the feeling. "Thank you," she said, sure her face was twitching as she worked to maintain a natural smile. "Are you ready?"

"I am."

Sitting in the cab, Alex tried to keep his mind off how much he wanted to kiss the beautiful woman beside him. "What's your meeting about?"

Kat shrugged. "I'm not really sure. I mean, I have a book in final edits, and several articles recently published, but he said this was about a new opportunity or something."

"Damn." He looked embarrassed. "I'm sorry, Kat. I knew you were writing professionally, but I guess I didn't realize how much."

"Why would you? We haven't seen each other in years until now."

She had a point; he stifled his disappointment. "What do you usually write about?"

"The socio-economic and political role of women in Hispanic countries," she said proudly.

Alex blinked, at a loss for words. "Wow. I don't see how I can ask an intelligent question about that."

Kat laughed. "Most people don't. My job is to spark interest about a hidden and powerless population."

Alex was mesmerized by her conviction. "If anyone can do it, you can. What are you doing afterward?"

"I may make a quick shopping trip. I'm not really thrilled with the dress I brought for the wedding."

"How about meeting me for a late breakfast afterward? Or an early lunch?"

Kat looked confused. "I thought you had a meeting to go to."

"I do, but I should be done by around ten. We could meet somewhere and grab a bite. And if you don't have time to shop before that, you could go shopping after."

Kat searched his face. "Are you asking me out?"

Alex sensed the worry in her voice, so he thought before answering. "Maybe," he ventured.

Kat looked into his eyes while hesitation and fear clouded her own. The corner of her lips lifted in a wry smile as her eyes cleared. "If it's a date, then I'm not interested. But if it's as friends, I would love to."

He did not care how they phrased it, as long as he got to spend more time with her. "Fine—just friends."

"Great. When and where?"

Alex was both shocked and delighted that she had accepted so easily. "Well, how about the café in the Citicorp? It's close for both of us."

"Great. I'll meet you there at ten?"

"Sounds good. Give me your phone for a minute."

"Why?' Kat pulled it out of her purse.

Alex quickly punched in several numbers and hit "send". Within seconds, a soft chime was heard from his pocket. "There. My number is the last one dialed, so if you need to call, just hit the send button. That way, if you are delayed or need to find me, you can."

Kat felt a thrill race through her. "Thanks."

The cab pulled up in front of the office building and Kat handed Alex several folded bills.

"What's this for?"

She rolled her eyes. "For the fare."

"I'll take care of it," he said, attempting to put the bills back in her hand.

"No," Kat said, pushing the money his way once more, "you asked me to breakfast, so you'll pay for that, and I'll take care of this."

"I'll take care of both," he asserted.

Kat was exasperated. "Alex, take the money." She tucked the folded bills into his shirt pocket, trying to ignore the warmth of his skin through the fabric. "If you hadn't been around this morning, I still would have paid for my own cab."

Alex smiled and ran his finger lightly down the side of her face. "You win. I'll see you in a bit."

Without thinking about what she was doing, Kat leaned forward and kissed his cheek. "See you then."

Chapter Five

Almost two hours later, as Kat negotiated the crowded sidewalk, she chastised herself for the kiss. Why had she kissed him right after saying it was not a date? Did he realize her confusion?

Approaching the restaurant, she spotted Alex in a booth at the window. She knew she was at least five minutes early, and a small tingle ran up her spine at the thought of him wanting to see her. Stopping to fix her hair in the vestibule, she muttered to herself. "Pull yourself together, Kat. This isn't a date; stop acting like an idiot."

As she reached the table, Alex looked up. "Hi, you're early."

"So are you."

He beamed as she sat down. "I left early to make sure I got here on time. You shouldn't be late for breakfast with a friend."

Kat knew he was baiting her. "That's right."

"Besides, I used the spare minutes to call and make sure Peter didn't need anything while we were out."

"Oh? Does he know we are having breakfast together?" she said, her voice now void of its jovial tone.

"No." His grin was devilish. "I just told him I had made friends with a gorgeous woman, and I asked her to join me for a late breakfast."

Kat rolled her eyes. "He's probably on the phone with Luke right now."

His voice lost its humor, hearing the note of concern in her voice. "Would that bother you?"

"What do you mean?"

Alex struggled for the right words. "Does it bother you that they know we're eating together? Or is it being here with me that bothers you?"

Kat touched his hand gently. "Alex, I wouldn't be here if I didn't want to be." She paused as she chewed on her bottom lip. "It's just that they'll think something is going on between us, and it isn't. We're just friends."

"You keep stressing the word *friends*. Are you trying to convince me, or yourself?" he said in a gentle yet seductive way.

In her heart of hearts, Kat had wondered the same thing. "Oh, never mind. Let's stop talking about it. You promised food, and I'm famished."

Once they ordered, Alex turned his full attention on Kat. "So, how was your meeting?"

She chewed her lip as she decided how much she was willing to disclose. What Leo had proposed was so major, she was not sure she was willing to talk about it with anyone yet.

When she did not answer, Alex looked at her strangely. "Kat, it was a pretty simple question. How was your meeting?"

"It was okay," she said, shifting uncomfortably in her seat. "I mean, it was good."

"And what was the big idea he wanted to talk about?" Alex held up a hand. "Wait, you don't have to tell me if you don't want to."

"No, it's okay." Kat searched for a truthful answer that would not give too much away. "He wanted to talk about the book going to print, and some new ideas about articles. More than anything, he just wanted to make sure we had a shared vision."

"And do you? I know my agent is usually about a million miles ahead of me."

"Yeah, I guess we do have a common view. It's just that I want to write more than anything and I don't always remember to worry about the money part." She shrugged. "I guess it's because I can always survive if…"

Alex knew she was about to say she could live off her inheritance. "Sorry, Kat, I didn't mean to open a sore topic," he said gently.

"You didn't. Anyway," she said, perking up, "my meeting went well. What about yours?"

At that moment, the food arrived, and as they ate, Alex regaled Kat with stories about preparing for his fall recording sessions.

The plates had been cleared when Kat looked at her watch. "Shit, I didn't realize it was so late. I still want to look for a different dress."

"What's wrong with the one you brought?"

"It's not a dress for a wedding on the shore. It's better suited for a city wedding, I'm afraid." Working up her nerve, she swallowed. "Do you want to go with me?"

"What?"

"Shopping, I mean." Kat scrambled to justify her idea. "We're both heading back to the house anyway. Bloomingdales is just around the corner, so we could run in there and I'm sure I could find a dress fairly quickly, and then we could grab a cab home."

As far as Alex was concerned, there was no explanation needed. If she was inviting him to do something, it was as good as done. "Do I get to express my opinion during the selection process, or am I expected to stand by and be quiet?"

Kat giggled. "Your opinion will be most welcome."

Kat flipped through dresses with the barest of glances at each one as Alex slipped aside and pulled a dress from a rack. "Try this one," he said.

"What?" Kat looked at the dress skeptically before waving a hand to dismiss it. "I don't wear pink."

He sighed. "Well, you should. Just try it on. Please?"

Kat reluctantly took the dress and headed to the fitting room. Inside, she looked at her reflection and rolled her eyes. "Why the hell am I trying this on? Because *he* wants me to? Everyone knows I don't wear pink."

His voice floated over the door. "Hey, Kat? If you don't want to try the dress on, don't. But I think it would look fabulous."

"How do you know what size I wear?"

"I took note of the area you were browsing," he said, bordering on exasperation.

Kat could not help her sulky tone. "Fine."

She quickly disrobed, then stood in front of the mirror in her lacy bra and panty set and high heels. Eyeing the dress, she removed her bra, realizing the two would not work together.

Alex's selection was pretty, aside from the deep rose hue, she thought. She slipped it over her head and the fabric slid seductively down her body. The drape of the neckline caressed her breasts; her arms were bare, as was most of her back. It was hard to deny that Alex was right; this color complemented her hair and eyes in a way she would never have imagined. And the style was... well, perfect. It was the perfect dress for the wedding.

Kat stood in front of her reflection, part of her wanting to pretend she had never tried the gown on; it was one she would have passed over without a second glance. Now she had to admit no dress had ever made her look this good.

A deep voice broke her reverie. "Kat, if you don't like it, just be honest, and we'll keep looking."

Kat closed her eyes for a moment and swallowed hard before emerging from the fitting room. Alex leaned against the doorframe, his back to her. She admired the way his broad shoulders stretched the soft blue fabric of his shirt. She cleared her throat.

Alex turned around, and it was in that instant that Kat knew, by the look in his eyes, that her own perception was real. She looked damn good.

Alex let a low whistle escape his lips. "Shit, Kat," he whispered. "I'm speechless."

Kat offered a sheepish smile. "Thanks," she said. Her mind screamed at her to be honest with him. "Thanks for the suggestion. I admit I would never have looked at this, but I really like it."

He moved closer and touched her arm. "You look amazing. Thank you for trying it on."

"Of course, now you can gloat over the fact that you were right," she said, trying to lighten the moment,

"Oh, I will. I plan to tell everyone I'm your personal stylist now."

Kat swatted him on the arm. "Perfect," she said, "that would be just friggin' perfect."

Chapter Six

Peter and Luke were getting ready to leave for the beach when Alex and Kat returned to the townhouse. Kat quickly ran upstairs and came back down dressed in jeans and a black fitted tee.

The bags were stowed into the cargo area of the car with Max. Peter volunteered to drive, and Luke sat in the passenger seat with Kat sitting beside Alex in the back.

Kat found herself getting sleepy as they drove beyond the city. Alex quietly reached over and unbuckled her belt. "Slide over," he whispered, "you can fall asleep on me."

In her mind, Kat knew she should stop giving Alex mixed signals, but she could not stop herself. "Okay," she said, sliding over. She tried to stay awake, but it was not long before she drifted off, her head nestled on his shoulder.

Alex was surprised when Peter turned into a driveway at the shore. "This is the house?"

"Yeah, why?"

"It's huge," he exclaimed. "How the hell did you guys buy this place? It must have cost a fortune."

Peter shook his head and smiled. "Nah. The original house belonged to our grandparents, who bought it when no one wanted a place out here. Then our parents added onto it, and the three of us inherited it. Luke and I use it more than the girls do, so we have kind of taken over."

"They sure as hell have," said Kat. "They've even taken over the master bedroom." Her voice was raspy from her nap, and Alex found it sexy as hell.

Peter chuckled. "Any time you want to move home and start coming here regularly, we would be willing to talk about moving to another room." He glanced back at Alex. "Anyway, we sure as hell couldn't afford to buy it now." He motioned to a small cottage next to the house. "That's part of the property too. Our great-aunt built it as her summer home, and since she was a spinster when she died, she left it to our grandfather. We usually rent it with a year's lease; there's an architect from the city renting it now, but he only comes up occasionally on the weekends."

The house faced the ocean with a full wall of glass. Inside, the main floor had lots of open space, and the soft neutral decor played up the airy atmosphere. A staircase led upstairs, and from the bottom, Alex could see several doors opening onto a center hallway. "Alex, feel free to look around."

Alex wandered up the stairs, finding five bedrooms with unobstructed views of the ocean. One room, clearly the master bedroom, had a private bath. On each side of the master were two bedrooms each connected by shared baths. The staircase then wound up one more floor, and when Alex climbed the stairs, he found a small sitting room with windows in all directions. It was a gorgeous house, warm and light.

On his return to the main floor, he helped unpack groceries. "Where am I sleeping?"

Peter came in from the car with more bags. "Well, Luke and I have the middle bedroom, and Beth and Sasha have another. Josh and Kim will share the bathroom with them. So, I guess you can take the room next to Kat's." He grinned at his sister. "Be warned, she's a bathroom hog. I should know, I had to share that bathroom with her every summer."

Kat threw a package of paper napkins at him. "You schmuck-face! You spent way more time on your hair each morning then than I did."

He tossed the package back. "Yeah, I admit it, baby sister. Anyway, Alex, does that work for you?"

Alex nodded. "Sounds great."

Everyone contributed to meal prep, and soon after dinner, Kat slipped upstairs to watch the waves from her window seat. What was she going to do about the job offer? And what the hell was happening with Alex? Panic swelled inside her, and she fought the urge to hop the next flight to Spain. Life was simpler there. This was all too much; too many people, too many options. *And Alex.*

Kat took a deep breath, trying to quiet her mind. *Alex*. From what could only be called a teenage crush, to now, with everything that happened in between, there was no chance of anything other than a fling, nothing more.

No more screw-ups, she resolved, like kissing him or falling asleep in his arms. And again, what the hell was she going to do with the job offer?

She tiptoed from her room and sat undetected on the top step to watch the three men. Alex was stretched out on a couch. Kat inched herself to the edge of the step to get a better look, and he looked up and winked. Mortified, she ducked out of sight and sat in the darkness for a while. What was he doing to her? Now she was experiencing all sorts of forbidden feelings and acting like a stupid teenager.

Taking a deep breath, she knew she had to go downstairs and pretend like everything was okay.

She walked into the living room and before she knew what was happening, Alex's hand had already snaked around her wrist. "Hey, come sit with me," he said, pulling her toward the couch.

Kat blushed. "I need to check on something in the kitchen."

"What?"

Her mind raced to find a plausible answer. "I need to make sure I set the dishwasher to run later."

"I'll check it in a minute," he said. "Come sit with me." He pulled her onto the couch and turned to look at Peter and Luke. "Does anyone want a beer?"

Three voices answered in unison. "Sure."

Alex jumped up and grabbed beers for all of them. After twisting the top off one, he handed it to Kat and sat down on the couch.

The group talked for hours, just enjoying each other's company. Finally, around midnight, Peter rose to set the security system and then came back to rub Luke's shoulder. "Goodnight, sis. Goodnight, Alex. Sweet dreams."

Luke planted a kiss on Kat's forehead. "See you in the morning, sweetie."

Once the guys were upstairs, Alex turned thoughtfully to Kat. "You're lucky to have Peter and Luke." He smiled. "Then again, they are lucky too."

Finally, a safe topic, she thought. "We are lucky. We have laughed about it a lot because Peter met Luke only because I dragged him to the gallery one day. They used to talk about it being luck, but it wasn't- it was fate." Kat's tone conveyed her envy. "They're a perfect match."

"Did it ever bother you that Peter is gay?"

"No. Peter is Peter," she said, looking intently at Alex. "Do you have any brothers or sisters?"

He shook his head. "No, my mom had several miscarriages before me, so I'm it. It's a shame too because Mom wanted a huge family." He ran his fingers through his hair. "I'm not quite sure why they didn't adopt, but I think owning the restaurant had something to do with it—it's a difficult lifestyle."

"Do they still have a restaurant?"

"Yeah, there's a manager now, but Mom and Dad still go in every day."

Kat suddenly remembered their conversation while making dinner the first time. "And to think I asked if you knew how to cook; you're probably a pro, right?"

He shrugged. "My cooking isn't bad. I'll make you dinner sometime," he said, running his fingertips over her toes. She smiled in response to the shiver he evoked. "So, why were you watching me?"

Kat was genuinely confused. "What do you mean?"

"You were sitting on the stairs watching me," he said playfully.

She tried to collect her thoughts before giving an honest answer. "I don't really know. I guess I was thinking."

"About what?"

"Our friendship."

"There's that *friend* word again. I think you like to hide behind it." He brushed his fingers slowly over her ankle. "This isn't a bad thing, Kat. I won't hurt you."

"What isn't a bad thing? There is no 'thing'," she asserted.

"Bullshit. You can deny it all you want, but something *is* happening between us, and you know it."

She knew he was right, and her voice was laced with panic as she sat up and wrapped her arms around her knees protectively. "Alex, I can't do this. I mean, I really can't. I'm not looking for a romance, I just need a friend-nothing more."

"I am your friend." He stroked her arm, seeing her eyes darken. "I'm just saying you shouldn't rule out something more. I won't hurt you."

"I know, but I'm just here for a few days. If anything was to happen, it would be nothing more than a fling." Kat hesitated, realizing she had just opened the door to this option. "I'm exhausted," she yawned. "I'll think I'll head to bed."

"Me too," he said. "You don't mind me sharing your bathroom, do you?"

"Of course not." She rubbed her eyes tiredly.

Kat gestured to the stairs. "Come on."

Once in his room, Alex quickly changed and realized he had not yet heard Kat in the connecting bathroom. He walked through and knocked on her door.

"Yes?"

"Can I come in?"

"Okay."

Alex opened the door to find her sitting cross-legged on her bed with her laptop. He told himself to disregard the way her breasts were so clearly visible through the black camisole. He instead placed his focus on the small flowers on her pajama bottoms. "I just wanted to see if you needed the bathroom first."

Kat looked up at him, trying to hide her reaction to seeing him in a snug tee and loose drawstring pants. No matter how many times and ways she denied it, she still found him painfully attractive. She wondered what it would be like to share a bed with him. Would he sleep in that shirt? Furthermore, would he sleep in those pants? Maybe he slept in nothing at all. Kat swallowed hard and dug her nails into the comforter, trying to stop her train of thought. "I'm all set," she said. "I'm just adding a bit to this chapter, then I'm going to get some sleep."

"Okay." He moved closer to touch her hair and one curl wound around his finger. "Sweet dreams. If you get cold, I'm right through that door." He leaned over and chastely kissed the top of her head.

Kat turned red. "Goodnight, Alex."

Alex awoke several hours later, feeling something was amiss. He quietly headed into the bathroom for a drink of water. After shutting off the faucet, he turned to go back into his room.

The soft sound from beyond Kat's door was nearly obscured by the sound of the plumbing. Without thinking, he opened her door, expecting to find her sound asleep.

Even in the dark, he could see the bed was empty. He looked around the room and discovered her huddled on the window seat. "Kat, you okay?" he whispered.

She did not turn to face him. "I can't sleep. I'm fine."

"Do you want company?"

"No," she said sharply. "I mean, no thanks," she said, now whispering.

Alex stood helplessly in the doorway, sensing she was upset. "If you want to talk, I'm here."

"Thanks, but I'll be fine. Sorry to wake you." Her tone was cold.

"Sure you don't want company?" he said, confused by her iciness.

"I'm sure. Goodnight, Alex."

As he turned to leave the room, Alex caught sight of a tear on her cheek catching the moonlight. Unaware he was still watching her, Kat's gaze remained fixed as tears trickled down her cheeks. "Kat?"

The sound of his voice made her jump. He sat cautiously beside her on the bench. "Talk to me."

Her eyes were awash with pain and sorrow as she looked at him fully. "Go back to bed," she said. "I'll be fine."

"Are you kidding," he said, "you're in tears. I'm not going to knowingly leave you like this."

"Why do you care?"

"Huh?"

"Just take a hint, Alex, and leave me alone."

"Maybe I can help."

Kat grew angry as her eyes welled with new tears. She knew she could not tell him and damn him for making her want to. No one had prompted her to feel this way in years. "No, you can't," she asserted, "no one can. Just leave me alone," she said tiredly. "Please."

Alex instinctively pulled her into his arms. She tried to resist but when he did not let go, she buried her face in his shirt. Alex rocked her until her tears subsided.

Kat raised swollen, combative eyes. "You should go now," she said.

He grinned, suddenly hopeful that she had let her guard down enough to cry in front of him. "Nope, you're stuck with me. Who knows, maybe you'll learn to like me too."

"I never said I didn't like you. I just don't want to *date* you. I don't want to date anyone; I just want to be left alone." Her voice broke again. "All alone. I just want to be left alone. I can handle things alone."

Whatever it was so close to the surface, Alex fought the urge to keep pushing, hoping to break through to her. But she looked so fragile; he could not be the cause of any additional pain. "Someday I hope that will change. Right now, though, please come to bed."

"I can't."

"What do you mean?"

"I can't sleep." She sounded weary and sad. "I shouldn't have come here. This is too much."

"Why? Talk to me," he said, his voice caressing her. "Tell me why you need to stay in Madrid. You looked so happy and relaxed walking around Manhattan today. Why don't you live here?"

She rested her head on his shoulder, wondering what it would be like to tell him everything. But she knew how revolted he would be. "I can't. I'm sorry, Alex, but I can't tell you."

"Okay." He squeezed her hand. "Well, whatever it is, it can't be as bad as you think."

Oh yes, it was, she thought. She had seen the look people found impossible to hide, even so-called friends. And they had not known it all, just pieces. In her heart, Kat knew she could never tell him. Only her sister, Peter, Luke, Josh, and Mariah knew almost everything. And her parents. *Her parents.* A fresh wave of grief washed over her as she realized anew how much she wished she could see them one more time. *Just once more...* Struggling to hold back tears, she realized she could never, ever tell him. But he was being so kind.

"Maybe," she said, yawning and exhausted from the emotions swirling inside her.

"Ready to sleep now?"

Kat offered a weak smile, silently stood, and took his hand as he led her to the bed, where he smoothed the blankets over her. "Goodnight again, Kat."

"Good night."

Chapter Seven

The sun was already high in the sky when Kat awoke. Moving quickly, she dressed in faded jeans and a black top and headed to the kitchen.

When she found no one there, she poured herself a cup of coffee and walked out onto the porch where the three men were sitting. Alex and Peter were reading the newspaper while Luke worked a crossword puzzle in ink, as always.

Peter was the first to spot her. "Good morning. I wanted to get you up earlier, but Alex wouldn't hear of it. He said you two stayed up late talking, and you needed sleep."

Kat sat down on the step to sip her coffee. She eyed Alex cautiously. "Hi."

"Good morning." His smile was gentle, and Kat instinctively knew he had not mentioned last evening's behavior to anyone. "How'd you sleep?"

Kat felt her face flush. "Fine."

Sitting in the sun, she began to relax. She snuck glances at Alex, and he met her gaze with a warm little smile that made her skin tingle every time.

Finally, she stood up and brushed off the seat of her jeans. "I'm going to see if we have everything we need for dinner."

"Need help?" Alex's voice was hopeful.

"No," she said quickly, frightened by the thought of having to make conversation with him. "I mean, you enjoy the sunshine."

A half hour later, Kat emerged from the house and looked at the men, "Okay, I need to do something physical. Anyone want to go for a walk?" The four of them set out on a three-mile walk along the shore, with Max running freely down the beach.

The long walk tired everyone out, and so the group sat in the sand and watched the waves. Kat sat off to one side, barely saying a word.

Kat's phone chirped as they walked back into the kitchen. She glanced at the caller ID. "Hey, Josh."

His voice was subdued. "Hey."

Kat's voice turned sharp. "What's wrong?"

"How do you know something's wrong?"

"I know your voice. What's the matter?"

Josh swallowed. "I had to go to Tiffany today."

"Okay, get to the point. You're scaring me." The three men in the kitchen all turned to watch her, unsure of what was happening. Alex fought the urge to swipe the phone away before Josh could upset her more.

"Well, as I was paying, I heard my name called. When I turned around..."

"What? Who was it?"

"It was Nate," he said. "I talked to him just a few minutes ago and he says he's here for the wedding."

Kat closed her eyes as panic hit her. "You're kidding, right?"

"Shit, Kat, I wish I was, but it's true. I almost keeled over when I saw him. He was picking up a gift, then heading straight out there."

Kat steeled herself by pursing her lips and drawing a deep breath through her nose. It was a weak attempt to keep the little white panic dots from clouding her vision, so she sat on a stool before her knees gave out.

Josh waited for her response. "You okay?" he called through the phone.

Kat shook her head. "Yeah, I'm fine," she croaked. "I have to go." She hung up, cutting off any reply Josh could offer, and buried her face in her hands.

"What was that all about?" said Peter.

Kat's face was ghostly pale, causing her freckles to appear garish. "Nothing. I'll be fine, Pete."

Peter pulled a chair up next to her. "What the hell is going on, Kat?"

She looked at her brother and sniffed as tears pooled in her eyes. "Nate will be at the wedding."

As Alex watched on, the shock of Kat's words hit Peter. His look of disbelief was complete. "What? Nate is coming to the wedding? How the fuck did that happen?"

Kat jumped up, nearly knocking her chair over in haste. "I have to get some air."

Peter shot up and grabbed her hand. "I'll go with you."

She freed her hand from his grasp and turned toward the door. "No. You can't. I need to be alone for a couple minutes."

Peter started to argue but Luke put a quieting hand on his arm. His tone was gentle but firm. "Alright but call us if you want company. I'll keep Pete here; we'll start lunch or something."

"Thanks, Luke." Kat rushed out of the house, leaving the screen door to bang shut behind her.

Peter turned on Luke, anger clear on his face and in his voice. "She shouldn't be alone right now," he exclaimed. "Why didn't you let me go with her?"

Luke's voice was certain. "She *needs* to be alone for a minute. This shocked the shit out of her, and the last thing she needs is for you to be all puffed up in anger. She needs to breathe for a minute and figure out what she's going to do. Period."

Knowing he was right, Peter sat in sullen silence until Alex cleared his throat. "Somebody want to tell me what's going on?"

Luke sighed, tired of all the secrecy. "Well, the short version is that Nate and Kat dated for a while in college, and toward the end of her senior year, he …" His voice faltered as he tried to find the words.

"The sonofabitch totally fucked her over," Peter cut in.

Alex tried to imagine what Nate could have done to illicit such a reaction from even-tempered Peter. "What did he do?"

Peter wanted to tell Alex the whole story, but Luke interceded one more time. "Alex, we're not trying to hide anything from you, but it wouldn't be right for us to tell you. Only Kat can do that when, and if, she feels ready."

Just then, Kat entered the kitchen. She was still pale but seemed calm. "I'm sorry, guys. I overreacted." Her voice was falsely bright. "I mean, it doesn't matter if he's here or not, right? That was a long time ago, and I'm here for 'Riah, nothing more."

Peter looked at her carefully, trying to gauge how much of an act she was putting on. "Are you sure?"

"I'm sure. Anyway, I don't feel like making lunch," she said. "Let's go into town."

Alex watched with guarded concern as Kat picked at her salad. After lunch, she looked at Peter. "You said you need to go for a final fitting, right?"

"Yeah. I need to be there at two. Luke's going with me—he says I have no idea what I'm doing. I'll drop you at the house first if you want."

She shook her head. "No. I need a few things and a walk will do me good." She looked at Alex for a moment, unsure of her feelings. "You want to walk back with me?" she asked him.

Was she volunteering to spend time with him? Alex tried to hide his delight. "Sure."

They wandered through several shops, Kat barely saying a word. At one point, Alex took her hand, and she looked at him in surprise. He expected her to pull away, but instead, she stopped in the middle of the sidewalk. "You know I'm messed up right now, right?"

He shook his head. "I don't think you're messed up. I think you got walloped by some shocking news this morning."

She reached out to brush a small leaf from his hair, her hand brushing the side of his face. "C'mon," she said as she pulled him toward a bench. Once they were seated, she looked him in the eye. "Yeah, this morning threw me for a loop, but frankly, that's just the tip of the iceberg as to how fucked up I am. All my 'I'm fine' comments aside, I know I'm a mess. I already told you, I don't date anymore. I'm no good at relationships and I'm okay with that. I don't want to lead you on or anything."

He grinned. "Would I like to ask you out? Hell, yes. But I realize we're on a mini vacation, in an odd situation, and you live half a world away. Besides, there's obviously a lot about you I don't know." He touched her face. "I'd be lying if I said I wasn't interested in seeing where things could go."

Kat tried to ignore her body's response to his touch. "And what if it doesn't go anywhere?"

"Then no harm, no foul."

That sounded too relaxed. "You're not going to push?"

"I won't push. But you can't blame a guy for wanting to."

"Okay. Just as long as we understand each other."

Five minutes later, they were shopping for sunscreen in the drugstore. Alex wandered off in search of gum and it was not long before Kat appeared next to him, her cheeks flushed, her eyes glittering. "What's the matter?" he said.

"I need a favor, right now," she said, taking his hand.

Whatever it was, she had touched him first, he thought. "Anything."

She tried to keep her voice light. "You may regret saying that."

"What do you need?"

"You know how I don't date and all that?"

"Yeah, we literally just talked about it."

"Right. There's no time to explain but I really need you to pretend you're my boyfriend, lover, whatever."

"Huh?"

"We're going to run into people in about thirty seconds, and that includes Nate. I can't stand having him think I'm a loser, going to the wedding alone." Kat sounded desperate. "Please?"

Alex struggled to follow the conversation. "You need me to pretend to be your lover? Are we talking just for right now, or through the wedding stuff?"

Kat's eyes darted nervously. "I guess through the wedding stuff. They're all going to be there, so I can't very well have a drugstore lover, then be alone at the wedding."

This could be fun, he thought. "Okay, on one condition."

Time was running out and Kat was getting flustered. "What?"

"After the wedding is over, you go on a real date with me."

He was asking her out *now*? "Deal." She took a deep breath. "Now, I'm going to walk down the next row, and I need you to come down the aisle, acting all lovey-dovey."

"My pleasure."

As she walked away, Alex fought the urge to tell her it would not be an act.

Kat turned into the next aisle, feigning concentration in the row of hair products. As she examined the bottles, she moved closer to the familiar figure in front of the shampoos. For a moment, her mind conjured up the countless times she had run her fingers through his hair, or kissed his lips, or felt his arms around her. Anger over his betrayal sparred with the mournful loss of a young love.

She suddenly felt old and sad but knew she had to go through with this. Out of the corner of her eye, she watched Alex move to the end of the aisle, keeping his eyes on her. He winked, and Kat fought the urge to giggle. At that moment, she picked up a bottle of gel and turned away from Alex, knowing instinctively that he would be at her side when she needed him. Putting a bright smile on her face, she feigned surprise. "Nate!"

Nate looked shocked. "Kat." He swallowed. "What are you doing here?"

"I could ask you the same thing."

Alex started down the aisle, amused by her.

"I'm here for Mariah's wedding, of course. What about you?"

Just then, a warm hand settled on her waist and Alex moved to stand behind her. Kat felt her body respond to his touch. His voice was soothing as he pointedly ignored the man standing before them. "Find what you were looking for, babe?"

Kat looked up at him adoringly. "I did." She turned in an offhanded way. "Oh, Nate. This is Alex. Alex, Nate and I went to college together."

Alex extended his hand. "Nice to meet you. I assume you're headed to the wedding then too?"

"Uh, yes." In all the time Kat had known Nate, she had never seen him at a loss for words, even when he had sold her out. "Nice to meet you too. Anyway, Kat…" He stared at her. "You look great."

"Thanks. So, we'll see you at the wedding? I'm sure we'll have time to catch up then."

While Nate tried to formulate a response, Alex figured they had better get away. With a sure arm around her shoulders, Alex said, "We should head back, love. After all, we have the house all to ourselves."

Her smile said it all, and Nate watched on as Kat took Alex's hand. "We do, don't we?" she giggled. "See you around, Nate."

After leaving the drugstore, the two of them strolled down the sidewalk in silence. Once they had moved out of earshot, Kat said, "Thank you."

"For what?"

"For doing that. I know I sprang it on you."

Alex stopped, and before Kat realized what he was doing, he had pulled her into his arms. "Let's be clear, sweetheart, playing your lover was fun." He leaned down to hover his lips over hers. "But I would rather *be* your lover."

Kat wanted to lean forward and touch her lips to his, but she pushed him away with a sigh. "Very funny," she said.

Back at the house, Peter and Luke were starting dinner. "Hey sis, Alex. How was town?"

Kat put her bags on the counter. "Fine." She washed her hands at the sink. "We saw Nate."

"What?" Peter coughed, nearly choking on a carrot.

Kat whacked him on the back and laughed. "We were at the drugstore, and we saw Nate. So," she grinned at Alex, "I asked Alex to act like my boyfriend, and we went over and said hello."

"No shit." He paused. "Wow."

At that moment, the phone rang, and Peter picked it up distractedly, still focusing on what his sister was saying. "Hello?"

"Hey Peter, it's Dan. I need a favor."

Peter was completely confused, still thinking about Kat's news. "Sure, what?"

"Becky and I checked into the hotel earlier today. All they had was a smoking room, and now her allergies are going nuts. Any chance we can stay with you guys?"

Peter's eyes widened. "Oh shit, I'm not sure. I need to see what's going on. Can I call you in a couple minutes?"

When he got off the phone, Peter explained the situation. "But we don't have any room, unless they sleep on the couches."

Luke looked around the kitchen, noticing how Alex was looking at Kat. A glimmer of an idea began. "Kat, you know how you said you and Alex pretended to canoodle at the drugstore?"

"Yeah."

"Do you plan to keep the charade going through the wedding?"

She shrugged. "Yeah. I mean, I asked Alex if he would. I can't very well lie today, and then be at the wedding alone."

Luke tried to keep a devilish grin off his face. "So, Dan and Becky need a place to stay. And if you guys are really playing this romance thing up, wouldn't you be staying in the same room?"

Kat felt panic bloom as she realized what he was suggesting. "I guess so."

"What if Alex moves into your room? If you don't want to share a bed, the couch there pulls out. That way, Becky and Dan can stay in Alex's room."

Luke continued to slice vegetables, keeping his voice neutral. "I'm just saying that if the two of you are going to the wedding as a couple, it's likely you would be sharing a room." He glanced at Alex, knowing he understood the game and was enjoying every second.

"Alex, I think everyone would think it was a bit odd if the two of you are snuggled up at the wedding and then come back here to sleep in separate rooms. I mean, who doesn't get horny at a wedding, right?"

Peter frowned but nodded.

"That seems to make sense," said Alex.

Kat turned to him with narrowed eyes. "Of course, it makes sense to you."

His voice was patient, but his eyes were twinkling. "Kat, you're the one who asked me to play along today. I'm just saying I'll make the sacrifice of sharing a room with you to make it all look legit."

"*Sacrifice?* Sharing a room with me is a sacrifice? Fine, I'll share a fucking room with you." With that, she flounced out of the room and slammed the front door behind her.

Luke laughed and pointed his knife at Alex. "You owe me."

Alex chuckled. "We'll see."

"You better go make peace, or she'll stab you in your sleep."

Alex stepped out onto the porch where Kat was sitting on the bottom step, staring out at the ocean. He sat beside her. "I meant it as a joke."

Kat kept looking at the waves. "I know. I overreacted, but…"

"But, what?"

Her voice was small. "It hurt my feelings for a minute. I couldn't hear that you were picking on me; I only heard that I was asking too much."

Alex put his arm around her. "You should recall we've had conversations about how interested I am in you. Hell, we've talked about it twice just today. Look, I was being a wise-ass, nothing more." Knowing he was taking a chance, he leaned over to kiss her hair. "I'm sorry I hurt your feelings. I only meant to tease you, nothing more."

She leaned against him. "I'm sorry I acted like an idiot again."

"You didn't," he said. "I can see it was too soon for a joke like that."

Kat slid her arms around him and gave him a quick hug. "Thank you."

"My pleasure, roomie."

Chapter Eight

Guests began to arrive around five o'clock that afternoon, and it was not long before the house was full of people, noise, and laughter. After a raucous dinner, Beth, Kim, and Luke decided to watch the news while Sasha and Peter read the newspapers and Dan and Becky opted to take a stroll into town. Kat disappeared outside. About five minutes later, Josh opened the screen door and walked over to sit beside her. "Can we talk about Nate?"

Kat maintained her distant look. "No."

"We need to," he pressed.

"No, we don't."

"Yes, we do." Josh moved to touch her hand, but Kat recoiled and continued to stare out at the water. "C'mon, Ducky," he said, "look at me."

Kat made the most minimal effort to turn her head. "Happy now?"

Josh fought his frustration. "Stop being so childish. We need to talk about this. Nate is here, I think we should be on the same page as far as knowing how to act." He paused. "What can I do to help?"

"You don't need to do anything," she said quietly. "I've already seen him."

His shock was visibly apparent. "What?"

"After you called," she said, "Alex and I went for a walk after lunch, and we ran into Nate at the drugstore."

"And?"

"And nothing. I went over and said hello. I decided it was going to be on my terms, not his. We played the game by exchanging forced pleasantries, then we walked away."

Josh's eyes narrowed. "And how does Alex fit into all of this?"

Kat looked directly at him for the first time. "I don't have the foggiest fucking idea."

"What do you mean?"

"I mean, he hasn't been shy about expressing his interest in me, and then, in a moment of panic, I asked him to pose as my boyfriend at the drugstore, and now with everyone here, we're… well, we're…"

Josh laughed. "You're playing house by sharing a room? I noticed that." He nudged her playfully. "Shit, Ducky, it took me almost six months to get invited to your bedroom."

"Very funny," she said, jabbing him with her elbow.

"Okay, so I need to say this." He put his arm around her and searched her eyes. "Some of us know the whole story and still love you. Hell, maybe we love you even more than before. You need to let it out; grieving is part of the healing process."

The two sat in silence a long time before Kat spoke. "I don't know how to," she said timidly. She took his hand and gripped it tightly. "I don't know how to open that door anymore." Her voice was so small, it was hard to hear her. "I'm afraid of what's behind it. Maybe it would be too much. I don't know if I could handle it."

Josh was shocked; this was more than he ever anticipated her saying. "We would be there for you. You know that, right?"

"I know." Her voice rose defensively. "I've made a pretty good life for myself in Madrid."

This was a touchy subject, and Josh knew he needed to remain calm, but his sarcasm still came through. "So, you keep telling me."

"What do you mean?" Her voice crackled with anger.

"Well, are you living there or hiding out?"

Alex's heart constricted as he waited in the shadows to hear her answer.

"I don't know," she said. "Six weeks ago, I would have said I'm living. I guess I don't know now."

"What's changed?"

Kat sighed. "Did I tell you I interviewed Alex when he was in Madrid for a concert?"

"Yeah."

"We went out for a drink, and he said some things about how I have changed over the years. Needless to say, I got pissed off."

"Let me guess. You stormed out?"

"Bite me," Kat chuckled. "Of course, I stormed out. But I did take his words into consideration, and it made me realize I need to get my life in order."

"And what about Alex?"

"I don't know. He's certainly good looking, I'll give him that."

In the darkness, Alex grinned, pleased to hear she felt *something* for him.

"He makes me laugh. And he puts up with me being a nut case- so far, anyway."

"You're not a nut case."

"Anyway," she said, ignoring his comment, "maybe in another world, in another time, I would be doing everything I could to start something with him." She grew quiet; Alex almost missed her next words. "Like I tried to years ago."

Confused by her last statement, Josh focused on the earlier revelation. "Why not now?"

"I'm too fucked up right now. I need to figure some shit out and get myself out of this funk. Besides, he's Peter's friend, and they work together. I can't screw that up, and let's face it, I totally suck at dating." She squeezed his arm. "I mean, you loved me, and I managed to screw it up."

"You were a great girlfriend, I just loved you too much. Besides, this is now. I think you just need to find the right guy. Who knows, maybe that guy is Alex."

"Maybe." Kat took a deep breath. "Josh, I love you. And I am glad you came out here tonight. I need a break though, so I think I'm going for a walk."

Josh kissed her cheek. "Okay, I'll see you when you get back."

Once Kat was far enough away from the house, Josh walked into the shadows. "Well," he said, "you heard her admit she's interested, so get off your ass and follow her."

"You knew I was here?" said Alex.

"Of course. Now get going."

Alex followed Kat's footsteps in the sand and found her sitting on a dune gazing out at the black ocean. The moon sent slivers of yellow light through the clouds to glisten off the waves as they rolled toward the beach.

"Hi," said Kat.

"Hi," he said, "may I join you?"

"Seems like you already have," she said wearily. "Be my guest." She watched him settle into the sand. "By the way, don't you ever give up?"

He shook his head. "No, why should I?"

She sighed as she pushed her hair out of her eyes. "You're persistent, I have to give you that."

Kat shivered, and Alex put his arm around her. She stiffened, and he felt like kicking himself until she moved to lean against him. Minutes later, he maneuvered around her, so she was sitting in front of him, and he wrapped his arms around her. She was shivering, but whether from cold or fear he could not tell.

"I won't rush you," he whispered, "but I'm not pretending either. I know this is real."

"Okay," she said, sounding tentative.

"Wait, you're not going to make an argument?"

She shook her head. "It doesn't seem to matter if I state my case or not, it does seem to be happening."

"And how do you feel about it?"

"I'm scared out of my mind," she said as her voice caught in her throat. "I'm completely fucked up and I'm heading back across the Atlantic soon. If you're okay with all of that, then-"

"I am okay with that," Alex cut in. "Let's just see what happens." He nuzzled her neck. "You set the rules of engagement."

"Engagement? Well, *that* might be moving a bit fast," she teased. They shared a laugh and Kat leaned back into him, relaxing in his protective warmth. They watched the waves in amicable silence for almost an hour before they realized they were cold and damp from the sea spray.

"C'mon, let's go get warm," Alex suggested.

Alex and Kat held hands as they walked back to the luminescence of a full house. When they got to the steps, she began to pull away, causing Alex to stop. "Kat," he said, "you started this, but if you still want to keep up appearances for this weekend, you need to play it through."

She stood one step above him, putting her at his eye level. "I thought we just decided we weren't pretending."

"What?" he said.

She leaned forward and pressed a brief but sure kiss on his lips. "I thought we agreed we both feel something. This isn't a game, right?"

He cradled her face in his hands. "It's definitely not a game; it never has been, to me."

His response took her breath away. "Okay then." She took his hand and pulled him toward the front door.

Six sets of eyes greeted them inside. Josh wasted no time throwing a set of dice at Kat. "Hurry up," he said, "we want to play Trivial Pursuit and we've been waiting for you. We already established teams: me and Luke, Peter and Beth, Alex and Kim, and dammit, Ducky, you and Sasha."

Having caught the dice neatly, Kat grinned. "C'mon Sash, it shouldn't take long to beat them *again*."

As the game progressed, the group yelled, competed mercilessly, drank copious amounts of wine, and laughed.

Kat and Sasha beat the rest of the competition easily and gloated mercilessly.

It was growing late; everyone quietly shared a nightcap as the couples cuddled on the couches. Alex placed his hand on Kat's and smiled when she entwined her fingers with his.

Some time later, Kat excused herself to go to bed, squeezing Alex's shoulder as she bid the others goodnight.

When Alex got upstairs, she was sitting on her bed. He closed the door and leaned against the dresser. "Hey."

"Hey," she said, chewing her lower lip. "I didn't know which you wanted- the bed, the couch..."

"What do you want?"

"I don't care," she said with a shrug. She stood up to look out the window. "This is silly, don't you think? I mean, we should be able to sleep in the same bed, right?"

"Of course." He stood behind her and placed his hands on her shoulders. "I certainly have no plans to force myself on you." He felt her breath catch as he spoke. "I promise."

Kat tried to act unfazed as she turned around to face him. "Okay," she said, "I'm ready to get some sleep if you are."

Once in bed, Kat hugged the edge of the mattress and became aware of just how tense and rigid her body was. She did her best to feign sleep.

After nearly a half hour, Alex whispered. "I know you're awake."

Kat turned over to look at him. "I'm sorry," she said, "it's been a long time since I slept next to someone." Even in the moonlight, Alex could see the blush travel across her cheeks.

"What about Tixi?" he said. "Is that his name?"

"Yeah, that was years ago. We stopped being… intimate more than three years ago." God, this is so uncomfortable, she thought.

"Really? Peter made it sound more recent."

"No," she said, suddenly needing to explain, "Tixi and I have known each other since high school when my parents sent me to Spain for the summer. We were just friends then. When I moved to Spain four years ago, we dated for a bit. It wasn't passionate, if that's what you're thinking. It was more like two friends who occasionally…"

"Scratched an itch?" Alex laughed.

Kat gave him a playful shove, immediately aware of the hair on his chest under her palm. "That's one way to explain it."

"True though, right?"

"True," she giggled. "And not to change the subject, but I'm really bad at sleeping next to anyone. I worry about whether I'm snoring or drooling or stealing all the covers. So, I pretend to fall asleep. Once my 'companion' is asleep, I get up and write."

"How about this," said Alex, "if you snore or take the covers, I'll give you a shove or steal them back. I think I can manage to handle anything you dish out."

"Deal," she laughed. With that, Kat leaned back on her pillows and reached over to take his hand. "Thank you, Alex. Sleep well."

He leaned in closer. "Sweet dreams," he said, leaving her with a gentle kiss on the tip of her nose.

Chapter Nine

Kat awoke the next morning to find she was completely entwined with Alex, her head resting on his chest. Her stomach clenched as this realization set in, but before she could extricate herself, his voice rumbled beneath her ear. "You sure seem to have conquered those worries you were talking about."

Kat pulled back to look at him. "Huh?"

He grinned mischievously. "Don't worry, you don't snore or drool. You didn't even steal the covers. And better yet, when I moved in closer to get warm, you smelled great."

His words made her blush, but a wide smile crossed her face.

Kat ate a light breakfast and then went for a long run; as she did so, she let her mind think about the job offer and Alex. It seemed too simple to think she could take a job based in Manhattan and somehow manage a relationship with Alex.

As the anxiety began to lick at the back of her brain, she started a second loop, knowing she needed to keep running until the fears took a back seat. What if moving home made the anxiety worse? What if she gave up her life in Madrid only to find she hated the job? What if living with Peter and Luke was not like it used to be? Would she be able to bring a man home and have sex, with her brother under the same roof? Wait, why the hell was she thinking about *sex*?

Kat could feel her heart beating harder at the thought of Alex naked. It had been a long time since a man had this effect on her. Her chest tightened as she realized she was living in a dreamland if she thought things could work out with him. The best she could hope for was a few fun days.

She slowed to a walk, more confused than ever. As she walked down the beach toward the house, she spotted Alex jogging toward her from the opposite end. As he neared, he called out to her. "I wish I had known you were going."

Kat grinned, suddenly hopeful. Instead of worrying about the future, why not just have a good time now? "I would have lapped you," she said.

Alex laughed, thrilled to see her smile. "How about we test your theory tomorrow morning?"

She bounded up the steps. "You're on."

The rest of the morning and early afternoon passed in a blur.

After hanging out and talking music with Peter for a while, Alex went upstairs to find Kat sitting on the window seat, typing away. He stood in the doorway for a moment, admiring the way the sun glinted off her hair.

When he cleared his throat, she looked up in surprise. "Hey," she said, "I didn't hear you come up."

"Would it be fair to say that an elephant could stampede through the room when you're writing, and you wouldn't notice?"

She moved to stretch her back. "If I'm in the groove, that would be a fair assessment. If I'm not, I get bothered by every little sound."

"So, it's going well today?"

She nodded happily. "Last night I worked out a sticky bit, and now I can't type fast enough."

"Then I'll let you be." He turned to leave the room but stopped short. "Kat?"

"Yes?"

"You know how I made you promise to go out with me?"

"Yeah."

"How about tonight? The guys will be at the wedding rehearsal, so I thought you and I could go out to dinner."

Kat grinned. "I'd love to."

Alex felt his entire body relax with her words. "Great, I'll make reservations."

Kat took Max for a long walk in the early evening. She returned to find that Peter and Luke had already left, and everyone else seemed to have gone out as well. With only fifteen minutes to freshen up for her date, she sprinted up the stairs. Entering the bedroom, she found Alex poring over a sheaf of music, mumbling to himself as he made notes. He looked up at her. "Fifteen minutes," he exclaimed.

"I know, I know," she said. "Go downstairs, so I don't have to worry about you seeing me naked."

He leaned back and looked her up and down. "What if I *want* to see you naked?"

"Get out," she said, rolling her eyes, "or I won't be ready on time."

Once she had showered, Kat looked at her watch and ran into the bedroom to slip into a black sundress. She stepped into her favorite black heels and combed her hair, leaving it loose so the waves could cascade down her back. Knowing she had just minutes to spare, she quickly spritzed herself with perfume, applied a bit of mascara, and topped it all off with a pair of gold hoop earrings. She stepped out onto the porch to find Alex waiting in a rocking chair, his feet resting on the railing. He looked casually refined in dark gray slacks and an ivory linen shirt.

"You look great," he said, "And I'm impressed; I expected to wait for at least ten minutes."

"You look nice yourself."

With the small talk out of the way, they suddenly did not know what to say to each other next. From inside the screen door, Max barked, breaking the tension.

Just then, Kat's phone rang from her bag, startling them both. She answered, and Alex stood and listened to a rapid-fire Spanish exchange, an apparent argument. Finally, she reverted to English. "This better be damn good, Manuel. It's Friday night and I have a date." Kat looked at Alex and winked. "Of course, I know who the Shining Path are. Yes, I know they are active again. No, I don't want to fly to Peru, let alone hike around with a bunch of revolutionaries later this month. Why are you in such a rush?" Kat crossed her eyes at Alex.

"Yes, Manuel, I know. Fine, here's what I can do. I need the next two weeks to finish some rewrites. If after that, you still want me to go, I'll consider it. That's the best I can offer right now."

"Sorry, Alex," she said, hanging up the phone.

"Don't worry about it. Are you ready?"

Kat slipped a pashmina over her shoulders. "Ready," she said.

Stepping out onto the sidewalk, they headed toward a restaurant at the base of a lighthouse down the beach. Once there, they were shown to a booth in a secluded alcove where a bottle of red wine was already waiting.

Kat touched his hand. "Ahh, you called ahead."

"Of course."

After ordering, they settled in with their wine, and after taking a sip, Alex looked intently at her. "Okay, tell me *your* version of your life story. I only know bits and pieces from Peter and what I've picked up over the last few days."

Kat smiled, suddenly feeling hopeful. "Full name, Katherine Ann Weston. Twenty-six. I'm named after my great-grandmother Ekaterina. I was scolded in Russian as a child." She rolled her eyes. "We moved to New York when I was eight because Dad sold the family mill and wanted to work as a financial advisor. By the time we moved, Jess was in college, so it was really just me and Pete."

"Was that a good thing?"

She shrugged. "Not good or bad. Jess is great, but she's so much older that we've only grown close over the last few years. I have always been close to Peter."

"Other than art and writing"—he paused— "and running, what do you like to do?"

"Wow, I don't know. A lot of things, I guess. I love to travel…"

"But not fly."

"Correct. I hate flying. I love to hike, ski, and cook."

"And after we met, you went back to school?"

"I did. I graduated that May, and after that, I lived in New York for a while before moving to Spain." She shook her head. "But enough about me… Your turn."

"Well, I'm thirty-two." He grinned. "I like all types of music, although some more than others."

"What got you into music?"

"My mother made me take piano lessons when I was seven. What shocked everyone was that I was good at it and loved it. One day I started writing my own music and building a portfolio."

"How did you form the band?"

"You know Peter and I met in college… He answered an ad I placed on the board. Thirty other drummers auditioned but he was the best. I saw Dave in a little bar in the Village. Will came along when our old bass player got pregnant.

"And the band's name?"

Alex laughed. "Before my first meeting with a recording executive, I called my father. I was so nervous I was actually throwing up; he said I sounded like a basket case. I went into that meeting without a name for the band, but when I was asked, his words must have been echoing in my brain, because I blurted 'Basket Case'. Dad still gets a kick out of it."

"And you obviously still perform solo."

"Yeah. Like Peter, I enjoy doing other things too. The solo tour was something I had thought about for years."

He sipped his wine. "Tell me about your writing. How did you get started?"

Kat thought for a moment. "I always wrote, even as a kid. In college, I needed a piece for an English class, so I spun a short story from a discussion I had with a Basque woman when I was in Spain for my junior year abroad. Ironically, my professor was editing an anthology about women, and she asked if she could include my piece. Of course, I said yes—I knew I wanted to be a writer. And then the publisher called and asked if I wanted to develop it into a book. I'm still astonished by how lucky I have been."

"So, what exactly do you focus on now?"

"I generally write magazine and newspaper pieces, usually covering socio-political movements in Hispanic cultures."

"And why specifically Hispanic women? Why not all women?"

"It is where the opportunities come from, I guess. I'd be happy to write about women from any place, I just haven't really thought about it because I have so much fodder as it is. I also write fiction loosely based on actual events or situations involving strong women."

He thought back to her earlier phone call. "And the piece you were asked about tonight?"

"An article on the women of Peru's Shining Path. They need a woman specifically—I would stay with them for a while to write about the feminine role and lifestyle there."

"Who are the Shining Path? I know I've seen the name, but I know nothing about them."

"They are a far-left guerilla group trying to bring down the Peruvian government."

"Is that considered a dangerous assignment?"

"It could."

"Is your job dangerous a lot?"

"It can be," she said. "It can also mean ordering room service in a lovely hotel in Buenos Aires before a cocktail party."

"Why do you do it?"

"Mainly because these women have the right to be heard. Unfortunately, due to the male-dominated social structure, women are not generally permitted much power. Providing them a platform on which to be heard is imperative. Besides, I admit I enjoy the thrill."

"Do you think you'll take the assignment?"

Kat shook her head. "I don't know."

They wandered down the beach after dinner, holding hands in amicable silence as the brightly lit house came into view, music drifting over the sound of the waves. "We obviously have company," said Alex.

Kat squeezed his hand, knowing they were both struggling with disappointment. "Yeah," she said, "but I had a great time tonight."

He stopped, reaching down to touch her cheek. "Me too," he said. "I don't think either of us realized our evening would end this abruptly."

She rested her head against his chest. "It was nice while it lasted."

"Want to walk a bit more?"

"Sounds great."

They continued beyond the house until Kat realized she was cold, despite her pashmina.

Alex put his arm around her and pulled her close. "I suppose we have to let the world back in," he said.

"We do."

At the house, they quickly joined the festivities as music played on and guests laughed. It was around one o'clock in the morning when Kat quietly excused herself, unbeknownst to all but Alex, to retire for the evening. He knocked on the bedroom door ten minutes later.

"Come in," she said.

He shut the door behind him. "You okay?"

"Yeah," she answered from the window seat. "You know how I said I don't feel like I fit in when I'm here?"

He moved closer and sat beside her. "Yeah?"

"Sometimes it hits me, and I have to get away from everyone. I can't explain it; it's like everyone becomes too loud, and I don't have anything to say."

Alex picked up her hand. "That's okay, it's easy to get overwhelmed by a crowd."

She smiled. "Thanks."

Chapter Ten

The house was crazy as everyone got ready for the wedding the next morning. Alex went upstairs to get dressed and found Kat just coming out of the bathroom. Seeing her in the dress they had selected together, paired with heels, and her hair cascading down her back in a twist, took his breath away. "You look amazing."

Kat blushed. "Thanks."

He came close and took her hand. "No," he said, "I don't think you understand. You are beautiful beyond words every day, but you are absolutely stunning today." He tried to sound playful, "I mean, Mariah may get pissed to have you at the wedding— all eyes will be on you."

Kat met his gaze and was sure she recognized desire in his eyes. "Thank you."

"You are going to stay by my side, right? I don't want anyone to whisk you away."

"I won't go far," she replied. "But you're bound to want to escape from me at some point."

"I don't see that happening."

Kat leaned in and rested her head on his broad chest, finding comfort in their blossoming intimacy. "Thank you," she sighed. "I don't really want to go, you know."

Alex put his arms around her, trying to ignore the effect her perfume was having on him. "Why is that?"

"I'm scared," she whispered.

"Of what?"

"Of seeing people like Nate's parents and not fitting in."

Alex rubbed her back, noting the tension in her muscles, and tried in vain to tamper his body's reaction to touching her bare skin. "I'll be right there with you."

"Promise?"

"I promise."

Over the course of the afternoon, Alex never left Kat's side as they found themselves seated at a reception table with Josh and Kim, and several strangers. After introductions, the group dined on a sumptuous meal, washing each course down with champagne. Throughout the meal, Alex kept Kat entertained, and at times, rested his hand possessively on the back of her chair.

Once all tables were cleared, the band began to play. Alex slid his chair back. "Dance with me?"

Kat hesitated; she was a bit self-conscious at the thought of being close to him after drinking so much champagne. She knew her guard was down. His eyes conveyed warmth and safety, and her anxiety soon evaporated. "Okay, sure," she said.

They danced and danced, never questioning whether they would stay for the next song. Some songs were fast, and the younger couples danced energetically, while others were soft ballads that brought everyone onto the floor.

The band played on, turning to softer, more romantic songs as the stars began to dot the sky. Alex pulled Kat close and whispered, "Why didn't you ever call me after that night at the opera?"

Kat pulled back in order to look up at him. "I did," she said.

He shook his head. "No, you didn't." Somehow, it was suddenly imperative that he hear the truth about this. "I'm not mad, I'm just asking why."

Her voice was certain, but for a moment Alex thought he detected sadness. "Yes, I did," she pressed. "I called you Saturday night, January twenty-first—That was the Saturday after the opera. Will answered, and I left a message. He said you would be back in less than a half-hour and would call me back. You never did." She pulled away from him. "I'll be right back; I need to use the ladies' room."

Shocked by her conviction, down to the exact date, Alex did not know what to do. "You called?"

"I did."

Kat quickly crossed the ballroom, arriving directly at the ladies' room. She stepped into a stall, pulled the door shut, and leaned against the wall as she closed her eyes, willing the tears back. Clenching her fists, she pursed her lips so hard she could feel her teeth beginning to cut into them. She took a few deep breaths and tried to collect herself.

Just as she had set her mind to leave the reception through a back hallway, she heard voices coming toward the restroom. "Have you seen Kat?"

From the safety of her hideaway, Kat recognized Mariah's voice.

"I'm trying to find her to get a photo of us with Josh. You know, with the college banner."

An unrecognizable voice responded, "Shouldn't you include Nate, since he went there too?"

"No," Mariah countered from her stall, "Nate didn't start with us in a freshman hall."

Kat smiled. Leave it to Mariah to find a simple reason to avoid forcing them together. She stepped out to face her best female friend in the world.

Mariah looked at her searchingly. "You okay, Ducky?"

"Of course, why wouldn't I be?"

"Hmm, let's recap. Your friend called you shit-faced drunk, begging you to come home for her wedding, then your ex-motherfucking-asshole-snake-in-the-grass of a boyfriend shows up, not to mention your distaste for crowds and social shit. To top it off, I just found you in a bathroom stall, knowing you have a history of hiding in such places when the mood strikes. *That's* why I asked."

Love so strong it almost took her breath away filled Kat. "I love you, 'Riah. Yup, it's a bit much, but I love you, and I'm here, so let's go do the banner photo thing."

Five minutes later, the three friends sat on the railing with the ocean behind them, holding the banner for the photographer. When done, Mariah handed them each a glass of champagne. "To never-ending friendships."

When Kat located Alex nearly fifteen minutes later, her face was pale, but she smiled. He took her hand. "You okay?"

"Fine. I think I should take a break from dancing for a while though."

"Of course. Do you want to sit on the terrace for a bit?"

"Sure."

As they walked across the crowded room, Peter caught up with them. "Alex, we're almost ready to play."

Alex immediately looked apologetic. "Kat, I forgot that we're going to play for a few minutes. Why don't you come over near the band?"

Kat considered running away and going home, but as she started to make mention of a headache that may cause her to leave, she saw Nate out of the corner of her eye. Shit!

Alex noticed what was about to unfold before him, and without thinking, he pulled Kat close, wrapped his arms around her, and leaned down to whisper, "It's okay. Just stay here with me, and when I'm done, we can head home."

Feeling Nate's eyes on them, Kat took a deep breath, slid her arms around Alex, and leaned into him. "Okay, thanks."

Alex and the band were fifteen minutes into their set when Kat needed some air. She leaned over and touched

Luke's shoulder. "Hey, I think I'm going to step out onto the deck."

He stood up immediately. "I'll go too."

She was touched by his steadfast loyalty. "I'm okay. You listen to the band."

Luke took her hand and pulled her to her feet. "C'mon, kiddo, I'm not letting you go alone, so you either stay here or take me along. No arguing."

After enjoying the view and cooler air from the balcony for a few minutes, Kat leaned on the railing and rubbed her temples. "Headache?" said Luke.

"Yeah. It's been a long day." She smiled. "And let's face it—I'm not usually around so many people."

"I'll get you a water and see if the bartender has aspirin or something."

Kat thought about arguing but decided relief from the pounding pain was too inviting. "That would be great," she said. "I'm going to walk that way for a bit of quiet," she said, motioning to her left.

"Sounds good. I'll be back."

Kat slipped further down the balcony, and once in the shadows, she leaned against the railing again and closed her eyes, willing the throbbing to stop. Why, after all this time, had Alex asked about that phone call? Furthermore, why had she gone into such detail with the exact date she called? Was she subconsciously trying to get him to ask more?

She was so wrapped in her thoughts, she did not notice Nate approaching. "Hi, Kat."

She jumped in surprise, then felt a wave of anger she tried to ignore. "Nate."

"Alone at last," he said. "I was hoping we might get a chance to talk." He stepped closer, his slight misstep and slurred speech indicating he had been celebrating hard.

She tried to sound nonchalant. "Really? What would we have to talk about?"

"Well, we could start with how fucking hot you look tonight. We should spend time together again. What the hell do you see in that guy from your brother's band? No offense to your brother, but you can do so much better than that."

As Nate rambled on, Luke and Josh stepped onto the balcony and realized what was happening. Luke rushed forward but Josh held him back. "Wait," he said, "let's see what she does."

Kat succumbed to the anger she could feel bubbling. "Do you really care who I'm with, Nate?"

He ran his hand down her arm, not noticing when she bristled. "Oh, come on, Kat, let's talk about us. Remember what we had?"

"Nate, you're here with a date," she said, her voice eerily calm.

"Who cares? So are you." He moved his hand back up her arm and reached up to touch her face, but she pulled away. He looked at her strangely. "Oh, I get it. You're still mad about that little misunderstanding."

"Little misunderstanding?"

"Yeah, you know—the mix-up with Reid. You aren't still mad about that, are you? I mean, he's my DKE brother. I had to help him out."

"You *had* to lie?"

"I didn't lie," he said, "I just embellished the truth."

"You said I liked rough sex and that I wanted to be hit."

He shrugged. "So, I guess I lied. Although you did let me tie you up once with your scarf; I just made it sound like more. There was no way I could let Reid get in trouble." He rubbed her arm again and moved closer as if to kiss her. "You understand, don't you, baby? Let's put that behind us. We could get out of here and go have some fun."

Luke started toward them again, but stopped as Josh whispered, "Oh, shit, I know that look on her face. He should back the hell away."

"I understand," Kat said, standing straight and planting her feet.

As Nate looked at her in anticipation, she grasped his arms, took a half-step back, and jammed her knee into his groin with every ounce of strength she had. Shocked pain crossed his face as he groaned and dropped to his knees before rolling over and vomiting off the edge of the balcony. Kat leaned over him, her voice low and threatening, "I understand fully, you fucking sonofabitch. I understand that you sold me out to save a drinking buddy, and if you ever come near me again, I will make your life a living hell."

With that, she turned and walked away to stride confidently by Luke and Josh. "Did you two enjoy yourselves?" she said.

"Sure did," they laughed. Kat held out her hand, took the two pain relievers, and swallowed them.

Returning to her seat at the table, Kat focused on the band, and before long, she felt herself relax and genuinely enjoy herself. When the set ended an hour later, Alex pulled Will aside. "Congrats again."

"Thanks, man, I can't believe she finally married me."

"What do you mean?"

"Shit, I've loved her for years, but she always shot me down." He grinned happily. "But look at us now, huh?"

"Awesome, man, congrats." Alex took a deep breath. "Hey, this may sound stupid, but is there any chance you might remember Peter's sister Kat calling me, like, about five years ago?"

Will's eyes grew wide. "Say what?"

Trying to remain calm, Alex knew he sounded impatient. "I need to know if Kat called looking for me one Saturday night, about five years ago. It would have been in the winter—January, I guess."

Will's eyes narrowed as he tried to recall something so trivial from so long ago. "I don't think so."

"Are you sure?" Why would Kat lie about such a thing?

"Let me think." Slowly, he nodded. "Wait a second... You know, I do remember that. I was eating sushi, and I'd had a big bite of wasabi just as the phone rang. Man, I really needed to wash it down, and she was saying something about just calling to say hi. I think I said you'd ring her back when you got home, but dude, seriously… I needed to get my hands on some milk, you know?" He shrugged, "Didn't I give you the message?"

Alex tried to hide his annoyance. He had spent months wondering why she had never called and fighting the urge to call *her*. It suddenly dawned on him how hard it must have been for her to work up the nerve to call. She had to think he was blowing her off at the time. Why hadn't she ever tried again?

"It's no biggie, Will. I was just wondering." He gave his friend a hug. "I think we're going to head out, but we'll see you at brunch tomorrow."

Alex returned to the table and smiled as Kat looked up at him. "Ready to go?" he said, extending a hand.

She placed her palm in his and wasted no time gathering her things. "Am I ever."

As they left the ballroom, Alex noticed Nate at a corner table, looking sullen and unusually pale.

Mariah had planned every detail of her wedding, including hiring a fleet of cars and drivers for anyone who needed a ride home. Kat gave the driver directions and sank into the back seat next to Alex, her headache finally waning.

They rode in silence back to the house, and once they arrived, Kat stopped to immediately slip off her heels. Without them, Alex towered over her. He smoothed a curl back from her temple. "How about a glass of wine?" he said. "We could sit on the porch, or in here."

She smiled broadly. "At this point, I might take several glasses of wine. Let's sit on the porch so we can listen to the waves."

Kat pulled an afghan off a couch to wrap around her shoulders and the two of them settled into Adirondack chairs facing the ocean. Alex opened a bottle of Merlot and poured two glasses. "I know how much you didn't want to go," he said, raising his glass, "but you did it. Congratulations."

She sighed heavily. "Thanks," she said, clinking her glass against his. "I'm so glad it's over. Thanks for escorting me, and for keeping me company, of course." She looked down nervously. "I had a really good time with you."

He reached over and squeezed her hand, "Me too."

The two of them sat watching the waves, talking occasionally, and without fully realizing it, continuing to hold hands. The bottle of wine was almost empty when Peter and Luke got home. As the two men got out of the car, Peter noticed the couple sitting on the porch. His voice rang through the darkness with glee. "You kneed the son of a bitch in the balls, making him puke? That is awesome," he exclaimed.

"Geez, Luke, thanks for keeping it under wraps."

Luke leaned down to kiss the top of her head. "Hey, at least I waited until we got in the car," he chuckled. "Besides, he knew something was up. Nate seemed to have trouble walking."

Peter came up the steps and opened his arms to his sister. Laughing, she jumped up and hugged him tightly. "Wish I could have seen it," he said, kissing her hair.

She nodded. "You would have enjoyed it. I don't know what came over me."

Luke squeezed her hand. "Josh predicted the whole thing; he knew exactly what you were going to do. It was awesome."

Alex looked up at the two men from his chair before turning his gaze to Kat, who had resumed her position, feet tucked under her. "What's all this about?"

Kat shrugged and smirked, and for a moment, Alex caught another glimpse of the girl he had known five years ago. "It's nothing to be concerned about. Nate came on to me-"

"He hit on you?" Alex blurted. "That asshole knew you were with someone."

Kat reached over to squeeze his hand, oblivious to the interested looks Peter and Luke were displaying. "Yeah, he came on to me, but I declined his invitation by rearranging his genitals."

Chapter Eleven

The rest of the weekend passed in a blur, and the group closed it out with a Sunday night bonfire on the beach. Alex watched Kat in the glow of the firelight, the flames reflecting off the old sweatshirt she wore, just hinting at the curves that lay beneath the heavy fabric. Alex moved closer and put his arm around her. Kat smiled tentatively before resting her head on his shoulder.

He traced the silver ring on her middle finger, rubbing his finger over the piece of onyx. "That's an interesting piece. Where did you get it?"

"I bought it years ago in Spain."

Detecting an intensity in her voice, he wound his fingers through hers. "Does it have any special significance?"

"I bought it because it made me feel invincible." She looked down and thoughtfully twisted the ring around her finger. "It still does."

"How so?"

"It's kind of a long story."

Alex looked around at the other couples deep in their own conversations. He stood up and pulled her to her feet. "We've got time, let's go over to the dunes."

Kat followed him to where they could sit by themselves. Alex sat on the hill, indicating she should sit in front of him. He wrapped his arms around her. "Okay, now tell me about the ring."

Kat leaned back, relishing the warmth of his arms, despite the warnings of her rational mind. "My parents sent me to summer school in Spain when I was sixteen."

"That's pretty young to be so far away on your own."

She nodded. "They said it was to teach me Spanish, but I know it was meant to get me out of my social circle."

"Why?"

"Let's just say my friends valued partying."

Alex wanted to know everything about her. "Were you partying with them?"

"No, that's the funny part. My parents were worried, but I hung out with those kids because they were into art and theater; they didn't think I was weird for carrying my writing journal around."

"So, it was guilt by association."

"Yeah. They thought a change would be good, and I knew I wanted to study Spanish in college, so I was okay with going."

"And the friendships? Did they stay intact when you returned?"

Kat shook her head. "No, they had moved on by the time I got back, which was fine; I had stopped caring if people thought I was weird."

"I see."

"The beginning of that summer was surreal. I was going with a school program for the summer. You know, live with a family, take classes, that sort of thing. So, anyway, we got to Madrid to find the airport had been bombed."

"*Bombed*?"

"Yeah," she nodded, "the Basques had bombed it just about the time we took off, so we had to land away from the airport and walk all the way to the part that was still standing."

Alex hugged her. "What an experience, when you were only sixteen."

"We got on buses to drive to the city on the northern coast where we would be living. Everyone was so nervous; the air smelled metallic and it made my tongue feel funny."

Her voice grew distant as she relived the memories.

"We arrived at the school hours later. I remember the sunset shimmering on the ocean; it struck me because the ocean was on the opposite side, compared to what I was used to. When the buses pulled up, there was a crowd waiting, with a couple standing off to one side. The man was tall with black hair shellacked into an Elvis-style wave, and he wore an oversized Confederate flag belt buckle and a studded leather vest. The woman next to him wore a floor-length black and purple paisley coat.

They were awe-inspiring—a cross between the Dukes of Hazard and the Munsters."

"Let me guess. that was your host family." He sounded amused.

"You got it. My stomach was rolling as I approached them."

"You must have been terrified."

"I was so scared, I couldn't breathe. It was funny, in a way, because when I was little, I needed an asthma inhaler but outgrew it. I really felt like I needed it again that day," she chuckled.

"Everyone else left with nice, normal looking families, and I was left living with Elvis and Morticia in a small apartment. The only word I really understood that first night was *plátano*. I was so thrilled to understand anything, and I ended up saying I *really* liked bananas. Which I don't. But to this day, they buy bananas for me when I visit, and I eat them."

"They wanted to make you happy."

"Yeah." She paused as she thought back, "I cried when I went to bed that night; I was already homesick. Once I cried it out, I began to look around, realizing I was in the daughter's bed while she slept on the couch." Kat's voice caught in her throat as she continued, "I was so upset. It was only a two-bedroom flat, and Ana had sacrificed her room for me. I tried to convince her to move back into her room, but she insisted."

Alex rubbed her arms. "That was her choice."

"I know, but I felt guilty about it. Anyway, on my second day, Ana invited me to go out, and she did my hair and makeup and chose an outfit for me that I would never have thought to put together. I looked completely different by the time she was done with me."

"How so?"

"She chose a black miniskirt from her closet and paired it with a red silk pajama shirt I had found at a thrift shop in the Village. It was all topped off by a pair of strappy sandals."

"Damn, you must have looked incredible," he said, picturing her in such an outfit.

"It was certainly a change of pace. Remember, I was the baby in a family of conservatives."

"How did you feel?"

"Like I had a split personality," she laughed. "Part of me wanted to hide under the bed because I had been such a sulky little bitch who cried over scratchy towels while Ana had given up what little privacy she had. Looking in the mirror that day, I realized I could be anyone I wanted."

"And?"

"Javi, the guy with the Elvis-do, was Ana's boyfriend. They introduced me to their friends, and we went to a fair outside the city where a huge Ferris wheel glittered, and loud music blared. I was so overwhelmed. Everyone was speaking Spanish a mile a minute, and I was lost. Luckily, Tixi was without a date, so he kept me company."

"Tixi, the artist?"

"Yes. Anyway, that night at the fair, Tixi taught me some common words and gestures, which helped. Around two in the morning, he offered to share his cigarette. Needless to say, I nearly choked to death, having never smoked before—no one in my family did any such thing. Tixi thought it was hysterical, and thus, a great friendship was borne. Sitting at the top of the Ferris wheel made me feel powerful and free. That was one of the most profound moments of my life. I guess you could say that was when I became my own person."

"And he helped you." Alex tried to keep his jealousy in check but struggled with the idea of this man being so important to her that she posed nude for him.

Kat eyed him quizzically to gauge his reaction. "I guess you could say that."

That seemed too simplistic. "Okay."

"So, I woke up with a purpose the next morning, and I set out to explore. I walked into a store, picked out this ring, and carried on the conversation needed for the transaction. When I look down and see this ring now, it's a personal reminder of my independence and how it all began."

Alex stroked her hand. "Wow, that's a pretty powerful ring."

"You asked," she shrugged.

He squeezed her shoulder. "Well, thank you for sharing the story; I love it when you feel comfortable enough to talk to me. You're quite an interesting woman."

He leaned close to whisper into her ear, the heat of his breath making her tingle. "And a beautiful, sexy, bewitching one, at that."

Chapter Twelve

As houseguests departed the next morning, everyone remaining pitched in to clean up the house. Kat was carrying towels and bedding to the laundry room when she passed Alex on the stairs. "We need to talk about something," she said.

"About what?"

"My niece and nephew are arriving soon, and… Well, I'm afraid they might assume you're my boyfriend." She tried willing herself not to blush, but her face turned crimson.

"Well, *am* I your boyfriend?" he teased.

Kat remained stoic. "I'm not sure what you are. What *we* are, I mean. But kids are naturally curious, and they are going to want to know."

"Okay, so if they ask, we could say we are boyfriend-girlfriend… I mean, for their purposes, right?"

"That would work."

Alex looked at her, seeing how important this seemed. "Would it be easier for you if we weren't sharing a room?"

"Oh, shit, they'll think we're sleeping together. How did I not think of that?"

He dropped the linens in order to take her in his arms. "Stop being sorry. It's not a problem."

Kat reached up to put her palms on either side of his face and kissed him. "Thank you."

"You're welcome. Now let's go move me out of your room."

It was early afternoon when a gray Volvo wagon pulled into the driveway. Kat was standing at the kitchen sink when she heard the crunching of tires on gravel, and Alex watched in amusement as she burst out the door.

"Aunt Kat," a young girl's voice rang out.

"Aunt Kitty-kat," called another young voice, just as excited.

Moments later, Kat returned to the kitchen with a little towhead boy on her hip while she held the hand of a blonde girl, both kids talking to her at once. Behind them followed an amused couple, the woman bearing such a striking resemblance to Kat that Alex immediately knew it to be her sister Jess.

Kat quickly introduced Alex to her niece Lily, nephew Noah, sister Jess and brother-in-law Brian. Luke and Peter returned from walking the dog just as introductions were finished.

That afternoon, the adults sat on the porch while Kat played in the sand with the children. Just before dinner, Kat's phone rang on the table next to Peter. He shouted down to his sister, "Kat, it's Leo."

Kat quickly stood and brushed the sand off her legs before coming up the stairs to take the phone. "I'll take it inside."

Peter looked at her quizzically. "Okay."

Kat moved as far from the porch as she could. "Hi, Leo."

"Kat. I thought I'd hear from you by now. Have you decided?"

"Leo, I told you I need a few days."

"It's already been a couple days," he pressed.

She sighed under the pressure. "Give me forty-eight hours, okay?"

"Forty-eight, but not more. You'll call me?"

"Yes," she said, "I'll call you."

"I look forward to hearing from you. You really should do this, you know."

"Bye, Leo."

When Kat came into the kitchen, everyone was there, and all eyes were on her. She rolled her eyes. "You can all relax, he's just my agent, for God's sake. We talk, that's it."

Her sister eyed her suspiciously. "Bullshit."

Kat shook her head. "It was just a typical check-in."

After dinner, Kat took the children upstairs for a bedtime story before tucking them in across the hall from her room. Returning downstairs, she sat down next to Alex, and her sister watched with great interest as they intertwined fingers. Jess sat quietly listening to Brian,

Luke, and Peter chatting until she could not resist any longer. "Okay, spill it, Kat. Alex, what's the deal?"

Kat looked at her sister and then at Luke, who was checking his watch and laughing. "Time?"

"Eight fifty-nine."

Kat pumped her arm. "Yes! I win."

Jess looked annoyed. "What's going on?"

"I bet Luke that you would ask about Alex and me before nine tonight. I won by one minute. Luke said it would take you until at least nine-thirty with several glasses of wine."

"Well done," Jess laughed. "So, tell me…"

Kat looked at Alex. "I head back to Madrid in a couple days, but we decided to have a fling while we're both here."

"You said fling," Alex corrected, "not me."

Kat's eyes widened, oblivious to the others now watching on with great interest. "We agreed we both understood the parameters."

"I agreed you had your parameters. As I recall, I told you we could take it as it came, remember?"

Jess, realizing she might have started something, tried to regroup. "Okay, fling, not-fling. Just wondering. So, Luke, since you lost the bet, don't you need to get us all some wine?"

As the conversation moved on to other topics, Kat sat in silence. She maintained her hold on Alex's hand but she appeared to withdraw from the group. Finally, around midnight, she stood up. "Good night, all. See you in the morning."

Kat came out of the bathroom to find Alex sitting on the window seat in her room. He looked at her but averted his eyes from the taut nipples that pressed against the fabric of her tank top. "We need to talk," he said.

"No, we don't," she said, focusing her attention on turning down the bedsheets.

"Yes, we do, and you know it."

She shook her head without looking at him. "I can't do this right now. Please, Alex, not now."

"No, Kat, not this time. I'm doing everything I can to make you feel safe, but I have to say I'm not okay with a fling." He paused, hoping she would turn to face him. "Dammit, Kat, would you look at me?"

Kat took a deep breath and turned to face him; he was shocked to see tears in her eyes. He took two quick steps to wrap her in his arms. "Don't cry. Look, I'm sorry. It'll be okay."

She leaned against him, her tears now falling. "No, it won't be okay. This can only be a fling, Alex. It ends when I leave, no matter how we feel. It has to."

"Why, Kat? Why does it have to end?"

She wrapped her arms around him, willing herself to stay the course. "Because it does. No matter what, there are things you don't know about me— things that will keep us apart. Please, Alex, I wish it were different."

As frustrated as he was, Alex focused on to what Kat was not saying—she was not denying she wanted to be with him. He sighed and rubbed her back without saying a word. He sensed her despair moving to desire. "Alex, don't."

He smiled, his hands stroking her back sensually. "Don't what?"

"Don't try to change my mind. That's not fair."

His body reacted immediately to her words. "You want me?"

"Of course, I do. But this isn't going to work between us." Mustering all her willpower, she pulled back. "Good night."

Alex wanted to shout in frustration. "Seriously, good night?"

"Seriously," she said with finality.

Alex knew enough to leave the room before he said something he would regret. In his heart, he knew she was not rejecting him per se, but rather the idea of them being anything more than a fling. "Good night," he said.

Alex stood at the window of his room, watching the waves, trying to calm his mind. What the hell happened to her all those years ago? What could be so bad? Was there a way he could get through to her?

The creak of a floorboard prompted him to turn, and Kat quickly padded across the room to stand in front of him. "Don't say a word," she said, "not a word." With that, she stood on her tiptoes and kissed him with all her pent-up desire.

Alex felt himself immediately respond and he pulled her into his arms hungrily. The kiss deepened within seconds as tongues teased each other and hands roamed.

Minutes later, Kat pulled back and looked up at him, her face flushed. "That's how I feel. I don't know what to do with these feelings, but no, I don't think I want a fling either."

Alex smiled. "Okay, then."

"Okay, then." She bit her lower lip. "So, can I sleep with you? My room feels pretty empty."

"Of course, you can." He leaned down to kiss her. "Same rules, you set the pace?"

"Same rules."

Kat slid out from under the covers just before daybreak as Alex struggled to wake up. "Where are you going?"

She kissed him briefly, fighting the urge to slide back under the covers and kiss him more thoroughly. "The kids will come looking for me soon."

He growled in frustration. "Come here for a second," he said, holding out his arms.

Kat sat down and leaned in. "What?"

Alex kissed her gently. "Good morning," he said. "It's only because I think those kids are great that I am not pitching a fit about you leaving me like this."

"Thank you," she said, "and good morning to you too."

Chapter Thirteen

Jess and Brian left after breakfast, and the rest of the day was spent playing in the sand and surf. Peter and Luke offered to pick up pizza for dinner, and Kat stayed on the porch with the children while Alex set the table. Kat was in the hammock when Noah came over and climbed up to cuddle with her. "Aunt Kitty, I wish you could go to my soccer games. I'm really good. Sometimes I score goals."

"I know you're good, No-no. Mommy sends me videos, remember?"

"But I want you to be there, not just watch videos."

Lily was sitting on the porch, building a skyscraper with LEGO bricks. "Noah, remember, Mommy says to not ask Aunt Kat about coming home."

Kat's stomach clenched. "What do you mean, Lily?"

"Mommy says asking you about moving upsets you, so we shouldn't talk about it."

The idea that her beloved niece and nephew were being coached not to upset her hit Kat like a ton of bricks. Her chest felt tight as she hugged her nephew. "Lily, your mom is just trying to protect me like a good big sister, but you guys can always ask me *anything*. I love you to the moon and back, and nothing will change that."

Noah snuggled in closer, oblivious to her pain. "Good," he said, "I want you to move back and come to my games, and I could come over and have sleepovers."

Lily seemed to decide this was now a safe topic. "Me too," she said, "Mommy doesn't get pedicures, but you do, and my friends all go for pedicures with their moms, so I want you to do stuff like that with me."

"I'd like that too," Kat said, trying to keep her voice from cracking. "Hey, you know what? I think the pizza is here. Go see if you can help Uncle Peter, okay?"

As the kids ran into the house, they also ran into Alex, who was returning to the porch. He looked at Kat, then stopped. "What happened?"

"What do you mean?"

"What happened while I was inside? You're paper white. Is everything okay?"

Kat suddenly felt old and tired as she sat on the edge of the hammock. "No," she said.

"No what?"

She held her hand out to him, and when he reached her, she rested her head on his chest, welcoming the feel of his arms around her. "No, I'm not okay."

"Why not? What happened?"

She sighed. "Noah asked me about moving back to New York, and Lily reminded him that they aren't supposed to ask." Her voice broke, "I'm such a whack job that my own sister has apparently coached her kids on how to handle my triggers."

Alex hugged her. "Oh, baby, you aren't a whack job. She was just trying to protect you."

"She shouldn't have to. The world will tell them soon enough who they can talk to and how they can act; I'm supposed to be someone they can talk to."

"I don't know what to say."

"How about I need to get my shit together."

Alex leaned down and kissed her. After a moment's hesitation, she kissed him back. When he pulled back, he stroked her hair. "Okay. How about you get your shit together. Anything I can do to help?"

Kat looked at him and her eyes filled with tears. "Don't give up on me, even when I tell you to."

Alex was shocked by her answer and brushed her tears away. "I won't, I promise."

Just then, Noah burst through the door. "Dinner!" he called out, "Everyone get washed up for dinner!"

Kat barely said a word all through dinner, but when they were done, she approached her brother. "You good here, Pete? I need to make a few calls."

"Of course. Is everything okay?"

"Yeah," she nodded. "I'm just going upstairs to take care of a few things."

Luke walked by and put his arm around her on the way. "We'll all take the monsters for one last walk so you can have some privacy."

Kat sat in the window seat of her room, looking out at the ocean, and watching Luke and Peter swing Noah between them as they walked, while Alex gave Lily a piggyback ride. It was time for her to decide.

Fifteen minutes later, Kat came downstairs and pulled some cookie dough from the fridge. She was making ice cream sandwiches out of the warm cookies when the group returned.

Within minutes, all were seated at the table, enjoying the treats while ice cream dripped everywhere. Kat turned to Noah as she licked her fingers. "Okay, No-no, so when do you play soccer?"

"Not till kindergarten in the fall," he said through a mouth full of ice cream. "That's when I start real school."

"Oh," said Kat, "so, would it be okay if I came to some of your games? I can't go to all of them, but I can go to some."

Noah was oblivious to the collective interest being piqued around the table while Kat remained focused on her dessert. "Aunt Kat," Lily said matter-of-factly, "you would have to be here a lot to go to Noah's games. Are you coming back for vacation or something?"

Kat lifted her eyes to look directly at her brother, her face flushed with nerves. "Well," she began, "if it's okay with Uncle Peter and Uncle Luke, I was thinking I might move home to live with them again. If that can be arranged, I should be around for some of Noah's games and be able to get pedicures with you."

Peter gasped, nearly choking on his cookie. "What?" he exclaimed.

"I mean, is it okay if I move in with you guys? I don't want to screw up your lives."

Luke and Alex looked on in shock as Peter set his plate aside, still digesting the news. "You're serious about moving home? Holy shit!" He jumped up and lifted her in a bear hug. "Yes!"

Mayhem ensued for the next few minutes as the kids and Peter and Luke hugged and danced around. Kat stood up amid it all to wipe the table down. "Okay, monsters, you need to go in the living room and find something for us to watch, okay?"

The children ran from the room, still giggling and chatting with excitement. Once the kitchen was quiet, Luke looked at Kat. "Now explain the details. What happened since your little tirade last night about moving back to Madrid?"

Kat sighed and sat down. She took Alex's hand and squeezed it. "When I met with Leo last week, it was because *Newsweek* was offering me a fulltime role as their New York based Latin America/Hispanic correspondent. The deal would mean my primary loyalty would be to them, but I could still freelance and continue to write books." She smiled at Alex. "It really hit me today that it's time to come home."

Peter kissed the top of Kat's head. "How about some champagne?"

Kat squeezed Alex's hand again. "Sounds great."

Hours later, everyone turned in for the night. Kat quietly slid into Alex's room and sat on his bed. "We need to talk."

He had been waiting for this opportunity for hours. "That would probably be a good idea," he said from his spot on the window seat.

She rubbed her temples as she searched for the right words. "Here's where I'm at: I just agreed to take a job here, move back, and move in with my brother and Luke. I just turned my life upside down in a matter of minutes."

"Uh-huh."

"And…"

"And what?"

"Shit, Alex, I really like you, and I don't want just a fling. But now I need to make sure I will be doing all this for the right reasons."

"Meaning?"

"I have to go back to Madrid to pack before I move here in a few weeks. And once I'm here, I will need time to settle into my new job and into living with Peter and Luke again."

"Of course." Alex was not sure where she was going with this conversation.

"What I am asking is, would you be okay with us tapping the brakes a bit until you return to the east coast to record in the fall? We could keep in touch by phone or email in the meantime, but maybe we could see where we are at then."

Emotions raced through Alex. He was thrilled to hear her admit she wanted more with him but frustrated at the idea of being apart—It all swirled around in his head. "So, you want to take a break, essentially before we even get started, while you get settled?"

"Yes." She had to admit it had sounded better in her head than when Alex said it.

He stood up and held out his hand. She placed her palm in his, and he pulled her up to take her in his arms. He leaned down to kiss her forehead. "So, I get just a few more days with you, then you walk away, we phone and email for a while, then we plan for a fall reunion. What about dating others?"

Kat felt like someone had punched her, and it showed on her face. Did he *want* to date others? "I don't know," she said.

Alex leaned down and kissed her deeply, becoming painfully aroused as she responded with every bit of the emotion she felt. When the kiss ended, he looked at her tenderly. "I saw your expression; you thought I wanted to be able to date others with no strings attached. That isn't what I was asking." He nibbled on her lip, smiling as she tightened her arms around his neck.

"Let me be clear," he said. "I don't like the idea of putting us on pause. I would much rather go with you, help you pack, and get you back here as soon as possible. I understand your point, but I want you to know I plan on being nothing but monogamous. I'm not waiting to see if my feelings for you change; I will be waiting for you to get settled enough to feel comfortable about me being in your life. I'm not okay with this if it means you plan on seeing anyone else in the meantime."

Kat's relief was clear on her face. "I won't be going out with anyone else," she said. "I just need to get my life in order."

"Okay."

"Okay?"

Alex scooped her into his arms and carried her to the side of the bed, where he gently laid her down. "Okay," he said, "we'll do it your way."

Alex laid down beside her. "A couple more days, then we do the long-distance thing until fall."

"Thank you." Her eyes grew misty. "You know there are still things I can't tell you."

He kissed the tip of her nose. "When, and if, you are ready to tell me, you'll tell me. I can wait, even if you never tell me, as long as you aren't pushing me away."

She wrapped her arms around his neck. "I don't want to push you away anymore. Just give me time, okay?"

"All the time you need."

Chapter Fourteen

Kat was back in New York on Thursday night, organizing her bag while Alex sat on the couch. She looked up and noticed he was watching her with a bemused look. "What? What am I doing now?" she said.

"You've packed and unpacked that same bag three times."

She blushed. "I get so nervous, I need to have my stuff accessible, so I can get it quickly."

"I'd still go with you, you know."

She sat down next to him. "I know. And you know I would like that, but then it would feel like the biggest reason I'm moving home is to be with you."

"And that would be such a horrible thing?"

She touched his face. "No, it wouldn't. We both know you are part of the reason I'm coming home, but I need to feel like the primary reasons are family and work. I'm not ready to turn my personal and professional lives upside down over a relationship that is barely a week old. No offense…"

"None taken," he said. "But remind me how long I have to wait before I'm allowed to call you in Madrid?"

"I promise to call *you* as soon as I get there."

Kat had been back in Madrid for only a few days when Tixi called. "So, you're really moving back to New York?" he said.

"You know I am," she said, "we've talked about this."

"What about the opening?"

Kat silently acknowledged the uncertainty in her friend's voice.

"You said you would attend the opening, but if you leave for New York next week, you'll miss it."

Kat rubbed her forehead, torn between her promise to her friend and getting started on her new life. "You're right," she said, "I *did* promise. I'll be there, just let me figure out the details."

Kat hung up and searched flight options before deciding to call her brother. She smiled when Peter answered the phone, although his voice indicated she was calling too early.

"What?"

"Morning, Pete."

"You okay? What's wrong?"

"Nothing is wrong. I'm just wondering if you and Luke want to meet me in Barcelona for a few days next week. I'll even spring for the flights and hotel," she said, grinning.

"Barcelona, what the hell are you talking about?"

Luke grabbed the phone. "Barcelona, for the opening? Of course, we'll be there," he exclaimed. "You know I would love to go, but Pete would love it too."

Kat and Luke chatted for a few minutes, agreeing that she would make the arrangements and send them the travel itinerary.

After hanging up, she decided a run would help quiet her mind, so she pulled on some running clothes and headed out toward Retiro Park.

Kat returned to the apartment an hour later and found her message light blinking. *Kat, it's Luke. Just a thought, but what about inviting Alex to the opening too? If so, see if you can book us all on the same flight out of New York and we can travel together.*

Kat dialed Luke's cell. "Would that be too much?"

"No," he said, "you know how he feels. Hell, he wanted to help you pack; you're the one who said no. Besides, he might think it's a romantic gesture."

"I guess I could ask, or offer, or whatever. I mean, he may not be free, but at least would feel included." Her eyes widened. "What would I do about hotel rooms?"

"Good Lord, Kat, you sound like a prude. The two of you shared a room at the shore. Just do that again."

Kat leaned back in her chair. "But how long can I keep sharing a room with him without having sex? I mean, what's reasonable?"

"I don't know. That's between you guys. I guess when, or if, he has an issue with it, he'll tell you." Luke paused. "Is there a reason you don't want to sleep with him?"

"Oh, God, no. I really do want to, but you know as well as I do that the past will be an issue at some point, and …"

Luke suddenly realized where she was going with her comment. "And if you get naked, he'll see your tattoo, and then you can't keep it a secret." He took a deep breath. "Kat, listen… Alex is a great guy, and he genuinely likes you. You could tell him, and I'm confident he wouldn't run away."

"Luke, there is no way you know that for sure," she said quietly. "But I do know that if things really are going somewhere, I will have to tell him. I'm just not there yet."

"Or you can just make sure the lights are off when you jump him," said Luke, trying to lighten the conversation.

She laughed. "Hell no, that man is gorgeous. If I'm going to jump him, I want to see him."

"So, you'll invite him?"

"Yeah."

"Awesome. I love you, kiddo."

Kat's eyes brimmed with tears. "I love you too, Luke. Thanks for listening."

Kat sat at her desk with the phone in her hand. Should she call, or email? She wanted to hear his voice but calling would put him on the spot. An email would allow him to think and respond without the pressure. Maybe she should check out flight information, work on hotel rooms, and then send him an email. She sighed, opened her laptop, and started googling. An hour later, she wrote an email.

Good morning— I have an idea, and I wanted to email you so you could think it over. I was wondering if you would like to fly to NY, meet Peter and Luke, and travel with them to Barcelona next weekend for Tixi's gallery opening. I thought we could all stay in Barcelona for a long weekend, see some sights, that sort of thing. Please don't feel pressured. I know it's a big trip for a long weekend, but I wanted to invite you.

Kat knew the email sounded awkward but could not figure out how to fix it. Once she worked up the courage to send it, she got up and grabbed her purse. She turned her phone off and headed to the Prado to lose herself in art.

Two hours later, Kat had to admit she was avoiding her apartment, and her phone, because she was nervous about Alex's response. What if he said no? What if he said *yes*? Was she ready for the sort of commitment that a weekend jet-away across an entire continent insinuated? How long could she continue to expect him to share a bed with no sex? Just thinking about him naked made her heart race. She shook her head and took a deep breath. "Okay, you sent the email… Let's see if he responded yet."

Opening her apartment door, Kat could see the light blinking on her machine. Three short blinks meant three messages. She pulled her phone out of her purse and turned it on; she had voicemails and texts there as well.

She sat at her desk, steeled herself, and hit play. "Hey brat," said Peter, "just want to say I love the Barcelona idea. Can't wait to see you."

The second message was from the owner of the apartment, inviting her to dinner before she moved. Kat started to feel silly about the anxiety she had felt over the lack of a response from Alex when his voice suddenly filled the room. *Hey. Where are you? You send me an email, then disappear? I tried calling, but your phone wasn't on.* He chuckled. *Call me.*

Shit, she thought, he did not give an answer. It looked like she was going to have to talk to him about this after all. She checked the voicemail on her cell. It was Alex again.

Good morning. Just got your email, trying to call you, but your phone is off. Call me.

Kat opened her texts and started to laugh.

If you want to know my answer to your invite, you will have to call and talk to me.

Kat tried calling him and was shocked when it went to voicemail. He had told her to call him, yet now he wasn't answering? "Hey, it's me," she said, trying to keep her voice steady. "I got your messages, so I'm calling you. Tag, you're it. Call me."

Thirty seconds later, her phone rang. He was laughing when she answered. "I was just messing with you," he said. "I knew damn well you were avoiding my calls this morning, so I figured I'd make you leave me a message."

Kat felt herself relax. "That is so mean," she cried.

"Yup." His voice deepened, "Tell me, did you honestly think I would say no? I practically begged to go pack you up in Madrid. Why wouldn't I come to Barcelona?"

When he put it that way, Kat realized how silly she had been. "I know, but I was overthinking, and I convinced myself it was too much to ask."

"I would love to meet you in Barcelona, and, no, you aren't picking up my fare."

"But I can order the ticket along with Peter and Luke's."

"Fine," he said, "and then I'll pay you back."

Kat smiled. "Okay. So, I'll book the tickets in a few minutes, including you flying to New York the day before, and I'll get hotel rooms."

"I will take care of getting to and from New York. You do New York to Barcelona and back. How's that?"

"That works for me."

"As soon as you have the info, let me know, and I will book the rest." His voice got softer, more sensual. "So, you are inviting me to an art opening to see naked portraits of you?"

Kat blushed and was grateful he could not see her face. "Yes, I mean no."

He laughed, and Kat tried to organize her thoughts. "I mean, yes, I am inviting you to the opening. And yes, there are pictures there of me naked. But no, I wasn't specifically inviting you to see *those* particular paintings."

Two hours later, Kat had all international flights booked, as well as two waterfront rooms in a seaside hotel. She then emailed everything to Peter, Luke, and Alex. Sitting at her desk, she–hugged herself happily, then called Alex. "Hey," she said.

"Hey. Are we all booked?"

"We are. The three of you will arrive Thursday afternoon, and I will meet you at the airport. We can relax Friday and Saturday; the opening is Saturday night. I thought we could go to the Sagrada Familia for a concert on Sunday, then you all fly out mid-day on Tuesday. I'll come back here and finish up with my packing, then fly back to New York the following Saturday."

"Do you want me to stay with you so we can fly home together?" he said.

"I would love that," she said longingly, "but I'm not ready for it. It was a really big step for me to invite you to Barcelona, and…"

"It's okay," he said, "I understand. If you change your mind and want me to stay, I would be happy to. Otherwise, seeing you for a few days like this is an unexpected gift." His words caressed her.

"I'm really glad you are coming," she said.

"Me too."

Kat took the train to Barcelona on Wednesday, and that night, she sat alone on the balcony of her hotel room, sipping wine while she watched the lights twinkle on the waterfront. She poured herself more red wine and put her feet on the ottoman as her phone chirped softly beside her. "Hello?"

"I'm sitting at your kitchen table," said Alex, "where are you? Remind me why I'm in New York without you?"

She pictured him there. "I'm sitting on our balcony, drinking wine, watching the water." Maybe the wine made her bolder, she thought. "And just thinking of you. Wishing you were here too."

"I'll be there in less than twenty-four hours." His voice softened, "We probably need to eat dinner with the guys tomorrow night, but how about a nice bottle of wine on that balcony afterward, just the two of us?"

"That sounds perfect."

The next afternoon, Kat was waiting at the gate when she saw the three men walking toward her. Her heart jumped and she felt like a teenager again. Peter reached her first. "I don't care about letting you kiss Alex first. He can wait." Peter picked her up in a hug before putting her down next to Luke.

Luke hugged her quickly. "Thanks for the invite, Kat. So glad we could be here."

Kat turned toward Alex, who was looking at her with a smile, his eyes darkening as he stepped toward her. "My turn?"

"Your turn."

He opened his arms, hugged her close, and then kissed her deeply. "Hi."

"Hi," she said breathlessly.

Peter laughed. "Okay, hotel, shower, beer, dinner… in that order."

Over dinner at a small seafood restaurant near the hotel, the men regaled Kat with stories of their last week.

Watching her brother and Luke, she suddenly realized how excited she was.

Alex squeezed her hand. "What?"

"What, what?" she said.

"You look like you just realized something."

She tipped her head as she looked at him. How did he know? "I did," she said. "I just realized how excited I am to move back to New York."

"Good," he said. "And me?"

How could she deny it? "And you." She paused, seeing his eyes light up. "You know…"

"I know. I know. Parameters, and slow."

Back at the hotel, Peter hugged his sister. "Night, brat. We aren't setting an alarm, so if you get up early and have something you want to do, no problem. Just leave us a message, and we'll catch up with you at some point."

"Sounds good," she said, turning to Luke. "Tixi asked if you wanted to stop by the gallery tomorrow during the final setup. He thought you might like time to look without a crowd."

Luke beamed. "I would love that. How about the two of us go by ourselves tomorrow afternoon, and these guys can amuse themselves?"

"Sounds like a plan."

Alex smiled upon spotting the bottle of wine and two glasses Kat had set out on the balcony. "Ahh, a woman who thinks ahead."

Kat looked unsure. "I just realized I never asked if you still wanted to sit out there. You've been traveling for days, so if you're too tired, I understand. I mean, we can always do that tomorrow night—the wine will keep." Even to her own ears, she sounded like an idiot.

Alex put his hands on his hips and looked at her steadily. "Katherine."

The use of her full name always got her full attention. "Yes?"

His frustration was clear. "I don't give a flying fuck if I've been up for three days straight, which, for the record, I haven't been. When I have the chance to be alone with you, that's what I'm going to do." He took a step toward her. "And, baby, you need to stop worrying so much." He reached out and placed his hands firmly on her hips, pulling her toward him.

"What I want right now is to kiss you senseless, then shower." He grinned suggestively. "You are welcome to join me, if you want. Then, I want to sit on the balcony with you and drink wine and listen to you tell me about Barcelona or anything else you want to talk about."

With that, he lowered his head and kissed her.

When the kiss ended, Alex gazed down at her. "I'm taking a shower. The invitation stands."

Kat felt desire rush through her. She swatted at him. "Take your shower. I'm pouring wine, and if you don't hurry, I'll drink it before you finish."

"Then we'll order more."

Kat woke early the next day and took her laptop out to the balcony while Alex slept. Several hours later, he emerged wearing only his pajama bottoms. Kat tried not to react, but before she could stop herself, Alex recognized the desire on her face. Whatever it was that was keeping her from being with him physically, he knew it was not lack of want. He stood behind her chair and leaned over her as he rubbed her shoulders. "Good morning," he said. "Have you been awake long?"

"Good morning. A couple hours." She smiled up at him. "How did you sleep?"

"Really well, despite the snoring going on next to me."

She grinned. "Oh, well, shit happens."

Alex laughed. "Come here."

Kat looked up at him, "Huh?"

He walked around to the front of her chair and held out his hands. Sunlight glinted off the hair on his chest, and Kat fought the urge to run her hands down the front of him. "Come here," he said.

She put the laptop on the table and stood up. Alex pulled her toward him, wrapped his arms tightly around her, and she stretched up on her tiptoes to kiss him. Within seconds, her hands were grasping his back. A noise in the hallway caused them to pull apart. "Just as it was getting really interesting," Alex said ruefully.

Kat straightened her clothes. "Good morning."

That day, the four went to the beach until Kat and Luke had to freshen up for the gallery. Back at the hotel, Alex watched as Kat put in her earrings. She stared at him; he looked uncomfortable. "What's the matter?"

"You'll laugh," he said, forcing a smile.

"No, I won't." She walked over to him. "What's going on?"

"It sounds stupid," he said, shaking his head, "but I feel jealous."

Kat was confused. "Of what? Or whom?"

He rolled his eyes. "I know you've explained the relationship, but I'm still jealous as hell that you are going to the gallery to see Tixi without me." He flopped back on the bed, feeling like an idiot.

A wave of giddiness washed over her. She climbed onto the bed on her hands and knees, beside Alex. "Look at me," she said.

He peered up at her, still embarrassed.

"That is the most beautiful thing anyone has ever said to me." Her voice softened, and he could see the raw emotion in her eyes. "I'm sorry you feel jealous—there is no need. But I'll admit it makes me feel…"

"Feel what?"

"Like a princess. Knowing you care so much is amazing."

Alex's smile lit his face. "Thank you. And yes, I am pouting out of jealousy. But if it makes you happy, I can live with it." He pulled her on top of him. "I want you here with me. Just me." He kissed her, feeling her body relax down onto his. His arms tightened around her as his hands roamed down her back.

Kat felt her heart begin to race, and she molded her body to his, feeling his manhood strain against her. She wanted nothing more than to make love to him. With a groan, she pulled back to look into his eyes.

Alex read her uncertainty and responded by rubbing her back as he tried to control his arousal. "It's okay, babe. I'm sorry I pushed."

She kissed the tip of his nose. "You didn't push. I want you more than I can tell you." She paused as she struggled to find the words. "I just— I'm not ready. I can't make love to you until I'm ready to tell you everything. And I'm not there. I'm trying, but I'm not there yet."

"But you do want me?"

She heard his need for reassurance. "Yes, I want you. So much it hurts."

"And you're okay with me saying I want you just as much?" His voice deepened. "That isn't going to make you run?"

She grinned. "Yes, I mean, I'd prefer if you didn't bring it up at dinner with my brother, but otherwise, yes."

Alex rolled the two of them in order to look down at Kat. "Then let me assure you, I want you so badly that I'm taking a hell of a lot of cold showers. And yes, I can wait as long as it takes until you're ready." He kissed her briefly. "Know that nothing you tell me will change how I feel."

The next evening, Alex was fumbling with his tie as Kat came out of the bathroom wearing a black sleeveless dress with a low back, and strappy black high-heeled sandals. His eyes widened. "Wow," he said, walking over to her. "You look amazing."

She grasped the ends of his tie and pulled his head down to kiss him. "So do you."

Wait staff circulated the gallery with trays of champagne, wine, and hors d'oeuvres. Soon after arriving, Kat, Alex, Peter, and Luke were standing in the main gallery sipping wine when they heard a woman's voice call, "Kat, *aqui. Aqui.*"

Kat turned and pulled Alex by the hand toward a very pregnant woman. Speaking in rapid Spanish, Kat hugged and kissed her before switching to English and introducing Alex to Monce, Tixi's wife. Peter and Luke hugged and kissed Monce, chattering about the last time they had seen her.

Just then, the man Alex recognized from the banner outside strode over. For a millisecond, Alex felt hostility fill him as he imagined Kat with the tall, dark, and handsome man. The look of joy on Kat's face as she saw Tixi made his jaw tighten. Tixi hugged Kat, kissed her on each cheek, then kissed her very briefly on the lips. Alex wanted to hit him. Taking a deep breath, he tried to hold on to Kat's assurances that there was nothing more than friendship between them. Besides, Tixi was married. Alex could not hear fully or understand their conversation, but Kat was clearly congratulating him on the show. Kat then again switched to English, and reintroduced Luke and Peter, before pulling Alex forward by the hand. "Tixi, this is my boyfriend, Alex. Alex, this is my old friend, Tixi."

The word "boyfriend" took all the anger out of Alex, and for a moment, he felt a swell of masculine pride. He extended his hand to shake Tixi's, but Tixi grabbed him and kissed him on both cheeks. In heavily accented English, Tixi said, "So glad to meet you. You're all Kat has talked about recently."

Alex was stunned by the comment. "So good to meet you," he said.

As Tixi moved on to greet other patrons, Peter and Luke wandered off to look at the art. Kat and Alex sipped champagne without talking. Kat raised a brow. "So, are we going to stand here all night, or do you want to look at the art?"

He grinned. "Do I want to look at the art, or search out the paintings of you?" He wrapped his arm around Kat's waist. "You know which ones I'm looking for, but yes, let's go look at all the art."

As they strolled around the gallery, Kat realized people were beginning to look at her with interest. She squeezed Alex's hand. "I guess they recognize me."

The nudes were all in one wing of the gallery space. The first painting Alex saw was of a pregnant Monce, seemingly getting dressed as she pulled on a shirt. As much as Alex did not want to be impressed by Tixi's work, he had to admit it was amazing. Turning a corner, he suddenly saw an almost life-sized painting of Kat standing atop a pile of rocks, looking toward a pond. Her body faced away from the artist, but she was fully naked. His breath caught as he saw the beauty of the painting- the way the light danced on her skin, the shadows hinting at her coiled movement like she was ready to dive off the rocks into the water below.

Putting down his now-empty glass, he wrapped his arms around Kat from behind, pulling her into his warmth. "It is amazing."

"Isn't it? Not because it's me, but because he's so good at what he does."

He nibbled her ear, trying to control his reaction when her nipples tightened under the thin fabric. "Yes, his talent is mind-boggling, and it's also amazing because it's you."

Just then, Peter and Luke joined them. Peter smiled, seeing Kat in Alex's arms. "Hey, Kitty Kat, so I admit it… This is amazing."

She grinned at him. "I told you."

The rest of the evening, the group walked the gallery and visited with Monce, Tixi, and the gallery owner. At one point, Alex excused himself to find the restroom. Kat was standing in the hallway nearby when he emerged. He walked over and brushed a wayward lock of her hair back from her face. "You okay?"

She ducked shyly. "Yeah. I'm better than okay. It's just…"

"What?"

She reached up to wrap her arms around his neck. "When you walked away, I realized you've had your arm around me all night, and it felt funny when you left." She looked down, and he could see a blush rising on her cheeks. "You've been a little possessive tonight, and I like it."

Alex pushed her back against the wall so their bodies were touching. "I'm trying like hell to not growl at men looking at you, and I almost punched Tixi when he kissed you. I love touching you, and there is no way on God's earth that I'm going to let the guys who are salivating over these paintings think they can hit on you. You came here with me tonight, and …" He leaned close, so she felt the heat of his breath on her lips. "You're going home with me tonight."

It was well after midnight when the two couples left the gallery. Kat offered to get a cab, but the guys were happy to walk, as was she. At the hotel, they said goodnight and went to their rooms.

While Kat changed her clothes, Alex stood on the balcony and looked out at the water. How could he get her to trust him? What could have happened to her? He jumped as he felt a hand on his shoulder, not having heard Kat cross the room. He turned, towering over her in her bare feet. Her tank top and pajama shorts made her look so young, yet so sexy.

He cleared his throat. "Hey."

"Hey." She stepped forward, stood on her tiptoes, and wrapped her arms around his neck. "So, are you ready to sleep, or do you want to sit out here for a bit?"

"Sitting out here sounds great. You?"

"Perfect. Do you want me to order some wine?" she said.

"Please do," said Alex, "I'll get changed."

The wine arrived minutes later as Alex came out of the bathroom. Kat carried the tray of wine and a small plate of olives out to the balcony. Alex poured and raised his glass. "To the star of tonight's show."

Kat laughed. "Hardly." She smiled at him. "Thanks for coming, and for going to the show. I know it was a weird thing to ask, but I'm really glad you're here."

"Me too."

They talked quietly, making plans for the next day, avoiding the topic of Alex leaving Barcelona. Finally, when the wine was gone, he stood up. "C'mon, princess. Time to get some beauty sleep."

The next morning, the four went out to brunch, then headed to the Sagrada Familia for a chamber concert. Leaving the cathedral, Kat turned her phone on and seemed surprised to hear a text notification. She looked at the message and shook her head.

"What's up?" said Alex.

"Monce sent a message regarding tonight's plans."

"Why?"

She rolled her eyes. "She's eight months pregnant, but she wants to go out dancing tonight; she wants us to go with them."

Peter answered before Alex could. "Sounds great. How about we take them to dinner first?"

Kat stopped walking to look at her brother. "You want to go dancing?"

"Of course. Well, really, I want to hear the music." Peter looked at Luke. "What do you think?"

"Sounds like a great plan. Alex?"

Alex looked at Kat, then at the other men. "If Kat wants to go, I'm happy to."

"Fine," she said with exasperation.

Back at the hotel, Kat was standing at the balcony railing when Alex came up behind her. "What's up? Why don't you want to go tonight?"

She shrugged. "It's not that I don't want to go. They're my friends and I love them, and I love being with them, and in a couple days, I'm moving away. But…"

"But what?"

"But I wanted to be alone with you tonight, not with a crowd."

He wrapped his arms around her, rubbing her crossed arms. "Me too. But we can go out, eat, dance, and then come back here to be alone."

She leaned back against him. "Okay."

He leaned down and gently kissed the side of her neck. "Besides, I get to dance with you, and holding you close for hours sounds like a great idea." He kept nuzzling her neck, feeling her breathing change.

She turned in his arms. "And what if the music is fast?"

Alex dropped light kisses on her shoulder and neck. He could feel her nipples harden as they rubbed against his chest, and he fought the urge to stroke her breasts. "Then I'll pull you into a dark corner so I can kiss you as much as I want."

Kat tipped her head, allowing him easier access to the hollow at the base of her neck. When he kissed her there, she moaned softly. "Okay," she said, "cold shower time."

Alex did not let her go. "Why? I know the rules, and I agreed to them. I'm not going to push this too far. I can control myself no matter how much I want you, so why not enjoy it."

Kat tightened her arms around his neck and kissed him. When she pulled back, she looked up at him and said, "I know you won't push, but I can't say the same for me." He looked confused, so she continued, turning bright red as she spoke. "I can't say that I can stop. But I know it's not right for this to go too far if I can't be completely honest with you. And no matter how much I'm trying, I'm just not there yet."

He looked at her intently. "Have you been lying to me?"

"No."

"Then what have you not been honest about?"

He could see her struggling to explain.

"Maybe that's not the right way to say it. Maybe what I'm trying to say is, until I'm ready to be open about my past, I can't do more than we already are. And every time you touch me ..." She looked down in embarrassment. "Damn, every time you *look* at me, I become a hormone-crazed idiot."

Alex grinned. "Hormone-crazed?"

She swatted at him. "Stop looking so smug."

"Hormone-crazed..."

Kat emerged from the bathroom ready to go out. Alex felt his mouth go dry. She was wearing a dark maroon dress, lower cut than some of her other dresses, and when she turned, he realized it was backless. He swallowed. "Shit."

She smiled and walked toward him. "I'll take that as a compliment."

He pulled her toward him and kissed her until they were both breathless. "Hell, yes. And I will kill any guy who hits on you tonight."

She put her hands on his chest, feeling his body heat through the fabric. "And how exactly is anyone going to hit on me when you said I was going to be dancing with you all night?"

"Just saying."

The two couples walked down to the waterfront to meet Tixi and Monce for dinner. Alex had to smile when he saw Monce, so obviously very pregnant but in a slinky dress and high heels. After dinner, the six walked to a nearby dance club.

Over the next several hours, the couples danced, laughed, and all but Monce drank lots of wine. Finally, Monce pulled Kat aside to say something in her ear, then went to find the bathroom. Kat began to laugh before telling the men Monce wanted to go to a local tango club.

Peter chuckled. "She wants to tango at eight months pregnant?"

Kat nodded. "Yeah. You've seen her tango before. Besides, she's been dancing all night, and still has more energy than the rest of us."

Luke nodded. "I'm game. Pete? Alex?"

Peter nodded and looked at Alex, who agreed.

As Monce returned to the table, Kat said, "Let's go."

At the tango club, the group sat on overstuffed couches facing the dance floor, enjoying the less raucous music. As soon as a new tango was ready to start, Monce and Tixi went dancing, and Alex was amazed at how graceful Monce was despite her condition. Watching Tixi look at her, he fully understood what Kat had been trying to explain to him. The look on Tixi's face was raw with love for his wife.

Finally, Monce pulled Tixi to the table and sat down. "I'm done." She kissed Kat on the cheek and said something to her in Spanish that Alex could not fully understand. Kat shook her head. Monce said it again, now with more vehemence. Kat shook her head and responded sharply in Spanish. Monce then turned to Alex. "You don't mind, do you? If Tixi and Kat dance once? Do you?" Before Alex could answer, Kat shot back a response that made Monce laugh.

Alex looked at Kat quizzically. Kat could tango? Well enough to dance with Tixi who, even to Alex, was a damn fine dancer? Seriously? Alex looked at Monce. "Of course not. I'd love to see Kat tango."

Kat's eyes widened, but it was Peter who spoke first. "Awesome! We haven't seen you dance for years. Go for it."

Kat squeezed Alex's hand and leaned closer to him. "Are you sure you're okay with this?"

He stroked the side of her face. "Do you want to?"

Her smile was broad, and for a moment, he saw childlike joy in her eyes. "Yes," she said.

"Will you teach me to tango sometime?"

"Of course."

He lowered his voice. "And who is taking you home tonight?"

"You are."

"Then dance."

A few seconds into the dance, Alex felt like he had been punched in the stomach. Nothing could have prepared him for the beauty and raw sexuality of Kat dancing the tango. It was obvious that she and Tixi had danced together often, but as Alex looked at Monce's face for any sign of jealousy, all he saw was joy in her face. Clearly, Monce felt completely secure in her husband's love and in her friendship with Kat. Feeling him looking at her, Monce slid over next to Alex and put her arm through his. "Don't they dance beautifully together?"

"They do."

"You aren't jealous, are you?"

Alex laughed. "No, but only because you aren't."

Monce tipped her head, focusing on him intently. "Kat and I are good. Better than good. We are old friends who just happened to have slept with the same man. Long ago, we openly talked out the weirdness, and moved on." She rubbed her belly. "I felt so comfortable with it that I asked her to be in our wedding. Besides, I've never seen her look at a man the way she looks at you."

Alex fought warring emotions as the song ended; he wanted her to sit with him, but he also wanted to watch her dance some more. As she walked toward the table, Tixi grabbed her hand and motioned back to the floor.

Monce waved them both back to the floor, and they danced again.

The song ended and Kat kissed Tixi on the cheek, then strode purposefully toward the table. Leaning down, she kissed Monce. "Thanks for letting me borrow your husband."

"My pleasure. Good to see you have not forgotten how to dance."

Kat slid into the seat next to Alex and smiled when he wrapped his arm around her. "Aren't you full of surprises?"

"Huh?"

He kissed her ear. "Not only did I not know you could dance, but you tango like a pro," he whispered. "You were so sexy out there."

The next morning, Kat tried to smile as she watched Alex gather the last of his things. He stopped packing to look at her. "You look like you're about to cry."

"I don't want you to go," she said, her voice trembling.

"I told you I would stay."

"I know. But I need to finish up in Madrid and get to New York."

Alex tried to fight his frustration as tears rolled down her cheeks. "Alex, I can't even work up the courage to tell you things, so it seems stupid to change my entire life on a *maybe*."

Alex sighed, rubbed his temples, and then sat down next to her, wrapping his arms around her. "Okay. I'll stay your *maybe* and go home today. And in a month, I'll be in New York, and we can be together."

"Are you sure you're okay with this? I understand I'm complicating things. I'm sorry…"

He pushed her back on the bed and looked down at her. "I've told you… I'm not giving up on us." He leaned down and kissed her. "You're stuck with me."

Chapter Fifteen

Alex arrived in New York at the end of August, and for three days, life was almost perfect. Then, Kat's phone rang one night when all four of them were in the kitchen.

Alex listened intently to her side of the conversation as she scribbled notes on a legal pad. "Tomorrow? You want me to go tomorrow? You couldn't have said something before now?" She grimaced at the response. "Whatever. The flight leaves at six a.m.?" She paused in thought. "Okay, I'm on it."

Kat hung up. "I'm leaving for Brownsville in the morning. They have reports of witchcraft and Satanism among the women in the immigration detention camp."

There was silence as all three men stared at Kat. Alex sat shocked, fighting disappointment and then anger that she was leaving so soon after his arrival. How were they ever going to see if this would work?

Peter spoke, his voice strained. "Satanic practices?"

"Yeah. They want an article about it." Kat turned toward the stairs, humming cheerfully under her breath.

Peter shouted. "Dammit, Kat, do you ever think before you accept an assignment? I mean, it doesn't seem you'll be very popular looking into Satanism."

Her face reflected her shock. "Peter, this is my job. I don't interfere in your career, do I?"

"My career isn't a threat to life and fucking limb."

She was confused. "I travel all the time. Why are you squawking about this now?"

"Because I'm sick of wondering where you are, or when you'll come back, and if you're safe. I love you as my kid sister, Kat, but it drives me crazy when you take risks like this."

"I can't believe we're fighting about this," she said, her voice rising in disbelief. "I leave for Brownsville in the morning."

Peter whirled around and stomped away without speaking. Everyone else sat in silence. A minute later, Peter was heard angrily playing the drums.

"Son-of-a-fucking-bitch." Kat marched out of the kitchen and climbed the stairs to her room, stomping loudly.

Silence filled the kitchen as Alex and Luke looked at each other with wide eyes. Luke shook his head and laughed. "Shit, there's nothing worse than sitting in a room while other people fight."

"Yeah." Alex looked down at his hands, unsure of his next words.

"You okay?" Luke was concerned.

"Yeah, just frustrated," Alex said with conviction. "I'm falling in love with her, you know."

"I know," Luke said, smiling broadly.

"Is it that obvious?"

"Yes."

"And you're okay with it? What about Peter?" Suddenly, Alex realized how much he cared about their opinions.

"Truly, Alex, we're thrilled."

"Peter, get up here," Kat yelled from upstairs.

Peter whacked a drum before he responded. "No," he yelled, "I'm not climbing three fucking flights so you can tell me to mind my own business."

"Fine, asshole," she spat, stomping down the stairs.

Luke grinned at Alex. "This could be interesting."

Voices rose and fell downstairs for ten minutes before there was dead silence. Finally, the siblings reappeared. "Kat and I have reached an understanding."

Smiling at her brother, Kat was smug. "I'm going to Brownsville tomorrow, but I'll have my phone on and with me at all times and I'll go out of my way to be careful. And I'll call home a lot. And I will try to be better about giving travel details and making sure I can be reached, even when I'm traveling."

"And I'll stop playing mother hen," said Peter. Brother and sister grinned at each other as Peter called for pizza.

The next morning, Alex carried Kat's bag to the airport security gate.

"Thanks for riding out with me," she said, suddenly feeling shy.

"My pleasure. I'll see you Thursday?"

"Maybe sooner, if it goes well."

"I hope so. Be careful."

Kat looked at the security line, which was getting longer by the second. "I should go," she said. "Bye, Alex, I'll see you soon." She swallowed. "I'm sorry to be leaving so soon. You know it's not intentional, right?"

"I know." He stroked her cheek. "Go, do a great article, call me when you can."

"I will."

"Be careful." Alex leaned in and gave her a tender kiss on the lips. "Remember," he said, "I'm only a phone call away."

"I will." Kat stood on her tiptoes to kiss him and ran through the gate.

Chapter Sixteen

When Kat returned, Alex knew he had her undivided attention, and the days that followed were perfect. The phone rang one night as he came through the kitchen. Distractedly, Kat picked it up from where she sat at her computer, still typing with one hand. "Hello?"

She shot a glare at Peter and Luke, who were walking noisily into the room.

"Hello?" she said again into the phone.

"What the hell is all the mayhem?" The voice on the other end was clear, even with the accent.

Kat's voice rose happily. "Secu! I've been leaving you messages everywhere. Where the hell have you been?"

"I've been busy, darling. I just got home, and Ana gave me your messages."

"Don't *darling* me," she said, "I talked with Paco. I know you've been home." Kat could hear children playing in the background. "Is he there? Let me talk to him."

"Hold on. I need to tell you something first." There was a long pause. "I got it."

Kat gulped, her face suddenly bright red. "You didn't," she said. "You're lying."

"I'm not lying. Tuesday morning. I did it!"

Alex was trying to follow the conversation, but only Kat's distress was clear. "I still say you're lying. But I'll play along. When, where, and how?"

"I pulled some strings," he said casually. "I fly in on Monday and I have two hours with him Tuesday morning, and then a bit of time to look around and meet with the opposition and fly home."

She grumbled. "Fuck, Secu. I can't believe you did it. Congratulations."

Peter poured a glass of wine and took a long swallow as he leaned against the counter. "Hey, the rest of us are dying here, Kat. What's going on with Secu?"

She looked at him, clearly trying to control her unhappiness. "He got the Somosa interview."

Peter's eyes widened as he reached to snatch the phone from her hand. "Shit, Secu. Congrats! Kat's been salivating over that one for months. Good for you."

Kat reclaimed the phone, whacking Peter on the shoulder in the process. "Give me the phone." She spoke into the receiver, "You called to gloat? If you're done, let me speak to Paco, you impossible ass."

"In a minute," he said. "I need a favor."

"What? You gloat and beg in the same breath?"

"Yes. I have no honor, you know that." Secu chuckled. "Anyway, I need a complete set of your books, autographed to his wife, of course."

Kat was shocked and immediately furious. "What? You shit. You get the interview, but you need *my* books as a hostess gift?" Her voice rose. "You used my name to get the interview, for Christ's sake."

"Yes," he said, his voice deepening, "and it would be a great help if you-"

"If I what? Jesus, Secu, get to the point."

"It would be a great help if you could get your skinny ass to Managua on Monday because we need time to prepare."

"What?"

"You dope," he laughed, "I got his agreement under the condition we do the interview together."

Her eyes grew big. "We, as in both of us? We got it?"

"We got it. I can book you a flight and meet you in Managua. That is, if you want to go."

Kat bounced off the stool to dance around the kitchen. "Oh, my god. Of course, I want to go. Book me on anything. I'll be there!"

Chapter Seventeen

Alex ate in near silence as Kat enthusiastically steered the dinner conversation around her upcoming trip to Nicaragua. As dishes were later cleared, Peter and Luke excused themselves to walk Max.

Kat walked up behind Alex, where he sat on one of the stools, and wrapped her arms around him. "Hi," she said.

"Hi."

"You okay?"

"Fine."

She wriggled herself in front of him and wrapped her arms around his neck. "What's wrong?"

Alex sighed. This was not a conversation he wanted to have. "I'm struggling a bit," he said.

"What do you mean?"

"I understand the nature of your work, but you're always leaving just as I get here. I've been here for two weeks, and we've only been together for four of those days."

She closed her eyes. "I know, I'm sorry."

He leaned in to kiss her forehead. "I don't want you to be sorry. I want us to figure out how to make this work."

"Do you want me to cancel?"

"No, baby. I would never ask you to do that; it means too much to you. I just hate it when we're apart."

"Me too."

Kat was awake long before dawn the next day. Alex woke to her gathering her things from the chair in the bedroom. "Hey, leave that," he said. "I'm getting up; I'll bring it downstairs."

"You should sleep," she said, leaning over to kiss him. "You don't have to get up so early."

"I'm going with you to the airport. I'll be down with your bag in five minutes. Go ahead and make some coffee."

Kat's wanting to protect his rest warred with her desire to have a few more precious minutes with him, no matter how excited she was about her trip. "Okay," she said, "see you downstairs."

A few minutes later, Alex came into the kitchen carrying her bag. She smiled at him. "How do you get ready so fast and look so damn good?"

His hands were warm on her hips, despite the fabric covering them. "Are you saying you find me attractive?"

Kat placed her hands on his chest and was immediately reminded of his firm muscles. "You know I do," she purred.

"Hmm." He grinned. "So, I still make you crazy?"

Kat blushed. "Stop being so damn smug about it," she laughed. "C'mon, let's have a quick bite and get me to the airport."

The next four days were a whirlwind of activity. Kat could not recall ever having so much fun on assignment and simultaneously missing someone so much. Every minute of the trip had been filled with the interview and research, then with editing. Kat loved working with Secundino, but she looked for every opportunity to call or text Alex.

On her final night in Nicaragua, she and Secu sat in a café. Once the waiter delivered two cold beers, Secu raised his bottle. "To what I think is our best damn interview and article together, ever."

"To us," she said, clinking her bottle against his. "Damn, we're good together."

Secu took a swig. "So, is Alex the one?"

Kat rolled her eyes. "Don't start. It's too soon to know."

"Do you want him to be?"

Kat turned the cold bottle between her hands, the condensation wetting her fingers. "Yeah," she said, "I think I do."

Secu searched her face. "So, you'll need to tell him at some point. You know that, right?"

"I know," Kat sighed.

Chapter Eighteen

It had been almost a week since Kat returned, and Alex realized she was growing quieter each day. He decided to question her one evening as they watched TV. "Babe," he began, muting their movie, "what's going on?"

"What do you mean?" she said cautiously.

"You have been quiet for days. Is something bothering you?"

She shook her head but avoided his gaze. "No," she said, "just having a down phase." She squeezed his hand. "It happens around this time each year. Don't worry though, I'll snap out of it. I promise."

Later that evening, Kat excused herself to make a phone call. She kissed Alex briefly upon returning to the room. "I have an early meeting tomorrow, then some interviews, so it looks like I'll be gone all day." Her tone sounded odd. "I may not be home until after dinner."

"Everything okay?" he said.

She forced a smile. "Oh, yeah. I'm just tired, I guess," she said with a stretch. "We should probably get some sleep."

The next morning, Kat slipped out of bed long before dawn. Alex stirred as she came out of the bathroom, leaned down, and kissed his cheek. "I'll see you later tonight."

He rolled over to look at her, blinking the sleep from his eyes. "Wait," he said, "I'll get up and have breakfast with you."

"I'll grab something on my way. I have to get going." She kissed him, grabbed her bag, and left.

When Peter and Luke came into the kitchen two hours later, Alex was drinking coffee. "Where's Kat?" said Peter.

"She left a few hours ago, citing what she said was a very full day. She doesn't expect to be home until late."

"What?" said Peter, sounding concerned.

"That's what she said. Why?"

Luke put his hand on Peter's shoulder. "No reason," he said. "She just doesn't normally decide things like that at the last minute, that's all."

Four days later, Peter's phone vibrated in his pocket. Caught up in the music, he ignored it. When it started buzzing again seconds later, he knew he needed to answer it. "Sorry, guys, I need to take this," he said, stepping out into the hall. "Yeah, what's up? I'm in the middle of rehearsal."

"I know you are, but she's gone," said Luke quietly.

Peter was confused. "What are you talking about?"

"Check your voicemail. I bet she left you and Alex both half-assed messages about how she's gone on assignment and won't have cell service for a few days. I know because that's the message I got. She obviously just called voicemail to avoid speaking to me. I called home and she didn't answer. Then I called her phone, and it's off. I can't reach her." He paused. "I came home and hit redial on the house phone, thinking it might shed some light on whatever is going on, and the last call was to West Brookfield. Tomorrow's the anniversary, Pete. I think she's gone to Massachusetts for whatever reason, and she didn't want us to know."

Shock shook Peter so hard the room began to swim around him. He keeled forward and pressed his head against the wall as he tried to think.

At that moment, Alex came up behind him. Before Peter could say anything, Alex said, "Is everything okay?"

Peter turned to look at his friend, completely at a loss for words.

"Pete, you need to come home," Luke called into the phone. "If I'm right, we need to go too."

Peter nodded silently. "Get ready to go. I'll be home in ten minutes." He looked at Alex and knew it was time. "No, let me rephrase that. *Alex* and I will be home in ten."

When he got off the phone, Peter looked at Alex. "We need to go."

"What? Is everything okay?"

"Yes. No. I'll tell you on the way."

On the Uber ride home, Peter said, "Check your phone. I bet you have a message from Kat, stating she's going away for a bit."

"What? We saw her at breakfast—she didn't say anything about going out of town."

"Check your messages," Peter pressed.

Alex felt his heart sink as her clipped voice came through his speaker. "Hi, Alex. It's Kat. Listen, I'm going on assignment for a couple days and I won't be reachable by phone. I'll see you Thursday or Friday. Have a good week."

Alex looked at Peter. "What's going on?"

Peter sighed. "You know how Kat has a secret?"

Alex was tired of the secrecy, and his voice showed it. "You mean the secret everyone but me is in on? Yeah, I'm aware."

"Well, if Kat doesn't tell you in the next twelve hours, fuck it, *I* will."

The late afternoon sun was reflecting off the lake and filtering through the trees that lined the long driveway leading to a waterfront lodge with a large wraparound porch.

Peter emerged from the car as an older woman came out to greet them. "Peter, it's so nice to see you. How long has it been?"

Peter walked over to lean down and kiss her weathered cheek. "Mrs. Wyman, it's so good to see you. Thanks for finding room for us on such short notice."

"Of course, dear." She smiled. "Your cabin is the one closest to your sister. She always rents the one on the point, you know."

Peter tried to smile. "We can't wait to say hello to her. Where is she?"

"Well, she has a bit of a routine when she's here— She goes shopping and then has some sort of meeting. She usually gets back somewhere around six, I believe."

Luke and Alex watched the color rise in Peter's face, but he kept his voice steady. "Geez, Mrs. Wyman, I guess I'm feeling a bit silly because I can't remember… How many times has Kat been here now?"

"Oh, just the five times, dear. This is the fifth, I believe. She has a standing reservation for three nights, the same nights each year."

Once in his cabin, Peter dumped his bag on a bed, and turned to Luke and Alex. "I'm moving the car over here, so she doesn't see it."

"Peter, she's not trying to get away from you. For whatever reason, this is just something she needs to do each year, and-"

"And what? She's been flying home from Spain for the last *four* years, and never bothered to tell us she was in the country?" He stopped. "I'm moving the car, and then I'm going outside to wait for her."

"No," said Alex, "we'll all sit on the porch. We're in this together."

An hour later, a small black rental car drove slowly past the lodge on its way to Kat's cabin. Luke and Alex sat in rocking chairs on the porch, while Peter was positioned against the railing, coiled like a rattlesnake. A car door could be heard closing, and Kat appeared around the corner of the building so deep in thought the men went unnoticed. She turned the corner of the gravel path and glanced up at them.

As Alex watched her, he recognized what looked like panic cross her face. The color seemed to drain from her face and her body clenched as if ready to flee.

"Don't you dare think about running away," Peter barked.

Kat gasped. "What are you doing here?"

"We could ask you the same thing since we all got lame messages about you being off on assignment."

Anger flashed across her face. "What I do is my business."

"Bullshit."

Alex realized she looked quite out of place in a stark black dress, white scarf with red roses on it, and spike heels. What had she been doing?

Kat closed her eyes in frustration. "Anyway, do what you want. I'm going to change, and then get some food. If you want something, let me know."

"Well, you obviously know exactly where to get dinner around here—you've only been doing it for *four* years now," Peter spat.

Kat recoiled. "You know?"

"Yes, I fucking know," Peter exploded. "We drove all the way out here, worried as hell, to discover you have been doing this for years, yet never had the decency to tell us." He pointed his finger at her. "You never told us," he boomed. "Did you think we wouldn't support you?"

Alex and Luke waited for her to erupt in matching anger, but instead, her voice grew quiet and sad. "I knew you would try to help, but that's exactly what I *didn't* need. I needed to do this on my own. This is my burden, and mine alone."

"It was never your burden alone," said Peter. "Never. We all bore it our own way. All of us. Me, Luke, Mom and Dad. Jess, in her own way too. I was there, remember? I was in the room when you first saw her, when you first held her. I was the one holding you when she-"

Peter's voice broke. "I was there too, and it almost killed me. How dare you take this on alone. How dare you act as though none of us felt anything. I think about her every day too. I think about what could have been. And I know what tomorrow is because it still haunts me too. Damn you, Kat, how dare you shut me out!" He looked at Luke. "How dare you shut *us* out of this."

"I know you were there, both of you were there. I couldn't have survived it without you both. I know it impacted you too, but-"

"But what? Why all the fucking secrecy?"

Kat's shoulders sagged. "I..."

Peter's voice rose again. "What, Kat? What?"

"You all kept telling me I had to go on- that I needed to find my peace and go forward, and ..." Tears slid down her cheek in the twilight. "And I can't. And I couldn't tell you that. I couldn't tell you that despite you all urging me forward, it *is* destroying me." With a sniff, she wiped at the tears angrily. "How could I tell you I can't let go? That I spend every day wondering what I could have done differently. I wake up at night and sit with my guilt, knowing it's all my fault."

Even in his anger, Peter wanted to protect her and make her see the truth. "It wasn't your fault," he pressed. "None of it was your fault."

"Yes, it was," she said, her voice rising in frustration. "If I hadn't gone to the party… If I hadn't had anything to drink… If I hadn't gone in the taxi that day. All of it was my fault. All of it." She started to cry in earnest. "And I miss her, Pete. I miss her so much. I wake up at night, just wanting to hold her again. And Mom and Dad, too. I miss them so much. And it's all my fault. I pretend I don't think about it, but once a year I let myself come here and I let myself feel it. I let myself cry because if I allow myself that other than when I'm here, I'll never stop."

Kat turned on her heel. "I've got to go," she blurted through her tears, "I've got to go." She ran into her cabin before the men could react. The sound of the lock clicking into place divided the silence.

The three men sat in shock for several minutes. The silence was overpowering. Peter looked at Luke in surprise. "Holy shit."

A ghost of a smile crossed Luke's face. "Holy shit, indeed." He stood and took Peter's hand. "Less angry with her now?"

Peter rubbed a shaky hand across his face, "Shit. I didn't mean to-"

Alex's frustration took over. "What? Could somebody finally tell me what the fuck is going on?"

"I will," said a small voice behind him. Kat stepped out onto the porch, barefoot, in jeans and a thick cardigan. "It's time, I guess."

"Are you sure?" said Peter.

"I'm sure." She looked at Alex. "Ready?" She sighed. "It's a really long story. We might as well go inside and get comfortable."

As she turned, Peter made a move to follow her. She held her hand up in warning. "If you come inside, you need to shut up and let me tell it."

He held his hand up as if to promise. "I'll be quiet."

"Okay."

Inside the cabin, Kat lit the gas fireplace, now the only light in the room.

Before she could sit, Alex took her hand and pulled her into the small kitchen. Once they were alone, he pulled her tense body to his and wrapped his arms around her. "You don't have to do this," he said, kissing her hair.

"Yes, I do," she said, her voice muffled against his chest.

"Well, it doesn't have to be right now. We can do this another day." His hands stroked her back. "Or never."

She wrapped her arms around him and hugged him fiercely. "It has to be now." She looked up at him, tears glistening in her eyes. "Kiss me, please?"

He leaned down to kiss her slowly and deeply, feeling her desperation and sensing her saying goodbye.

With a sigh, she pulled away and looked up at him. She cradled his face in her hands. "Alex, I have to tell you that if it's over between us after this, I understand."

"Kat, whatever this is, it's not going to change my feelings for you."

She shook her head sadly. "You don't know that."

Chapter Nineteen

Peter and Luke sat on one couch, leaving the other empty. Alex sat down, assuming Kat would join him. When she chose to sit on the hearth, he extended his hand. "Come sit beside me."

"I can't," she said. "This is hard enough." She looked nervously at her brother. "Pete, there are some things you don't know."

Irritation crossed Peter's face and Kat saw it instantly. "Please don't be mad."

Seeing her fear, he smiled gently. "I won't, Kitty Kat. I promise. I love you."

"I know." She pulled her knees to her chest and wrapped her arms around them. She tipped her head and looked at Alex, taking a moment to savor him. Then she took a deep breath.

"I had a roommate during my freshman year in college. It was the only year I had one, and Kelly was okay. I mean, she was completely different from me— She was tall and gorgeous, with dark hair that made guys crazy. She started dating a guy named Reid, and she thought he was amazing. I didn't know why but he always made me uncomfortable. They dated from like October on and were even together the next year."

Alex wondered why any of this mattered, but he stayed quiet as she went on.

"They broke up in May of our sophomore year. After we stopped rooming together, Kelly and I had breakfast together once a week, so we were still in the loop on each other. That summer, I stayed on campus to get ready to move to Madrid, and Reid stayed on campus too because he was getting ready to go to Russia. During that time, he asked me out a couple times, and I kept saying no, which made him unhappy. But then I started dating Nate, who was set to go to Russia too. We dated casually through the rest of the summer, and when we came back for our senior year, things became more serious."

Alex was trying to follow, knowing that whatever had happened was at the end of college. Why the need for all the history?

"We broke up around Thanksgiving of my senior year, and soon after, Reid asked me out again, and I still said no. Then I came home for Christmas and…" Despite the dim light, Alex could see Kat's cheeks darken. "And I met you over that break."

"When we went to the opera," he said gently. "And then we stayed up way too late, talking that night."

"Yeah."

"And you called me on January twenty-first, right? That's the day you called my apartment while I was out running errands."

"What did you say?" said Peter, his voice cutting through the room.

Kat looked at him sharply. "Peter, I told you there were some things you were not aware of, so just shut up."

"And I never called back because Will never gave me the message," said Alex.

"Son of a bitch," said Peter, realizing the implications.

"Pete, shut up!" Kat closed her eyes, and when she opened them, raw pain radiated from them as she looked at Alex. "And you never called me. The thing was, well, it was *really* hard for me to find the nerve to call you. I really liked you. Looking back now, I had a hell of a crush on you, then you gave me your number and said to call, but I wasn't sure you really meant it. I kept telling myself you hadn't truly intended for me to call- you were just being nice. But then I decided the only way I would ever know was to just do it. And so, that afternoon, it was a Saturday, I made up my mind."

She rubbed her forehead. "It sounds really stupid, but once I decided, I took a shower, got dressed up and everything." She buried her face in her hands. "I was so nervous about calling, I guess I wanted to look good, as if you could see me or something."

Alex saw the pain on Peter's face but knew he needed to focus on Kat. "I'm sorry I didn't call you back," he said. He smiled, trying to convince her he was still there for her. "I kept hoping you would call. I promise, if I had gotten the message, I would have returned your call."

Kat sniffed. "I know. I mean, I know that *now*. But after Will said you were expected back, I sat and waited. Actually, I didn't sit. I paced and then I cleaned my room."

She stopped. "That's funny, I'd forgotten that part." The amusement left her face as quickly as it had come. "But after an hour, you still hadn't called, so I got up to use the bathroom. When I was out in the hall, I ran into Kelly and her friend Kaitlyn." She grimaced. "They invited me to a party, and I said I was busy. Kelly pressed until I said I was waiting for a call. When she heard how long I'd been waiting, she told me to get a life and go out for a change. Suddenly, I was mad at you for not calling me." Kat's face showed contrition. "I'm sorry I got mad at you, Alex. I thought you were blowing me off."

"There's no reason to apologize."

She looked down at her hands and rubbed her fingers like she did after writing for too long. "I went out with Kelly and Kaitlyn, across campus to Deke."

"Deke?" Alex knew the name was familiar, but he could not recall the context.

"One of the frats- the one Reid and Nate belonged to. There was a band, and purple punch, and everyone was drinking."

Alex recalled their first meeting. "And you didn't drink because you were still underage."

She shook her head ruefully. "No. Although life would have been different if I had been so virtuous *that* night. I didn't drink with you guys because I wasn't legal, but my morals left the building that night. I drank a cup of punch, which was basically vodka, rum, and a splash of grape juice. I danced for a while, and then Reid asked me to dance. I declined, which really pissed him off; he called me a cold bitch but then apologized and offered to get me a drink to show there were no hard feelings. By that time, the punch was already making me stupid, so I agreed."

Kat stood abruptly. "I need something to drink."

"I'll get it," said Peter, jumping up. "What do you want?"

She shrugged, "I don't care. Water, seltzer…." A smile flickered across her face. "Hemlock tea seems fitting." She turned and stared silently at the fire. As Alex watched her, he realized he had never seen someone as withdrawn as she was in that moment.

Once Peter returned with drinks, Kat took a long swallow, then sat back down. "And so, if the first punch made me stupid, the second drink was worse, especially since it had been laced. Obviously, I didn't know that at the time."

Alex's heart sank.

"Reid again asked me to dance, and I said yes. The next thing I remember is waking up in his room with most of my clothes off. He was raping me, and I tried really hard to stop him, but he hit me several times, and I passed out again." She paused to take a sip, keeping her eyes lowered.

"The next time I came to, I remember trying to get him off me. He said I deserved what was happening after all the times I had rejected him, and he called me a tease for showing up at the party dressed the way I was. I finally got enough leverage to knee him in the groin. He punched me in the head at least once that I remember, but in the end, I had a bunch of bruises, so I don't know how many times he struck me. I woke up half-naked, bruised, and in the frat's back stairwell, where they stored the garbage until trash day." She closed her eyes. "I guess I was considered trash at that point."

Alex searched for something to say, nauseous over what he had just heard. "Kat, I'm so sorry."

"You have nothing to be sorry for." She took a deep breath.

"I remember wanting to make sure I was covered; I didn't have my coat anymore, only some of my clothes. Luckily, my dorm keycard was in my skirt pocket. I wandered back to my room to call the only person I could think of for help—I called Josh. He came over with Mariah and took me to the hospital, where they examined me. I was informed they couldn't administer a rape kit because they were out of them."

"While I was doing that, Reid was clearly formulating a plan to cover himself; by the time the police were called, he had gone to campus security and thrown himself at their mercy, saying we were a *couple* and things had gotten out of control. He told them he was *worried* about me. Public safety came to the hospital and told me how *lucky* I was to have such a great boyfriend."

"You can't be serious," Alex shouted, coming off harsher than he intended.

Peter could not keep quiet. "Oh, it gets better."

Kat shot him a warning glance. "Josh called Mom and Dad, and they whisked me home for a couple days.

But amid it all, we never stopped to consider the hospital's failure to give me a morning-after pill. In the meantime, the police investigated, with Deke brothers giving affidavits about how I had been dressed that night and how I was seen drinking and dancing with Reid. One of the frat brothers even swore he heard me begging Reid to, and I quote, 'Fuck me hard.' Another said I was so drunk the bruises were from me tripping and falling. And Nate…"

Kat stopped, causing Luke to cross the room and place a hand of support on her shoulder. "Enough," he said. "the rest can wait."

"I've gone this far…" she said, looking at Alex. "It's time he knows it all."

"Are you sure?"

She shrugged. "I might as well get it over with."

Luke felt his heart swell with pride.—"Okay." He moved to resume his position next to Peter.

"So, anyway," she went on, "Nate provided an affidavit that said I liked rough sex when we were together. He even added that I liked being hit. Which, for the record, I don't."

Alex's heart ached as he now understood her visceral reaction to Nate. "Meanwhile, Reid's father was proposing plans for a new student center, so you can imagine the weight that carried in their favor."

"After spending a week at home, I returned to campus thinking I might have some support, other than Josh and Mariah, yet people only seemed interested in gawking and gossiping. Then the anonymous phone calls started- guys tormenting me. And maybe I could have made it through all of that, but then the police decided there wasn't a case, since Reid stated it was all a romantic evening that had gotten out of control. I completely fell apart." Kat leaned against the wall.

"Dad made arrangements for me to finish my senior year as an independent study at home so I could still graduate. Even then, the phone calls didn't stop until we got an unpublished number. In the meantime, the college announced that the Morgan Family Student Center would break ground the day after graduation, completely funded by Reid's father."

Alex closed his eyes. "Jesus, Kat, I'm so sorry."

"Oh, it wasn't over."

Alex tried to imagine what more could have happened.

"When I came home, I just wanted to hide, and lick my proverbial wounds, but then two months later, I-" Kat hugged her knees closer.

"Being a runner, my periods had never been very regular, so it wasn't until the end of March that I realized I was queasy a lot and my favorite jeans weren't fitting right."

Alex suddenly realized what she was saying, and his eyes grew wide.

"I went to the doctor and found out I was two months pregnant. I'd had periods since Nate and I had broken up—the rape was the only possibility. And so, I had to figure out what to do. My parents..." She looked at Peter and Luke adoringly. "...and Pete and Luke and Jess were wonderful. Mom and I spent many hours weighing options before I decided to abort the pregnancy.

"Mom was sick with strep throat on the scheduled day, so Dad took me, and he wasn't happy about it. I mean, he was a pro-choice guy, but not so much when it came to his little girl. He never said a word to try to stop me, but I knew how he felt.

"When we got to the clinic, Dad said he loved me no matter what and he offered to go in with me. I told him I needed to do it alone; I couldn't ask him to hold my hand through it, knowing how he felt."

Alex tried to imagine her father's pain as he watched her walk through that door.

"But it didn't matter in the end anyway because I couldn't go through with it; I called it off just before the procedure. We went home and discussed how I was going to have the baby and how we were going to make sure, as a family, that the baby never knew anything but love." Kat's eyes were full of tears as she looked to her brother. "She never knew anything but love, did she, Pete?"

"She was loved through and through," he said. "That is certain." His voice broke. "She still *is* loved; that never changes."

Alex's mind reeled as the pieces fell into place. When Kat had referred to missing "her", he had assumed she meant her mother. He now knew differently.

Kat's voice trembled. "Over the following months, my pregnancy became obvious." She paused.

When she resumed, her voice seemed stronger, "But we had figured it all out. I was going to have the baby and stay in New York with Mom and Dad. Once the baby was old enough, I could think about working. We even made a nursery out of the room off my bedroom. And then, Dad was contacted by Reid's father. They wanted to offer a financial gift—not as an admission of guilt, but because I had 'obviously misunderstood what had happened that night.'"

"Did Reid or his father know you were pregnant?" said Alex.

"No," said Kat, "we never told them."

"Did you accept the money?"

She shook her head. "I didn't want to. I wanted nothing to do with any of it—I just wanted to make a life for me and my child." She looked at Peter. "Remember how she used to kick in my belly when we watched TV at night?"

The pain on Peter's face was replaced by a smile as he thought back. "She packed a wallop," he said. "I remember watching your stomach move as she danced around."

"Especially when you played the drums."

"Yeah, that was the best." He gazed at Alex, suddenly so relieved to be able to share the memories.

"Peter was my birthing partner." She grinned, then looked at Alex. "But you asked about the money. I refused, but Dad convinced me otherwise. He said that by accepting their settlement offer, the baby would always have financial stability. I put it in a trust fund on his recommendation." She looked embarrassed. "It was a million dollars, and it seemed like a huge amount at the time, but frankly, Reid's father had spent eighteen million on the stupid student center, so it was nothing to him."

Kat's face clouded. "I had a doctor's appointment in late September, and I decided to take a cab that day because it was hot, and I was tired." Her shoulders sagged. "My cabbie was in a hurry to pick up his son at school, and he was driving like a bat out of hell. He flew up a side street and gunned it through a yellow light. As we went through the intersection, a moving truck plowed into the side of us." Her voice trembled. "I was thrown against the driver's side wall of the cab, fracturing three ribs and throwing me into labor."

Kat sat straighter and now leaned against the wall in exhaustion, her face ghostly pale. "I was rushed to the hospital and immediately whisked into a delivery room because she was ready to be born. When Pete got there, they were assessing whether I could naturally deliver with broken ribs. And then, several hours later-"

"And incredible pain on Kat's part," Peter interjected. He smiled at her with tear-filled eyes. "And you never complained."

"She was born several hours later. Five years and four days ago, Rose Belle, our Rosie, was born at three pounds, one ounce, and seventeen inches long."

Alex could not help himself from interrupting. "Four days ago, when you took off for the day?"

Kat nodded. "I needed to be alone. I'm sorry, but it was the best excuse I could think of." She wrapped her arms around her knees again to keep from crying. "Five years, four days ago. She was so little and the accident caused her to arrive too early. But she tried so hard..."

Kat laid her head on her knees as her shoulders shook with soft sobs.

The three men sat in silence. Alex looked up at Peter and Luke and saw tears running down their cheeks too, and suddenly realized his own were wet. Peter wiped his eyes.

She lifted her head and looked straight at Alex.

"But no matter how hard she fought or how hard we all tried or how hard the hospital tried, it was too much for her little system," she said. "She died five days later."

Alex thought of ways he could convey his sadness. "Oh, Kat…"

It was as if she did not hear him.

"We came here three days later for a private funeral." She looked at Peter. "And this is the rest of what you don't know, and I'm sorry for that, Pete."

"It's okay, Kitty, tell me now."

"That night, after the funeral, we came back here. And I was supposed to go to sleep."

"Yeah," said Peter, "because you needed it. We even sedated you so you could rest."

"You *thought* you sedated me," she countered.

"No, we literally did. I saw Mom gave you the pills. She made you show her your mouth after you swallowed, like you were a kid again."

"That's partially the way it went," she said. "I hid them under my tongue and spat them out."

Peter raised a brow. "What's the other part?"

"I snuck out that night to walk back to the cemetery while you all slept."

Peter looked horrified. "That's over three miles," he said in disbelief. "You walked there after being in a car accident and having a baby?"

"I couldn't let her be there alone that night," she said in a small voice. "I know it sounds stupid, but I couldn't stop thinking she would be afraid. And frankly, it was the first time I was alone since her birth. I never had the chance to say the things I needed to."

"We would have taken you," said Peter. "Well, I don't know about Mom and Dad, but I would have taken you. Or at least walked with you or something."

"I know, but I couldn't tell anyone. I needed to do it alone. She was *my* daughter—the little life I had dreaded and resented but become excited to welcome. I needed to talk to her alone, so I sat next to the grave for about an hour before a man came out of the shadows."

Luke's shock was clear. "Jesus," he exclaimed.

Kat continued, "Remember how there was another funeral there the day Rose was buried?"

Peter and Luke nodded.

"It was for a twenty-five-year-old named Jacob White. He had been killed by a drunk driver as he crossed the road near the post office. It was his father who had been sitting at his grave, doing the same thing I was. The two of us talked for hours. We lost children on the same day and buried them on the same day. So, we sat between the two graves and drank a couple beers, and cried, laughed, and shared our life stories. When the sun started to come up, he gave me a ride, and I snuck back in."

"We never knew," Peter said incredulously.

"You weren't supposed to. It was my secret." She was desperate for her brother to understand. "Pete, in having that few hours, I wasn't on display. And so, when Mr. White drove me back here, we made a pact."

"What?"

"Every year, on the day our children died, we come back. I bring dinner, he brings beer. Tomorrow, I'll pick up a pizza and meet him there at dark. We'll let ourselves mourn, catch up on the year, talk about what could have been, and then move forward again."

"Okay." Peter tried to assimilate this new information, his head still reeling with emotion.

Luke leaned forward, suddenly realizing something. "Kat, if you're meeting him tomorrow, why do you come up the day before, and what is the meeting Mrs. Wyman says you go to each year?"

Kat took a deep breath. "I…"

"What?"

She looked down at her hands, suddenly afraid they may not like her answer. "I started a foundation with the money. I come up each year to shop for the local women's shelters, and then I give them a donation from the foundation each year." She swallowed, and her voice was small.

"I'm sorry I didn't tell you. I just wanted to make sure her life stood for something. I give the gifts in her name." She stood up, rubbing her arms as if cold. "Guys, I really need a moment. I promise I'll be back."

She walked away, fading into the darkness away from the fire.

Peter looked at Alex. "Sorry, Alex, I..."

Alex shook his head. "You don't need to say anything. As a matter of fact, I probably owe you an apology."

Peter looked confused.

"I'm sorry, Peter. And Luke, you, too. I'm sorry I wasn't there to support you during all of this. I'm sorry." He stood.

"I need to go find her."

Chapter Twenty

The front door of the cottage was ajar. In the quickly fading light, Alex could see Kat standing by the shore, staring out at the black water. He quietly approached her, unsure of what to say.

She made no move to look at him when he stopped beside her. "You don't need to say anything," she said. "It was time to tell you, even if it changes things between us."

Without saying a word, he moved to stand in front of her, reached out to cradle her face in his hands, and leaned down, willing every ounce of his love into a kiss.

Kat held herself stiffly, not touching him, not responding. As he continued to kiss her, she moved closer, then tentatively wrapped her arms around him. The kiss deepened as their passion erupted. Tongues danced and hands roamed until Alex reluctantly pulled back, feeling the need to speak aloud.

"I love you," he said.

"You what?" she said in disbelief.

"I love you. I have probably loved you since that night at the opera, but I have definitely loved you since the wedding weekend. And after what you just shared, I love you even more."

Kat stepped back and looked at him warily, crossing her arms in front of herself defensively. "You can't love me," she said. "I just told you I was raped, knocked up, and lost my child. The part I left out is how I fell apart to such an extent that my parents had to care for me. They got so burnt out that they needed a weekend away—that's when they were killed by a drunk driver. So, in effect, I killed my child and my parents. You can't love me; the pity you feel for me is mistakenly translated."

In a strange way, Kat's words filled Alex with hope. She had not denied her love for him; she was only justifying why someone would not love *her*.

He smiled and pushed a strand of hair away from her eye. "Nope. I love you." He rested his forehead on hers. "I love you, but I don't think you love yourself. Truth is, that's okay, because I love you enough for the two of us. Now that this big secret is out in the open, we can move forward."

"You think that now," she said, "but you may feel differently in the cold light of day."

"Do you love me?" he said.

Even in the darkness, he could see her eyes glisten with tears. "Oh, God, yes, Alex, I love you."

He wrapped his arms around her and kissed her forehead. "Then it's settled—I love you, you love me, and we can figure out the rest."

Kat started to cry, and Alex picked her up, cradling her close as he moved them to an Adirondack chair. He tried to imagine her pain, and he tightened his hold on her, hoping she could feel his love. Finally, her breathing slowed, and the sobs quieted. She sniffled. "Your shirt's all wet," she said.

Alex was amused that this was her immediate concern. "Yup," he said, "and it will dry."

"I love you," she said, looking up at him.

He smoothed her hair back and brushed the remaining tears from her swollen eyes. "And I love you. Nothing is going to change that."

Suddenly her eyes filled again. "Shit, Alex, I miss her so much."

His own eyes filled with tears. "I know, baby, I know." He stroked her cheek. "I wish I had been able to meet her."

Just then, the porch door swung open. Kat took a deep breath. "That's Pete, being as patient as he can be. I guess we should go back."

"If you're ready. Otherwise, he can wait."

"Ahh," said Kat, sounding more relaxed.

"Ahh, what?" He nuzzled her cheek.

"Your protective side is back."

"Is that good, or bad?"

"It's very good," she said, shifting on his lap, then standing up. "We have to go back." She held out her hand. "C'mon."

As they neared the cabins, Kat dropped Alex's hand and ran up the stairs, into Peter's arms. Alex watched as brother and sister held each other and cried. He could only hear fragments of their conversation but Rose's name was mentioned several times over the next couple of minutes.

Finally, Peter stepped back with one arm still protectively around his little sister and looked at Alex. "You two okay? I mean, really?"

Kat tipped her head in thought, and then a slow smile lit her entire face. "Yeah. We're good— really good."

"Well then, let's have dinner to celebrate."

The four of them discussed dinner options, leaving Peter and Luke surprised when Kat voted for a local diner- one the family had frequented before Rosie's death.

After burgers, fries, and local draft beer, the four made their way back to the cottages. At the steps of Peter and Luke's cabin, Kat paused. "Alex is going next door with me, but we'll see you in the morning," she announced. "I am so glad you guys came up today and I love you both so much."

Peter's voice shook. "I am so glad too, Kitty Kat. And I'm glad we can talk about it. I feel like I can finally mention her name without being afraid of driving you away."

Kat looked down at her feet. "Would it be okay if we hung the photo of all of us in the sunroom when we get home?"

Peter immediately knew the picture. "Of course. We would love that."

Kat stood on tiptoe and kissed her brother on the cheek. "Night, Pete. Night, Luke."

Alex and Kat walked in silence to their cottage. Inside, Alex lit the fireplace to take the chill out of the room. He put his arm around Kat. "What picture were you talking about?"

"Do you want to see it?"

"Of course," he said, surprised she would have it with her.

Kat left the room and came back a minute later with a wooden box. The top of the box was carved with a rose and two dates under it. Reverently, she placed the box on the coffee table and sat down, motioning for him to sit beside her.

She opened the box to reveal a soft green baby blanket. "I made this for her. I knitted a couple of them; one was buried with her." She picked it up and held it to her face. "I can almost still smell her." She set the blanket aside. "This is the first picture of her."

Alex looked at the framed image of a perfect, tiny baby girl in Kat's arms. The bruises on Kat's face and arms were visible from the accident, but the look of pure joy and love was clear on her face. "She was beautiful, Kat."

At the bottom of the box was a framed family photo. The baby was held protectively in Kat's arms, with everyone else wrapped around the two of them. "This is the one I meant," she said, her voice breaking. "It was the last photo taken before she died." She wiped her eyes.

"They told us there wasn't anything more they could do. Her organs were failing, so they recommended we hold her and talk to her and sing to her and let her know how much we love her. She died in my arms with my whole family around us."

Alex pulled her close and kissed her head. "How beautiful."

Kat leaned against him wearily. "I am so glad you know."

"Me too. So many things make sense now."

"How so?"

"Well, you said you get down this time of year. And it explains your reaction when I asked why you hadn't called me." He paused. "Kat, I am so sorry."

"For what?"

"For not calling you back. Maybe things would have been different. I'm sorry for not being there as you and your brother were both going through hell."

Kat turned to look at him fully. "Alex, don't apologize. I'm only recently beginning to figure it all out. I wish I hadn't been raped, of course, but I will never regret having Rosie.

"Despite what happened, I wouldn't give up having those days with her. I'm her *mom* and I wouldn't change that for the world. I've hidden this part of me for so long, and I won't do it anymore. I want to hang pictures of her. I want to say her name. I want to finally let myself *feel* it." Her voice broke. "I will live the rest of my life with the guilt I feel for getting in the cab that day. If I had walked, she might be here now. I know I can't change that, so I have to live with the guilt. If I had handled things better, my parents may have had an easier time and might not have needed a getaway."

"Their deaths, all three of them, are not your fault." How could she blame herself? "Kat, truly."

She stroked his face. "We'll have to disagree on that."

"Okay," he said, believing he could help her let go of the guilt with time.

There was a quiet knock at the door. Alex opened it to find a bottle of wine and a bottle of champagne, with a note that read, *Love you both*.

Kat chuckled from behind him. "Peter and Luke strike again."

Alex carried the two bottles into the kitchen. "Would you like something?"

"Wine, please."

When he returned to the living room, Kat was standing by the fireplace, gazing into the flames. He handed her a glass. "To the future."

"To the past and to the future." She took a sip, then looked at him searchingly. "You really love me?"

Alex placed his glass on the mantle, then took hers and put it there as well. He turned to Kat and pulled her into his arms. "I love you more than I can express. I have loved you since you interviewed me in Madrid. You know… when you looked like you'd bit into a lemon upon realizing I was your subject."

"I did not," she exclaimed.

"Yes, you did. And it was one of the sexiest things I ever saw. You, all professional-like, looking fine in those black jeans, asking your questions without letting me know anything about you. When we went out after the concert, I can promise you, I hoped you were coming back to the hotel with me that night." He smiled. "But I felt a bit guilty about hitting on my friend's baby sister."

"That's not love, that's horniness."

"I admit you turned me on, but I wanted to make love to you. I wanted to sleep next to you and wake up and have breakfast with you." His voice deepened, "After all that time I thought you never called, it was like the universe was giving us a second chance. Believe me, I wasn't going to screw it up again."

"Oh."

"And then there was dress shopping. The nervous look on your face when you came out of the dressing room made me want to protect you." He nuzzled her ear.

"Yes, Katherine, I love you to the moon and back. I love you; I like you; you turn me on; I want to protect you. Sometimes you make me insane, but more than anything, I love you."

Kat's last reservation dissolved. She reached up and pulled him down, kissing him with all her love. For the first time, Alex felt no hesitation from her, but knew he needed to let her take the lead. She pulled him to the couch and laid down beside him, not breaking the kiss. She tugged his shirt free, needing to feel his skin on hers.

For long minutes, they kissed; hands roaming, tongues teasing. When she started to unbutton his shirt, Alex stopped her. She pulled back and he kissed her lips softly. "I promised you I would respect your boundaries. This is uncharted territory." He grinned and nipped at her bottom lip. "And as much as it kills me to stop you right now, I need to know what you want."

Kat was no longer afraid. "I want to make love with you," she said, her eyes glowing.

Alex stood up and took her in his arms. "Then we need to move to the bedroom."

Alex placed Kat gently on the bed. Silently, he laid next to her and caressed her face with his fingertips. Her breath caught in her throat as desire overwhelmed her. Stroking her hair back from her face, he kissed her deeply. He smiled as her tongue met his in a tantalizing dance. He rubbed her back and slid his hands under her cardigan to touch her soft bare skin.

Kat's hands wandered over his chest and she unbuttoned his shirt; her fingertips trailed across the hair on his chest. Alex gasped under her light touch. He looked into her eyes, recognizing her hesitation. He slowly nibbled on her lower lip.

"Kat, I love you. If you want to stop, just say so. I won't be mad."

"I don't want you to stop. I'm just-"

"What?" He stroked her face. "Tell me."

"It's been an intense day. My head is spinning."

"Do you want to take this slow?"

She ran her fingertips over his chest, suddenly realizing how much she wanted to touch every inch of him. "No," she said, "if anything, I can't wait much longer." She smiled.

"Well, then we should probably do something about that." He ran his hands lightly down her sides, feeling her breathing change.

She giggled, and he realized it was one of the sexiest sounds he had ever heard. Still giggling, she eagerly opened the rest of his shirt. He stopped to unbutton his jeans while Kat stood to pull hers off.

She now wore only her unbuttoned cardigan and a pair of silk bikinis. Blushing, she scurried to get under the covers, but Alex kicked them out of her reach as he lay beside her in only his unbuttoned jeans.

Reverently, he traced a line from the rapid pulse in her neck to the shadow between her breasts. Pushing the sweater aside, he drew a sharp breath as he saw her perfect shapeliness for the first time. Looking into her shining eyes, he kissed the shadow. "Kat, you are more beautiful than I imagined, and believe me, I've spent a lot of time imagining," he murmured.

His eyes went to a small tattoo over her left breast. He traced it with one finger. "A rose for Rosie."

Kat knew what he was thinking. "If you had seen it before you knew the whole story, I would have had to tell you, which I wasn't ready to do, or lie to you, which I didn't want to do." She blushed. "I also couldn't make love to you with a secret like that."

The small red rose rested in a heart with two dates on either side, representing the life of a beautiful little girl. "It's perfect," he said, looking uncomfortable. "Is it going to weird you out if I touch it when we...?"

Kat blushed at the intimate words. "No, it won't weird me out at all. Now please take off your clothes."

"With pleasure."

Alex stood and stepped out of his jeans while Kat lay on the bed watching. She had seen him naked from the waist up but seeing him totally naked for the first time made her heart race. His body was perfect in her eyes. He leaned over and kissed her parted lips. "Do you need help with the rest of your clothes?"

Biting her lower lip, Kat shook her head. She pulled her sweater off and then slid the wisp of black silk off her hips. Totally naked, she laid back on the bed, never taking her eyes from his.

The bed moved as Alex came to lie beside her and kiss her deeply. Where their bodies met, he could feel her racing heart. Murmuring words of endearment, he began to lightly kiss his way around her face and neck. Slowly, he kissed her shoulders and arms, smiling as she gasped when he reached the hollow of her collarbone.

He kissed every inch of her until he reached her swollen, rosy peaks. He skimmed his fingertips over the sensitive skin until she began to move restlessly. His tongue flickered out to tease them as she arched her back, giving him easier access. Slowly, he continued on to kiss her smooth stomach, and then he stopped. For an agonizing moment, Kat thought he was through, and perhaps her reaction had turned him off.

Then she saw the loving look on his face. He looked at her with passion and hope as he laced his fingers through hers. "Say it, Kat. I need to hear you say it."

With complete understanding, she looked into his eyes. "Please make love to me, Alex."

With the smile of a conqueror, he softly kissed her mound of reddish-gold curls. Lightly licking and nibbling, he became unbearably aroused listening to her gasps, until he heard her say, "Please, I need to feel you inside me."

Alex slowly slid into her warmth; the months of pent-up desire was called upon as soon as she wrapped herself around him. Bracing himself on his forearms, he looked down at her flushed cheeks and eyes that glowed in the lamplight. Slowly, he moved in and out, watching her look of wonder. He leaned closer to lightly lick her ear. She gasped and her muscles tightened around him.

"God, Kat, you feel so good." He slid back, so they were barely in contact. She bit her lip and opened her eyes. The fear in them caused him to pause. "Baby, what is it? What are you afraid of?"

"I don't know. I don't feel in control anymore. This is so different. I don't know what to do."

"Good different, or bad different?"

"Good different."

"Then enjoy it. Stop thinking so much."

He leaned down and began to lightly stroke her lips with his tongue. "Let go, Kat. Nothing that happens between us is wrong. Let yourself go and just feel. This is right. This is love."

She ran her hands down to his waist and pulled him closer. Alex watched the emotions play on her face as he began to move again. She closed her eyes and her lips parted as her muscles tightened around him and her breathing became ragged. He felt her fingernails dig into his back as she contracted around him. "Alex... Oh, God, Alex."

Smiling, he lost himself to the tide of passion as he poured into her.

Neither of them knew how much time had passed before Alex stirred. "Oh, baby, I must be crushing you."

Kat tightened her arms around him. "No, you aren't. Don't move. I don't want this to end."

He gently untangled himself in order to pull her into his arms. "Don't want what to end? Me crushing the breath out of you?"

"No," she said, smiling sheepishly. "Our lovemaking. I don't want it to end."

He kissed her hair. "I have to admit, I've spent an ungodly amount of time fantasizing about it, but it was better than I ever imagined."

Kat stroked his chest. "It was like I was being drawn to the edge of a cliff, and even if I had wanted to, I couldn't have turned around. Suddenly, the whole world was swirling around me and it was like freefalling… and then I felt you come with me."

Alex kissed her gently. "You just needed to trust in us."

"Trust and love. I trust and love you." Tears pooled in her eyes as she looked at him. "Oh, Alex, thank you so much."

He caught a tear on his finger. "No, baby, thank you. You trusted me. That means more to me than you know."

"Do you think we could do it again?"

Alex raised an eyebrow. "Try and stop us."

Chapter Twenty-One

Kat rubbed the sleep from her eyes, realizing she was a little sore from their activity the previous night. As she stretched, it dawned on her that she had slept through the night, something she had not done in a long time.

Just then, Alex kissed her shoulder blade from behind, gently trailing kisses to her neck. Logically, she knew it was time to get up, but the sensations were too delicious to pull away from. He snaked his arm around her, sliding up under one breast to hold her close. "Tell me you aren't thinking of getting out of bed," he whispered.

She rolled over, pressing her breasts against him, feeling his arousal. "I was, but then someone started kissing me."

"Hmm," he said, "what are you thinking of *now*?" He slid his hand from her upper thigh, over her hip, and up her ribcage. She shivered in anticipation.

"You," she said, stretching so he could stroke the skin beneath her breast. "I'm thinking of you."

He grinned, his fingertips now brushing across her nipple. "What about me?"

She arched her back, wanting him to continue. "At the risk of swelling your ego, if you don't make love to me now, I may scream."

"Really?" In one fluid movement, he rolled her on her back, gracefully resting on his arms above her, looking down at her lovingly. "So, you want to make love with me again?" he said, rubbing against her tantalizingly.

Her fingernails bit into his back, "Damn, Alex. Yes. Now."

She thought she would lose her mind in her need to feel him inside her again. She reached down to his lower back and pushed him toward her, urging him to enter her.

"Do you love me? Still? In the cold light of day?"

She looked up at him, recalling her own words from the night before. "More than I can tell you," she said with certainty.

"And do you believe that I love you too, and nothing will change that?"

Kat nodded. "I do. Now can you please, please make love to me?"

With a smile, Alex slid into her, hearing her sigh with pleasure.

An hour later, Kat rested her head on Alex's chest, listening to the reassuring sound of his heartbeat. "Okay," she said, "I think we should get up now."

"You're probably right," he said, stroking her back. "What do you want to do today?"

"I don't have the foggiest idea," she said. "If I were alone, I would be working today, then I'd run, and go to the cemetery."

"Do you still want to do that?"

"No, but maybe we could all go to the shelters, so you can meet the people I work with on this stuff. And maybe we could show you where our grandmother lived and take a walk before we go over to the cemetery."

"That sounds great."

Several hours later, Luke drove the Jeep into the driveway and smiled at Alex as Kat and Peter nearly jumped from the car. "You go ahead," he said, waving Peter on, "we'll be right there."

As the siblings walked away, Luke turned to Alex. "It's like now that her secret is out, she can't wait to show you everything."

Alex nodded. "I think she held it in so long, that now she wants to show you and Peter that she had a plan and followed it."

As they walked into the shelter, Kat happily introduced them to the directors of five women's shelters from around Massachusetts who were gathered there for their monthly meeting. The men sat stunned as the directors spoke of Kat's generosity to their clients, financial support, and personal time and attention. Peter's eyes brimmed with tears as he listened to how his sister had grown close to a rape victim, even traveling from Spain to accompany the young woman to court to confront her rapist.

They went out for a late lunch, then back to the cottages. Sitting on the porch, Kat looked at her brother. "Are you really okay with this? I'm going to get a pizza and eat dinner at the cemetery. That isn't too much?"

Peter looked at her seriously. "My head is already spinning; nothing you could say would shock me. Pizza and beer at the cemetery doesn't sound even remotely weird at this point."

Kat laughed. "Okay." She stretched. "I'm going to rest for bit. Meet here at seven?"

Peter and Luke nodded, and Alex looked at her quizzically, causing her to blush. "Seriously, Alex, I'm taking a nap, but if you want to join me…"

Kat kicked her shoes off inside the cabin, then stretched out on top of the comforter. Alex came over and laid down next to her. "Sleepy?" he said.

She smiled and reached up to tangle her fingers in his hair. "Sort of," she said. "I'm emotionally fried, more than anything. I needed a break."

"Do you want some time alone?" He caressed her face. "It's okay if you do."

"No. I want you here."

He could not help thinking she looked vulnerable. "Could you just hold me for a bit?"

"Of course," he said.

Kat snuggled into his arms, much like a child, while Alex held her and stroked her back. He could only imagine how painful all of this must be. No matter how cathartic it was, it drained her. Before long, her breathing slowed as she fell asleep.

While Kat slept, Alex worked to piece together the information from the last twenty-four hours while also working to ignore his physical reaction to her very presence. He had certainly had enough lovers in his life, but none of them had ever made him feel the way she did.

Two hours later, he stroked her hair and whispered, "Hey, Sleeping Beauty, it's time to wake up."

Kat blinked the sleep from her eyes, realizing the time. "Hey," she said, sitting up, "I need a shower."

"Okay, I'll just head over to visit with Peter and Luke."

"Alright," she said, pulling clothes from a drawer. She headed to the bathroom, clearly inside herself. She stopped, turned, and looked at him through stricken eyes. "I don't mean to shut you out, you know. I don't know how to do this any other way than alone."

He crossed the room and hugged her. "I don't know how or what to do, so we'll figure it out together. I'll give you a few minutes to yourself." He kissed her hair. "I love you."

"I love you too."

Next door, Luke sat on the porch reading a book while Peter stared off at the lake. As Alex walked up the steps, Peter looked at him. "Did she sleep?"

"Yeah, for about two hours."

"Good, she needed it."

"I know." Alex sat in the empty rocking chair.

Peter turned his attention back to the lake. "You know, Alex, I have no fucking idea how she has kept going. The shit those assholes did to her after the rape— the calls, the comments—they would have destroyed most people. Then when she found out she was pregnant, she was like a friggin' train— She plowed ahead, doing everything she was told. If they said walk three miles a day, she did it. She didn't drink a drop of alcohol or caffeine.

"When they recommended antidepressants for the stress, she refused. The doctor recommended yoga, so she took classes. She also listened to Mozart because the doctor said it was good for the baby. And talk? Shit, she talked to that baby constantly. She called her Bubba because she didn't want to know the gender, but you'd hear her telling Bubba how much she loved her and talking about all the things they were going to do together.

"She was hurt so badly in the accident, and it was like she didn't even realize it— Bubba was all that mattered. His voice cracked. "Shit, watching her push with broken ribs? Even the nurses were crying."

He looked at the lake, no longer seeing Alex as he recalled the past. "Then, for those five days, I don't think Kat slept one minute. I think somehow her soul knew Rosie wasn't going to survive, and she wasn't going to miss a minute with her. She held her, talked to her, sang... She made up songs about how much Mommy loves Rosie. When she died, Kat wouldn't let them take her away. She just held her— didn't cry, just held her. I swear I actually saw her heart break in two. Then, when Mom and Dad tried to make the arrangements for the funeral, Kat insisted on planning it herself. And fuck, now we know how much she went through here, after the funeral, all alone."

Alex tried to find the right words, realizing Luke had put his book down and was now watching the two of them. Finally, Alex spoke. "Pete, it had to be alone." He thought back to his own parents. "My parents lost several babies before I was born. My mom said the reason their marriage survived it was because they were the only two people in the world who shared the exact experience; they weren't alone in their grief. You all were there, loved Kat, loved Rosie too, but ultimately, Kat was the only parent. She had to do it alone to a certain extent."

"Maybe. When we came home, she became invisible. She stopped eating, running, and writing. She sat in the rocking chair in her room for hours. My parents worried that she was suicidal. I don't think she really was. I think the grief was so profound that she went into a sort of dormancy. But they didn't leave her alone for as much as a minute. When they needed to go out, they called us or Jess to step in. Kat was in hell, and our parents were in their own hell as they watched her fall apart. They mourned the loss of their grandchild and the fact that their baby had been raped and treated the way she was."

Alex shook his head. "Damn, Pete, I am so sorry I wasn't around when they died. I remember getting the call in Italy, but I couldn't get back in time for the funeral."

"Six months after Rosie died, Jess and I convinced them to go to the shore for a long weekend. You know, get away, sleep for a night, and not worry about Kat." He rubbed his face. "Luke and I were living together by then, in the apartment, and we offered to stay with her because Dad couldn't stand the thought of her not having someone with her at all times.

"We were staying there, and it was a good weekend. Then Mom and Dad called to say they were stopping for dinner on the way home. From what the police said, they were just leaving the restaurant when they were hit. The only blessing is that it was instantaneous."

"The other driver was drunk, right?"

"Drunk and high. Driving without a license too."

"Then what happened?"

"You mean with Kat?"

"Yeah."

"We all planned the funeral together, came back here to bury our parents. Then Luke and I moved into the house with Kat. It had been left to Kat and I equally. Jess inherited an equivalent amount of money, so we moved in. And Kat remained invisible, but frankly, no matter how much we wanted to be with her every minute, we couldn't. So, I guess you could say we all sort of limped along for three months.

"Then, we came home one day, and there was a suitcase in the hall. Kat was sitting in the kitchen and said she needed a ride to the airport. She was moving to Spain that night. And until you came back into her life, she never really came home again."

"You mean she literally announced she was moving to Spain hours before she left?"

"Yes. I think if we had been late coming home that night, we would have just found a note on the counter."

Just then, the three men heard the door of the other cottage open. A few seconds later, Kat came around the corner. Pete took one look at her and jumped to his feet. "You've been crying," he said. "Are you okay?"

Kat smiled tiredly. "Calm down, Pete. This was what I was trying to tell you when you arrived. This is what I do when I come here. I cry, sometimes I yell, sometimes I throw rocks. Regardless, for a couple days, I let myself feel it fully, let it out, then try to put myself back together to face the world. So, yes, I just cried, a lot. And it's okay."

Alex could see Peter trying to stomp down the urge to protect his little sister from any sort of harm. Finally, he sighed and opened his arms to her. "Okay. I just want to help."

She hugged him tightly. "I know you do. And I love you. And I'm trying to let you in." Letting go of her brother, she moved over to stand next to Alex, and picked up his hand. "Are you all ready? We need to go."

As they drove through the cemetery gates, Alex could feel Kat get apprehensive. "Are you worried your friend will be upset we're here?"

"No," she said, "he'd never get upset. It's just different."

Alex spotted a sedan parked along the side of the roadway. "He brought someone," Kat said, sounding stressed. Alex thought he detected a note of jealousy in her tone. "He brought someone, and he didn't tell me."

Luke turned in his seat. "Well, so did you. Breathe, it's okay."

Peter parked the car, and Kat looked at her brother in the rearview mirror. "Can you guys wait here for a minute?"

"Of course."

Kat got out of the car, noting a woman in the passenger seat of the sedan. Mr. White was nowhere to be seen at first, until Kat saw him over at her parents' graves, on his knees, pulling weeds. "Mr. White?"

The man stood slowly and turned, his face breaking into a wide smile. "Katherine, you made it," he exclaimed.

The men in the car watched as the two ran toward each other, tears running down their faces as they hugged. The conversation could not be heard but it was clear that something Mr. White said pleased Kat immensely. Kat turned and waved in the direction of the Jeep. "C'mon, Pete, Luke, Alex, come here," she called.

Over the next few minutes, introductions were made, and Kat shared that Mr. White's guest was his fiancé, Dotty. Dotty got out of the car and Kat's joy in meeting her shone clearly on her face.

Mr. White took Kat's hand. "Okay, Katherine. Now you take them to see little Miss Rosie for a few minutes and visit your parents. We'll set up for dinner on the hill."

Peter wrapped his arm around his sister and together they walked ahead to stop at the small marker. The tiny headstone was beautifully engraved with a simple rose, with the words "Rose Belle Weston, beloved daughter, granddaughter, niece."

Kat knelt. "Hi, Rosie. We're here. Mommy brought Uncle Peter and Uncle Luke and Alex." Tears started to roll down her cheeks. "We love you, Rosie, and we miss you."

Peter crouched down and looked at the small stone. "Hi, sweetie. I miss you an awful lot. I sing your song a lot because I know you can hear me."

Luke knelt and brushed some dried grass off the stone. "Hi, Rosie, we love you always."

Kat stood up and wrapped her arms around herself. "We'll come back again in a bit. Let's go see Mom and Dad."

Peter and Luke stood up and started to move toward their gravesites. Kat gazed at the small headstone, holding herself stiffly. Alex moved forward and wrapped her in his arms from behind. She leaned back against him, and he kissed her ear. "I wish I'd met her."

"Me too."

"I love you," he said.

Those words made Kat come undone. She turned and hugged him, sobbing convulsively. Alex held her until her crying slowed. Pulling back, she wiped her face with the crumpled tissue in her hand. "Okay, let's catch up to the guys."

The six of them sat on a hill, ate pizza, and drank Molson Goldens. They toasted to the memory of Jacob, Rose, Mr. White's first wife, Dotty's first husband, and Kat's parents. Then Mr. White and Dotty told Peter and Kat about how they had gone to high school with their mom and regaled them with stories of her. As the moon rose, the group cried and laughed together.

After packing up, Kat and Mr. White walked hand in hand to the graves of the two children. As they walked, Mr. White looked down at Kat. "I like him," he said.

"Who?"

"Alex. I like him. I've been hoping you would find the right man. Seems he's it."

"I don't know if he's it, but I like him a lot."

"You told him everything?"

She nodded. "Everything, start to finish. Other than you, I'd never told anyone the entire story."

"Good," he said, squeezing her hand. "And you promise you'll come back for the wedding?"

"I promise."

Chapter Twenty-Two

Back in New York, the group unpacked, and Alex offered to make dinner. Kat sat on a stool and watched him cook, saying little.

After dinner, all four went into the sunroom, and when Kat started to yawn, Alex pulled a throw pillow onto his lap. "Lie down," he said. Kat lay her head on the pillow and fell asleep as Alex stroked her hair.

Hours later, Kat awoke in bed, realizing that she had fallen asleep on the couch but was now tucked in bed beside Alex. She rolled over and stroked his chest. "Hi," he said.

"Hi." She moved her hand lower as she reveled in touching him. He moved to stroke her arm, but she stopped him. "No. It's my turn to play."

"Really?"

"Really. I want to touch you all over. You have to be patient." With that, Kat rolled so she could kneel next to him, her hands roaming to touch his shoulders, his legs, and hips— her fingers just skimming his skin. In the dim light coming through the window, she saw how aroused he was becoming. She bent down, her lips and tongue now tasting everywhere her hands had been.

Alex drew a sharp breath as she slid his boxers down his hips, then took him in her mouth, "Jesus, Kat."

"You want me to stop?"

"Hell, no, baby. Just let me touch you too."

"Not yet," she said, continuing to taste, lick, nip, and just barely run the tip of her tongue across his skin.

Finally, she leaned back to pull her tank top off, then moved to straddle him. His hands came to rest on her hips. "Patience," she reminded him, pushing his hands back to his sides. Slowly, she rubbed against him, feeling him strain against her.

"Kat, enough. I want to touch you."

She leaned down, her hair cascading around them like a veil. She kissed his lips briefly, still rubbing against him. "Why? You aren't enjoying this?"

"Yes, I'm enjoying this," he growled. "It's just…"

"What?" she teased, while slowing moving her hips.

Alex could not take it anymore and his hands grasped her hips possessively. "In this case, patience is not one of my virtues."

He moved to slide inside her, and Kat started the rhythm, loving every moment. Within seconds, passion overtook them, and conversation ceased as she continued to move.

Alex stroked her hair as their breathing returned to normal. "I don't know what I did to deserve that but thank you."

She laughed, tightening her arms around him. "I just wanted to touch you," she said sounding tentative. "You don't mind, do you?"

He shifted so he could look down at her. "I love touching you, babe. I love you touching me. You can wake me up anytime you want."

Kat was sipping coffee when Alex came into the kitchen on Monday morning. "Why didn't you wake me?" he said, kissing her forehead.

She smiled. "You were sleeping so peacefully; I didn't have the heart to disturb you."

He leaned down and pulled her hair aside to nibble on her neck. "Yeah," he said, "somehow mind-blowing lovemaking makes for deep sleep."

"Really?" She blushed.

He poured a cup of coffee and looked at her. "What are your plans today?"

"I need to get a revision to my editor by Thursday, so it's going to be a rush for the next couple days. You?"

"Planning session today, rehearsal tomorrow. We're recording on Wednesday and Thursday if all goes well."

"So, we are back to reality… busy, busy," she said mournfully.

"At least we're together."

"Yeah," she said, her gaze fixed on nothing in particular.

"Are you okay?"

Kat sighed. "Yeah, I'm fine. We just had so much change in our lives over the last few days, and now it's back to the mundane."

He pulled her to her feet and wrapped his arms around her. "I know," he said, "but we'll make the evenings special, I promise."

The week went on, and on Thursday morning, Alex approached Kat as she worked. "Done editing?" he said.

"Just about. It'll be done by noon today."

"Then what?"

"Then I can get back to writing for a bit."

"Any plans to work tomorrow?" he said, trying to sound nonchalant.

"Just writing, why?"

"Just wondering."

The next day, Alex kissed Kat goodbye in the kitchen. "What are you doing today?"

"Same ole, same ole," she said, "then running after work. Why?"

He pulled her close. "How about stopping by the studio around ten this morning?"

"For what?"

"I have a surprise for you."

"And I have to go to the studio to get it?"

"Yes."

"Tell me now."

"No." He grinned, his eyes twinkling. "You have to come there, or no surprise."

"I'll be there."

Kat walked through the studio door at exactly ten. Alex stopped the band and came out to kiss her. When he pulled back, she smiled. "I guess that falls under the category of making sure everyone knows our status."

"I love you," he said, stroking her arm. "That's what it means."

"So? My surprise?"

Alex pulled her into the hall for some privacy. "I was thinking we could go away for the weekend?"

Her eyes sparkled. "I'd love to, where?"

"Here. New York. I got us a corner suite at The Plaza for the weekend."

Her eyes lit up. "Really?"

"Really. I have your travel bag ready to go, here in the office, and a car is waiting to whisk you away. I booked you a pedicure at noon, a massage at one, and then I'll be there to join you at three." He ran his hands along her curves, resting them on her hips. "You, my lady, are going to go be pampered for the day, then we are going to have the entire weekend to ourselves."

"You arranged all of this?" she said, giddy with delight. "That sounds so nice."

"It does, doesn't it? You sounded so down about going back to the mundane, I wanted to do something special."

Kat stretched up to wrap her arms around his neck before kissing him passionately. His warm hands slid up her back, pulling her close. They both jumped as Peter whacked a drum.

Alex laughed and stuck his head into the recording studio. "Fuck off, Pete."

"Hey, that's my little sister, remember?"

Kat slid under Alex's arm to enter the studio and went over to hug her brother. "I kissed him first."

Peter rolled his eyes. "Don't you have somewhere to be?"

"You know?"

"Of course," he said, "we've been in on it all week." He kissed her cheek. "Have fun, see you Sunday night. Love you."

Alex carried Kat's overnight bag and walked her to the awaiting car. Handing her bag off to the driver, he turned to kiss her once more. "I will see you at three."

"At three." Kat squeezed his hand. "Thank you so much."

He pulled her close. "I love you—it was my pleasure."

Kat checked in at the hotel and a bellhop showed her to the suite. She walked around, delighted by the beautiful rooms with full views of the cityscape. The kitchenette was fully stocked with wines, beers, cheeses, fruit, and chocolate. Damn, he had really planned. A large crystal vase holding long-stem red roses was on the dining table with a card.

Kat,

As I said, I grabbed your travel bag, but take the card and go shopping if you want.

I love you, can't wait to be with you. See you in a bit.

Alex

Behind the note was a gift card to Bloomingdales. She laughed. Looking at her watch, she realized that if she left right away, she had time to shop before her pedicure. Something slinky would be perfect for tonight, she thought.

Alex was in the hotel elevator when he got her text. *By my watch, it's 3:03, where are you?* He smiled.

Two minutes later, he slid his keycard through the reader. Opening the door to the suite, the first thing he saw was a very sexy black negligee draped over a chair in the foyer, with a deep rose colored one on the next chair. A folded note rested on the table between them. Opening the card, Alex's eyes widened.

I couldn't decide which one to wear tonight—your choice.

At that moment, Kat appeared in the doorway, barefoot, wrapped in a white hotel bathrobe. She frowned playfully. "You're late."

Alex dropped his bag to gather her in his arms, kissing her hungrily. "Sorry I'm late, and damn, you know how to get my attention."

"Thank you."

Picking up his bag, he took her hand and pulled her into the living room. "How was your afternoon?"

"Absolutely perfect."

"Good, just as I planned." He looked around, then looked down at her. "Is the room okay?"

She swatted his arm. "It's perfect and you damn well know it."

"I'm going to take a shower, then, your wish is my command."

"Nope."

Alex was confused. "Huh?"

"I want you. Now," she said firmly.

"Baby, I want you too, but I need a shower first." He nuzzled her neck. "You smell amazing, and I smell like the studio. Five minutes is all I need."

"Fine," she groused.

As Alex walked into the bathroom, he called, "Five minutes."

As soon as Kat heard him shut the shower door, she slipped out of her robe and quietly entered the bathroom. As she walked toward the glass enclosure, she could see bubbles cascading down his tan, muscular back. She opened the shower door and smiled as he jumped with a start. "Hi," she said.

Alex smiled, pushing his wet hair off his face. "Hi, yourself. Decided you needed a shower too?"

She moved forward, relishing the feeling of the warm water. "No… I told you, I want you. Now."

He rested his hand on the shower wall while the other hand slowly caressed her breasts. "Really?"

Kat arched her back. "Really."

Alex picked her up so she could wrap her legs around his hips, and he slid inside her. "Damn, I love you."

"I love you too." As they slowly made love, the two of them murmured words of endearment.

Alex gently toweled her dry. Cinching the belt of the robe around her waist, he smoothed back her hair. "You are full of surprises," he said.

Kat sat on a chaise, watching him towel off. "Sorry, no patience." She looked down at her hands, suddenly quiet.

"What's the matter?"

"Nothing."

Shrugging on a robe, he crouched down in front of her to look into her eyes. "What's going on?"

Her cheeks grew red. "I'm sorry."

"For what?"

"I couldn't wait. I needed to know you needed me as much as I need you."

Once again, her vulnerability floored him. How could she be apologizing for this? Men dreamed of someone like her walking into the shower. How could he make her understand?

He stood and pulled up a chair. "Let me understand. You're apologizing for joining me in the shower?"

She could not bring herself to look at him. "I told you I wanted you, you said you wanted a shower, and yet I forced the issue."

He put a finger under her chin, lifting her face to meet his. "Look," he said, seeing the uncertainty in her eyes. "Listen to me carefully. I'm so crazy for you, I was like a teenager the whole ride over. And the little lingerie show in the hallway did nothing to cool my desire. I would have happily taken you right in the hallway, on the couch, or on the kitchen counter— Anywhere, any time. You smelled so good, and I felt like a grub. It's as simple as that."

He rubbed his thumb against her lower lip, smiling as he saw her eyes darken with desire. "Kat, I want you as much, or more, than you want me. I struggle to keep my hands off you. You turn me on so much it boggles my mind. You walking into that shower was just the sort of thing I dream about at night."

"Really?"

"Really."

He took her hand and pulled her to the panoramic windows in the living room. He wrapped his arms around her, resting his chin on the top of her head, amazed by how much just being near her affected him, emotionally and physically. They had made love only minutes before, and yet he could already feel the pull of his desire for her again.

"Okay, love of mine. What do you want to do? We can stay here and order dinner. We can go out to the hotel restaurant, or someplace else. We can get a drink, and come back, and eat here. What do you want to do?"

Kat felt loved and protected, wrapped in his arms. "I don't know," she said. "I'm so happy right now that I can't think of anything beyond the next couple minutes."

"Then we don't need to decide now."

Without warning, he scooped her up in his arms and carried her to the overstuffed armchair facing the window. Settling into the chair with her in his arms, he said, "We can sit here all night if you want."

Kat smiled. "No, you know me. I'll get hungry at some point."

Alex brushed a curl off her temple, then stroked the side of her face. "Do you understand how much I love you?"

"Yes, I do."

She leaned forward and kissed him, and within minutes, their desire had blossomed again. Still in the chair, Kat untied their robes and slid them open. The lovemaking that followed was gentle, slow, and sweet, punctuated by ecstasy.

Later, Kat stirred. "Okay, so now I want to get dressed, get some dinner, then drink wine and watch the city from here."

"Sounds perfect."

While at the restaurant waiting for their entrees to arrive an hour later, Kat excused herself to the ladies' room. Upon her return, she noticed two attractive young women in scant dresses approach Alex. Even from a distance, she could hear their giggles, and then heard one of them say, "Aren't you Alex Tamaro?"

Alex seemed surprised by the intrusion. "Yes, I am," he said.

"We are huge fans." One shoved the other. "Could we get a few photos with you?"

"Sure." He stood and stepped away from the table as Kat approached. "I'd be happy to," he said.

Kat sat down without saying a word while Alex patiently stood for photos as each woman vied for his attention. "Thanks so much for your support, ladies. Now please excuse me, but I am on a date."

"Oh." The taller woman looked at Kat haughtily. "We didn't realize you were with someone." She nodded at Kat. "Anyway, Alex, thanks for the pictures."

As they walked away, Alex took Kat's hand and kissed it lingeringly. "Don't you dare look intimidated by them."

She looked at him, shocked by how quickly and accurately he could read her thoughts.

"I love *you*. *You* turn me on. *You* are the woman I want to be with. *You*."

Back in their suite, Alex sat on the bed and smiled at Kat. "As I remember, I had a choice to make about what you were going to wear tonight."

"You do."

"The pink one."

"I'll go change," she said, "and you go pour us some wine."

Minutes later, Alex felt his mouth go dry as Kat walked toward him, clad only in delicate wisps of rose silk. He traced the neckline, trying to keep his voice light. "You have amazing taste in clothes."

"Thank you."

Going over to the chairs by the window, she smiled as she noticed the glasses waiting for them. "Perfect."

Alex sat in the chair across from her and handed her a glass. "To us."

"To us." She raised her glass. "I love you. Thank you for planning all of this."

"My pleasure." He pulled a small box from the side of his chair. "This is to go with your outfit."

Kat's eyes grew big at the sight of the small Tiffany box. "Alex, you are spoiling me rotten, you know."

He took her hand and kissed her palm. "I'm not spoiling you." He grinned. "I'm *accessorizing* you."

Kat laughed and opened the box. Nestled on the blue velvet was a gorgeous diamond and opal bracelet. "Oh, Alex, it's gorgeous." She looked at him. "You shouldn't have. You didn't need to do all this."

Alex stood up and came to kneel in front of her, reaching up to hold her face in his hands, "I didn't *need* to do anything. I *wanted* to do this. I love you, and I had more fun planning this than I've had in a long time." He stroked her lips with his thumb, and saw her body respond through the thin silk. "Figuring out the details of this was a blast."

He picked up the bracelet. "This was the first part of my plan this week." He slid it onto her wrist, then looked at her with twinkling eyes. "Unless you don't like it."

She leaned forward and kissed him passionately. Pulling back, she looked at her wrist. "I love it, thank you."

The rest of the weekend passed in a blur of luxury and passion. They woke up late Saturday morning and ordered room service before taking a long walk through Central Park. That evening, they ordered room service and watched movies while cuddling in the king-sized bed. They made leisurely love on Sunday morning before stepping out for breakfast.

Walking back into the suite, Kat sounded wistful. "I guess we need to think about heading home."

Alex pulled her to him and kissed her hard. Her immediate reaction was a wave of desire, and within seconds, they were shedding their clothes as they headed to the bedroom one more time. Afterward, he kissed her hair as their heart rates returned to normal.

"*Now*, we have to think about going home…"

Chapter Twenty-Three

Alex returned to California two weeks later. With that, they found themselves in a long-distance relationship. Kat flew west when she could, ultimately getting to meet his parents; then Alex came east. It was not perfect, but it seemed to work.

Kat began to gather her scattered belongings on a Monday, following a weekend visit to California. Alex had been playing piano for several hours as she worked. Just as she was shutting down her computer, he abruptly stopped playing.

"Kat," he called, "where are we going with this?"

"With what?"

"With us. Where do you see our relationship going?"

"I don't know what you mean."

"I mean what's our status?"

"We're a couple. We try to be together as much as possible. You visit me. I visit you. We talk on the phone. We're monogamous."

His voice rose, "I need to know if this is all you see for us, this long-distance thing. Do you see us commuting like this forever?"

"*Forever* is a long time, Alex. All I know right now is that I love you and love being with you. I don't know any more than that. We've been together less than a year. We can't exactly make life decisions yet."

He nodded slowly, looking unhappy. "I guess you're right. But I feel so helpless thinking we'll be apart again by tonight."

"I feel the same way. But we both have big things coming up soon. I have the new book, we're going to Spain in January, and you and Peter leave on tour in February. At least we're spending Thanksgiving together. We need to keep things as simple as possible."

"What about Christmas?" he said.

She took a minute to think as she continued to gather her things. "What if we invited your parents to New York?"

Alex grinned. "That would be okay?"

"I'd love it."

"Great," he said, "we'll work that out. What if I fly out before Christmas to help you get ready? That way I can also get some work done with the band."

"That sounds great, but I'll miss you between now and then."

Alex pulled her onto his lap. "I'll miss you too. I guess we'll have to settle for the phone and email until then."

Chapter Twenty-Four

A week and a half before Christmas, Kat woke up late on morning, and tried to figure out what she was going to do with an entire day alone, as Luke and Peter were in Boston for the weekend. Pulling on jeans and a sweatshirt, she opened her bedroom door and was shocked to hear the stereo playing. She walked downstairs, assuming her brother's plans had changed, only to find Alex making coffee in the kitchen.

With a shout of joy, she raced to him. "What are you doing here?"

"Well, Peter mentioned they were going to be away this weekend, so I decided to surprise you."

She kissed him passionately. "God, I missed you."

"Me too." He handed her a cup of coffee. "Come cuddle with me, we'll worry about food later."

Sitting on the couch, they watched the snow fall outside.

Alex nuzzled Kat's neck and laughed as she shivered, her nipples becoming erect under her shirt. He pulled her onto his lap and began to kiss any exposed skin he could find. "So, what's our plan for the week?" he said between kisses.

"Well, I fly to Madrid on Monday," she said nonchalantly.

He stopped what he was doing and straightened up, nearly dumping her off his lap in the process. "What?" he exclaimed. "Why didn't you tell me?"

"Because I didn't know until last night and you didn't call last night."

"Because I was on my way *here*."

"I'm sorry. I didn't know you were coming, so I thought I had time to make this trip before Christmas."

"Couldn't you have talked to me about it before you made plans?"

"I didn't know until yesterday that the only serious female presidential candidate is willing to talk to me. She'll see me Wednesday morning, and I need at least one day to do research there."

"You're going to Madrid on Monday, and I only found out about it because I happened to show up two days before you leave?"

"Alex, I told you, I found out just last night, and we didn't talk until I saw you today."

"Because I was flying *here*!"

"How the hell was I supposed to know that? Why are you so worked up about this? I'll be back next Friday, so there will still be four days left to prepare for Christmas."

"Why go for so long?"

"A friend happens to be getting married, and I originally didn't think I could go. Now, I'll be there anyway, so I can attend the wedding."

"Why didn't you invite me?" Alex knew he sounded petulant, but he could not stop himself.

Kat's temper flared, and she stood up to face him. "Jesus Christ, Alex. You keep telling me how busy you are, and how many details still need to be ironed out for your tour. I didn't want to make you feel guilty about being unavailable, so I just didn't ask. Why are you being this way? It's not a big deal."

"It is to me."

"Why? I don't blow up every time you have to go somewhere without me. I need to go to Spain because of my job, and you're upset. I don't understand."

"I don't understand why you run off to these places. You certainly don't need to work. Even if you didn't have money, you know I'd support you. You could stay in New York or California and write. Or do something else if you want."

Kat's eyes widened. "So, my writing is a *hobby*, while your music is a *career*?"

"No, that's not what I mean. You don't have to race all over the globe; you could stay here, or in California."

"Are you saying I should become your kept woman?" she said, her voice becoming shriller. "You want me to stay home, have a cute hobby, and be here waiting for when you find it convenient? God forbid I not be here when you need servicing."

"I can't believe you would say that! I never said I wanted to, as you so nicely put it, keep you. All I want is for us to be in the same country, and for you to write on topics that don't take you into godforsaken countries."

"Spain isn't exactly a third-world country. I'm going for less than a week. Again, I didn't know you were coming; I didn't think you would mind. I'm sorry if this bothers you, but I've already committed to the trip. Of course, I would love it if you wanted to go with me."

"Oh, now that we're discussing it, suddenly I'm allowed to go? If I hadn't shown up here, what would you have done? Left a message on my machine on Monday saying 'I'll be back in a week. Don't call me, I'll call you?'"

"No. I planned to call you today and tell you."

"It would be nice if we talked about things before you made decisions."

"Did you ask how I felt about you being on tour for two months? Did you ask me to come along? No. You assumed I wouldn't want to."

"That's why I'm here," he said, now exasperated. "I came this weekend because I wanted to talk to you about getting an apartment together. I am tired of living without you. I want us to live together, and I want you to go on tour with me."

"You came here planning to throw the idea of living together at me? You never brought it up before," she spat. "And you accuse me of not talking to you about things!"

"I'll do anything I damn well please. You sure do," he countered.

"You can't be serious. You're doing exactly what you are accusing me of doing," she exclaimed.

"I am not. I'm here to have a conversation about this, I didn't sign a lease or anything. This is completely different. You decided to go away, *again*, without talking to me. I am just a spectator in this relationship, not a part of it. I can't do this."

"What are you saying?"

"I'm saying I need us to be together, wholeheartedly, or not at all. I can't do the long-distance, half-assed thing."

"Are you giving me an ultimatum?"

"No." His voice became more certain, "Yes. I guess I am."

"Alex, Jesus, how can you do this? We aren't at that point yet."

"I think we are. And if you are hesitating, then your answer is clear."

"Don't do this," said Kat.

"I have to. I love you, but I need to know where we stand— We're either together or we aren't. You making major plans without even talking to me is total bullshit. Clearly, I'm more invested in us than you are."

"I can't believe you would say that." Kat stood and grabbed her jacket and keys. "I'm going to Beth's. You're welcome to stay until you can get a flight back home later today."

She walked over and put her hand on the side of his face. "I'm sorry," she said. "I love you, but I will *never* be dependent on anyone, and I will never ask permission for anything. My career is just as important as yours. I won't live my life to please anyone other than myself. Goodbye, Alex."

Chapter Twenty-Five

Kat hurried through the quiet streets to the subway station to catch a southbound train. She held herself together until she reached Beth's apartment. When her friend opened the door, she gasped. "Jesus, Kat, what's wrong?"

"Alex and I just broke up."

"You did what? I thought things were fine. What the hell happened?"

"He was angry about me going to Spain without clearing it with him. I yelled back, reminding him he makes decisions all the time without consulting me."

Beth just stood, listening in silence.

She continued. "He says he came to ask me to move in with him. I accused him of double standards, and he told me to give up assignments that take me on the road, so I walked out." Tears began to escape from the corners of her eyes.

Beth hugged Kat as she led her into the kitchen, where she poured her a stiff shot.

"Drink this."

"I hate brandy."

"I know, but it will help."

"Help what? To kill me?"

"Just drink it."

Kat downed it and shuddered. Beth poured a cup of coffee. "Okay, the brandy will calm you down, and the coffee will keep you from getting a headache."

Kat started to cry in earnest. "Shit, Beth. I fucked up. I didn't talk to him before accepting the assignment. Now he feels like he doesn't matter."

She shared every bit of the conversation with Beth, who sat in stunned silence as Kat recounted the argument.

Beth looked pensive. "Okay," she said, "looking at it from my old-married-woman standpoint, you should have told him as soon as you could, but he shouldn't expect he can choose your assignments for you. He can't expect you to be sitting around waiting for him when he decides to pop in for a surprise visit. As I see it, you both need to figure out what you want from the relationship, and then work together on it. It's that or break up for good."

"What do I do?"

"No clue. Either cancel the trip because it's a big deal to him-"

"Not happening, the fact that I got this interview is too big of a deal. Besides, if I cancel, that will get around and hurt my chances for future work."

"Then try talking to him. Tell him this is important to you, but you see how you blew it by not talking to him *before* you booked the flights. Tell him you'll try to be more considerate in the future."

"So, you think I screwed up?"

"Yes, you did, and so did he. Somehow— text, email, voicemail— you should have let him know as soon as the trip came up. His ego is bruised now."

"Should I call him?"

Beth shrugged. "Maybe he's still at the house, looking for a flight. I suggest you go talk face to face. If he's gone, *then* call him."

Kat opened the front door, not sure which would be worse: to find Alex had left, or to find him still there. Her eyes went right to a piece of paper on the counter.

Dear Kat,

I don't know how to say everything I want to say. We both said awful things this morning. I love you. I will always love you. You're right. I was expecting you to live by a code I wasn't willing to follow. I thought I was being romantic by surprising you with the idea of living together, and instead, you saw it as controlling.

For me, the bigger issue is that I was here to ask you to live with me, but I realize that what I really want is for us to get married. I want us to be joined, not just in our hearts, but legally, and to have a complete life together— kids, dogs, and all. Right now, I feel like this can't work, and it's breaking my heart. Ultimately, I think we both need time alone to think about us. Now you know what I want for us... Please look in your heart and see if you want it too.

I love you. ALEX

Kat picked up the phone and dialed his cell, which went right to voicemail. With a trembling voice, she said,

"Alex. I just got your letter. Please call me when you get in. Please. I love you."

It was mid-afternoon when the phone rang.

Kat's heart lurched as she answered. "Hello?"

"Hi, it's me."

"Hi."

"I got your message."

There was a pause. She took a deep breath. "I love you."

Alex closed his eyes and sighed. "I love you too."

"I wish you had stayed here, so we could have talked."

"You told me to get out," he said.

"And you believed me?"

"You took off to Beth's instead of staying to talk it out."

"So once again, it's my fault?"

"No, people talk in a relationship. You should have talked to me about all of it."

"So, once again, we're back to my inadequacies as a partner. You were here to talk about moving in, and you accuse me of not sharing?"

"Yes, I was, I was trying to be romantic. But you were planning to leave the country without even telling me.

"And I was trying to be supportive of your career pressures by not adding to them right now. It's not like I didn't want you to know about the trip; I was planning on telling you."

"But you didn't. That's what it boils down to, Kat. I need to be first in your life, and I'm not. I come in a distant second or third to your writing and other people."

"Alex, I need to go. I can't handle this conversation right now. I love you but I'm leaving for Spain on Monday."

"I know that now," he said, his voice cracking. "I love you, but I can't go on like this."

"I know. Goodbye, Alex."

Chapter Twenty-Six

Kat wandered around aimlessly over the weekend until leaving for Madrid. The interview went well, and then she traveled to the northern coast of Spain for the wedding.

Throughout the festivities, she stayed outwardly cheerful, celebrating until dawn with a large group of friends. Silently, she left the reception and went to sit alone on the sea wall, looking at the cold ocean. A noise from below caught her attention— it was Secundino climbing up to see her.

He sat down next to her and lit a cigarette. His pockmarked face scanned the ocean. "Are you going to tell me why your smiles haven't reached your eyes today? And why isn't Alejandro with you? You haven't even spoke of him today."

"Fuck off, Secu," Kat said tiredly, "I'm fine."

"You're always fine, lovely. But you just recently softened and opened up. Now you're back to shutting everyone out. Why?"

She sighed. "Oh, Secu," she said, "I fucked up, big time." She closed her eyes and shook her head sadly.

"I've never really been in love like this before, so I didn't consider Alex could feel left out."

Secu raised a questioning brow. "You love him?"

"Of course, I do."

"Then you should have stayed and talked it out."

"I know."

"Have you called him?"

"No, not since the day after our fight. He was still angry, so I gave up."

"Why haven't you tried again? Doesn't this matter to you?"

"Of course, it matters to me," she exclaimed. "He suggested some time and space to cool off, and I agreed."

Secu snorted. "You need to start trusting him and your relationship."

"What are you talking about?"

"You need to trust his love is strong enough for each of you to make concessions."

Kat was genuinely confused. "Explain."

"You need to start giving each other some latitude. Start asking if you need or want something. If I do something Ana Lucia doesn't like, she screams at me. And when I get mad at her, it works the same way. We work it out. But you two are so afraid of upsetting each other that you would rather lose him than stand your ground and fight it out. You would rather lose him than honestly tell him you were afraid to ask him to accompany you because you are afraid he doesn't love you enough to rearrange his schedule."

Kat reached over and took a drag from his cigarette. "All right, Mr. Know-it-all, what do I do now?"

"My, my, asking for help. You are softening."

"Really, Secu," she implored, "what do I do?"

"Call him. Just start with hello. C'mon, I'll walk you to the Telefonica because the cell service here is awful."

At the phone office, Kat cautiously punched in Alex's home phone number. As it started to ring, she hung up.

Secu rolled his eyes. "Why did you hang up?"

"It's the middle of the night. I didn't want to wake him."

"And you have never woke him before, perhaps to...?"

Her blush told Secu the answer. "Call him now," he said.

She resolutely dialed again, and Alex answered on the third ring. "Hello?" He sounded annoyed.

Kat slammed the receiver down.

Exasperated, Secu picked it up. "Now, *hija*, you've hung up on him twice. Call him back and at least let him know it's you."

This time, Alex answered on the second ring. "Whoever you are, I hope to hell you know what time it is, and I really don't appreciate this shit."

"Hi," said Kat.

"Katherine?"

With the use of her full name, her heart sank.

"Yeah. Hi, it's me. It was me before too. I'm sorry I hung up, but..."

"But what, Kat?"

"But I just wanted to tell you I got here safely."

"I'm glad." There was a long pause. "However, if we'd gone together, you wouldn't have needed to call; I would have known firsthand."

Hurt showed in Kat's eyes. "I know. I'm sorry, but I did what I thought was best."

"I know you did," he said, softening his approach. "But you need to think about what's best for us as a couple and talk to me, rather than making decisions based on what you *think* I want or need."

Kat's voice hardened. "I'm not the only one who screwed up, Alex. Anyway, I just wanted to hear your voice, but I guess this is too soon. Goodbye."

"Kat, wait!"

"No. I tried, and you aren't ready to meet me halfway. Now the ball is in your court."

"But Kat..."

"Goodbye, Alex."

Kat hung up and turned to her friend. "I tried, Secu. I tried..."

Chapter Twenty-Seven

Once Kat returned to New York, she fell back into her normal schedule, although every time the phone rang, she hoped it was Alex.

Peter, Luke, and Kat had decorated the house for the holidays prior to her trip. Now that she was back, she shopped and baked, but could not really get into the holiday spirit.

Meanwhile, Peter did not tell Kat that Alex had been in New York, staying at a nearby hotel, while the band finished up some cuts. Peter and Luke planned their annual Christmas party at the house, inviting all of Kat's friends, hoping to cheer her up.

Guests poured through the doors on the night of the party and Kat welcomed them as they arrived. As the crowd grew, someone requested shot glasses, causing Kat to climb up on the counter to reach them; her back was turned as Alex walked in. He agreed to attend the party only because Peter had begged him, but the view of Kat's toned legs as she reached into the top cupboard took his breath away.

Alex was filled with hurt and jealousy as an unknown man carefully lifted her and the glasses off the counter; he turned to leave just as someone grabbed him by one arm.

"Come on, Alex," said Josh, "let's talk." He tugged him into the mudroom, as it was the only room not teeming with people.

"What is there to talk about?"

"Your reaction to what you just saw, for starters. Second, the fact that you obviously still love her. Third, she's going crazy missing you, but is afraid to call you again."

Alex stared at him stoically.

"She loves you so much it's amazing, but she's afraid you'll reject her. Why don't you get over yourself and talk to her?"

"She seems happy enough without me."

"Oh, screw you. You know you can't avoid her forever."

Alex held his ground and worked to appear indifferent.

"Look, she's one of my best friends, and I've lived through most of her relationships. She's going crazy trying to figure out how to make things right with you."

Alex refused to give in. "I'll think about it."

"Damn, you're even more stubborn than she is," said Josh as he stalked off and left Alex alone.

The Christmas tree glowed in the corner while Alex fantasized about making love to Kat on Christmas morning before showering her with gifts. Never in his life had he felt this way, and the realization made him remove his coat, as he decided to stay.

He walked back into the fray to discover that many of the partygoers had moved on to the sunroom for dancing. He watched Kat dance with the man he had spotted her with in the kitchen, and before he realized what he was doing, he approached them. "This dance is over," he said.

The man looked shocked and became defensive. "What?"

"I'm going to dance with Kat now."

"Maybe you should ask her first," said the man.

Alex turned to Kat, who was standing in stunned silence. "May I have this dance?"

She looked at him searchingly before silently nodding.

As they stood there looking at each other, a new slow song started, and Alex cautiously pulled her toward him, waiting for any sign of resistance. He wrapped his arms around her and sighed contentedly as she tentatively returned his embrace.

When the song ended, Alex gazed down at her. "It feels so good to hold you again."

She smiled sadly. "I know."

"Please, can we dance again? This is the first time in two weeks that we haven't hung up or walked out on each other."

"Alex, I've always been the last one to want to talk, but we need to."

"We will. Later. Please, just dance with me."

Kat nodded slowly as he pulled her close again. They danced the next three songs, and then he pulled her over toward a buffet table. She went willingly, beginning to feel a shimmer of hope. Standing nearby, Dave slapped Alex on the back and said, "Wasn't the last remix a bitch yesterday?"

"It was. I thought we'd never finish."

Dave nudged Kat. "Hey, lady, we've missed you around the studio lately. You too famous to hang out with bums like us?"

Kat grinned at Dave. "Nah, I just… Wait, you guys were remixing yesterday? Alex never told me anything about a remix."

"Hell, yea, we finished it up late last night," he said, sounding apologetic. "Hey, my gorgeous date is waiting for me on the couch. See you later."

As Dave sauntered off, Kat turned to Alex with narrowed eyes. "You've been in town and didn't tell me?" Before he could answer, she yanked his hand and pulled him toward the stairwell. "We need to talk… now… upstairs."

"But Kat…"

"Now!"

In the relative quiet of her sitting room, Kat pointed to the couch. "Sit down," she said, "I have some questions for you."

"Kat-"

"Don't give me any bullshit right now. I want answers. How long have you been in town?"

Alex squirmed uncomfortably on the couch. "Basically, on and off since I came to see you. I flew home for a couple days for my mother's birthday, which was when you called me from Spain. Then I came back to New York."

"Where have you been staying?"

"At a hotel."

"And I assume Peter and Luke knew?"

"Of course, they did. Come on, let me explain."

"Wait a minute. Now it's my turn. You've been here over a week, and you never told me? I bet you didn't think I'd be here tonight, did you?"

His silence gave her his answer.

"You accuse me of not telling you things, then you're here in town, and you avoid me to the point that you come to my house only because you thought I wouldn't be here?"

"Kat, wait-"

"No, *you* wait. I've had it. I made the effort to apologize. I didn't question when you showed up tonight. But now I find it was just another game, another fucking power trip. In other words, *you* do what you want, and *I* do what you want. What part of this did you think was so good for the *us* you were harping about?"

"Kat, listen to me," he yelled.

"No, goddamn it, I'm through listening. I've taken the blame for the problem between us. I admit I screwed up about the trip to Spain. I admit it. But now this isn't my fault. I tried to make amends. I tried to call and apologize. But you're playing by different rules, Alex. It's not okay for me to make decisions but it's okay for you to do it. Do you have any idea how much it would've hurt to run into you on the street? I've been trying to deal with missing you, just trying to get through each day. And now I find out I could have bumped into you looking at Christmas windows. It would have destroyed me to run into you like that."

With her fists clenched, she looked at him. "It would have hurt almost as much as it does now. Do you care?"

She turned to face the windows before turning back to look at Alex. "God, Alex," she said, her voice softening, "I love you so much it's inconceivable. But..."

As she stood poised to finish her sentence, Peter knocked on the door and strode into the room. "Hey, sorry to interrupt, but we're ready to play, Alex."

Alex shifted his gaze back and forth from Kat to Peter. Before he could speak, Kat said coolly, "He'll be right down. We're through here." She looked pointedly at Alex. "And I do mean *through*."

Peter raised an eyebrow. "What's your problem?"

"You are such a motherfucking shit that you neglected to tell me Alex was in town," Kat snapped.

"Kat, we just-"

"Don't say anything right now, Peter. Get the hell out of here." She turned back to Alex. "Now you need to go downstairs and play. I'm not leaving tonight. But I'm warning you, Alex, stay the fuck out of my way, or I'll make an unholy scene that will forever tarnish that sensitive guy image you have."

"Kat, let me explain."

"No. Not now, maybe not ever. I'm tired of this game. Get away from me and stay away."

Alex stood helplessly in front of her.

"*Now*, Alex!"

Slowly, Alex followed Peter downstairs.

Kat stood silently and stared out the window. Finally, she walked into the bathroom to repair her makeup and fix her hair. Belligerently, she looked at her reflection, unbuttoned the top of her blouse, and adjusted her skirt to show a little more leg. Then she took a deep breath and walked down to the party.

She mingled with friends, pointedly ignoring Peter and Alex, and tried to avoid any deep conversations. With malice in her eyes, she danced with men in front of Alex, who stood at his synthesizer looking like he was about to explode.

It was around midnight when Kat kissed friends goodnight. As she stood at the edge of the room, looking around one more time to make sure she had said goodbye to everyone, Alex approached.

Imploringly, he held his hand out to her. "C'mon, Kat, just let me explain."

"Did you miss the part where I said I'd raise holy hell if you got anywhere near me?"

"No. I heard every word you said, which is more than I can say for you. You won't even give me a chance."

She took a deep breath and shoved a finger into his chest. "I've listened to you since we had the fight, more than you've listened to me. And I was all ready to try here tonight, but I got screwed." She smiled cruelly. "And I don't mean in a fun and dirty way— I mean screwed over. You made me feel like shit, and goddamn it, I will not allow myself to be treated that way."

She ran a finger along the side of his face. "I love you, but we need to be apart right now." She rose on her tiptoes to kiss his cheek. "Goodbye, Alex."

Peter knocked on Kat's door at dawn, holding two mugs of coffee. He was surprised to find her sleeping on the couch. Shrugging off sleep, she sat up and motioned him in.

"Are you still pissed at me?"

Her eyes were swollen and red as they looked at him sadly. "Yeah, but I don't know what to do about it."

Peter sat next to her and handed her a mug. "I'm so sorry, Kat. Alex couldn't really take off right after he arrived to see you. We needed him for sessions, so he moved into a hotel. And you went away, and then he asked me not to tell you because he said you wanted him out of here. I didn't know what to do; I thought I was helping. And then I thought you two could work it out if he came to the party." He looked at her helplessly. "I seem to have made it worse. I'm so sorry."

"You didn't really do anything wrong, Pete. I just needed to trust someone, and I felt like you set me up last night. I still don't know if we can work this out. It doesn't seem that way right now."

She picked up a pillow and swatted at him. "I was really ticked at you last night."

"So, I gathered."

Her eyes filled with tears as she leaned against her brother. "Oh, Pete. I miss him so much. I don't know what to do."

He hugged her close. "You wait and see."

Christmas morning, Kat awoke to find the world covered in snow. She pulled on a heavy coat, went for a long walk with Max, and then came home and hopefully checked the answering machine.

Peter, Luke, and Kat exchanged gifts and made their holiday lunch. At four, Kat was curled up in the deep armchair in the sunroom, when the phone rang.

Peter answered, "Hello? Oh, hi. How are you? Merry Christmas to you, too. Let me get her." He turned and held the phone out. "Kat, it's Alex's mom."

Kat took the phone. "Merry Christmas, Maria. How are you?"

"Merry Christmas, sweetheart. We wanted to tell you how much we loved the gifts you sent us. The pictures of Alex are spectacular, and the tea set is perfect."

"Oh, I'm glad you like them. Thank you so much for the sweater, I love it. As a matter of fact, I have it on right now," Kat said, looking down at the handknit sky blue Aran sweater.

"Good. Sweetheart, Alfonso and I were so disappointed that we couldn't spend the holiday with you this year."

Kat sat down and sighed. "Oh, Maria, I was so looking forward to the holiday with you all."

"Well, love, perhaps next year. True love always wins, even if it takes a while. Well, I must go. Alfonso sends his love. Merry Christmas, Katherine."

"Merry Christmas, Maria, please send my best to Alfonso."

As Kat hung up, she looked at the men. "I'm going out for a while, okay?"

"Sure, do you want company?"

"Nah. Just some time to think."

Kat and Max wandered up and down the streets, watching couples and families exchange holiday greetings. Windows glowed brightly in the dusk, and finally, the two of them started home.

Peter greeted her at the door. "Alex called."

Her smile was blinding. "He did?"

"About fifteen minutes ago. He said there should be an email for you."

Kat raced up the stairs.

Kat,

Merry Christmas. I love you more than anything. That I know. That part is easy. It is the rest that is so hard. I feel like you don't want to commit to me, only be part of my life when it's convenient. I want more than that. But, maybe with time, we can both compromise. I don't know how yet. But I wanted to let you know that more than I ever believed possible, I love you.

Alex

Kat immediately dialed Alex's home number and got voicemail. She listened for the beep. "Hi, it's me. I got your email and I just wanted to say I do understand, and I will wait forever, hoping." Her voice wavered. "And I will always love you. Always. Merry Christmas."

Out in California, Alex closed his eyes against the pain he felt in hearing her voice. Then he picked up his bag and left the house.

Chapter Twenty-Eight

Kat's life settled into a monotonous routine after the holidays, and it was in the last week of January that she received a call from a lawyer she knew in Madrid who was heading up a conference on the role of Hispanic women. She called to say that the keynote speaker had backed out, and they wondered if Kat would give the speech during the second week of February in Madrid.

Two days before the conference, Kat packed excitedly and left for Madrid to have time to prepare. She was to give the speech the night before the band kicked off their tour, and her plan was to fly home with just a few hours to spare before the opening concert. She hoped she and Alex could work things out that night.

An hour before the speech, a bellboy knocked on her door with a bouquet of tulips and a Hershey's bar. Attached to the flowers was a note: *Hey, the flowers are to wish you luck, and the chocolate is to give you a rush before your speech. We are so proud of you. Good luck -- See you at the concert. Love, Peter and Luke.*

Kat's speech went off without a hitch. Afterwards, she rushed to the airport only to find that her flight was delayed. She sat for two hours before she realized she would never make it home in time. With a sad sigh, she dialed his cell phone, hoping he would still have it on him as he prepared for the show.

His voice flowed through the phone. "Hey, where are you?"

"Madrid. Shit, Petie, I'm so sorry. My flight has been indefinitely delayed and there isn't any other option. I obviously won't be there for the concert."

"I understand. You did the best you could."

"But I'll be back tomorrow. How about lunch?"

"That sounds great. I miss you."

"I miss you too. Knock 'em dead tonight."

"We will."

There was a pause. "Is Alex there by any chance?"

"Yeah, I'll get him." He handed the phone to a shocked Alex, who was sitting on a nearby couch.

"Hello?"

"Alex? Hi."

"Hi."

"Good luck tonight. I really wanted to be there."

"Me too."

"You really wanted to be there tonight?" she mocked.

"No, I mean I wanted you here. Where are you?"

"Madrid."

"Why?"

"Why what?"

"Why are you there?"

"I was asked to give a speech."

"Oh," said Alex, "I didn't know."

"That's because I didn't tell you. How could you have known?"

"I should've asked Peter."

"Alex, relax. You don't need to know everything."

"Yes, I do," he exclaimed. "I need to know everything about you. And maybe if I had asked, then we could've worked something out for tonight."

"What do you mean?"

"So you could have been here."

Kat spoke slowly and carefully, enunciating each word but trying to keep her cool. "Listen carefully, Alex. As much as I love you, I just was the keynote speaker at an international conference on the role of Hispanic women. I was not over here doing my nails. I would not, repeat *not*, have given up the opportunity to speak, even if I had known I would miss the concert. This is not my hobby—This is my career. Until you understand that, I don't see the point in talking. I have to go. Good luck tonight."

"Kat, wait. I love you."

"I know, and I love you too. Let's see what we can do with that."

Chapter Twenty-Nine

The concert was a rousing success, and Peter and Kat had lunch together the next day before the band left for a concert in Saratoga.

Once Peter left the next morning, Kat and Luke moped around for the next week as they adjusted to daily life without him.

At the beginning of the third week of February, Kat was invited to Peru to report on the Shining Path. After starting the process to go, she went downstairs to the kitchen for dinner with Luke. Partway through the meal, she took a deep breath. "Hey, Luke, I'm going to Peru three days from now."

"You're going where?" he sputtered, nearly choking on his seltzer.

"To Peru, to work with the Shining Path. I was offered the assignment again."

Luke considered his next words carefully. "This has nothing to do with showing Alex you're in control of your own life?"

"No," she asserted.

"Bullshit. This has everything to do with it." He rubbed her hand gently. "Just make sure you're going for the right reason. They aren't exactly a vacation tour group."

"I know, Luke. Believe me—I'm going for all the right reasons."

Kat flew to Lima to meet Secundino that following weekend. Except for one call to let Luke know she had arrived; she did not contact anyone for the next three weeks.

When she flew home in mid-March, Luke was shocked by how thin and tired Kat looked. Her long braid was gone, and her hair now barely covered her ears.

On her first night home, she called Peter at his hotel in Amsterdam. After their conversation, Peter spoke to Luke. "She sounds exhausted," he said.

"She looks it," said Luke. "She even said she was going to take a few days off."

"Wow, that's not like her. Was the trip more than she bargained for?"

"I don't know, but she looks absolutely beat, and she says she got blisters that still hurt. Hopefully, a few days of rest will snap her back to normal. Did you tell Alex she went?"

"No. Kat forbid me from volunteering any information. Did she say anything about him?"

"No. She looked through her messages and then just sat there."

As the third week in March began, the band landed in London and prepared for the two concerts they were set to play in England.

The first concert was perfect for both the band and the crowd. It was late when the limo finally sped them back to the hotel. Peter was so quiet in the car that Alex finally nudged him. "Hey, what's the matter with you?"

"Oh, he's just lonely," Dave snorted. "He hasn't seen Luke in almost two weeks."

Peter shook his head. "No, this has nothing to do with Luke. I don't know, maybe it's just some nasty form of jet lag, but I feel jumpy."

As they entered the hotel lobby, Peter's phone buzzed in his pocket. Pulling it out, he looked at the text. His face grew grave, and he sprinted to the elevator.

Alex put his hand on Peter's arm as he passed. "Who's the message from?"

"It's from Luke. I'm sorry, Alex, I've got to go," Peter said as he slipped onto the elevator just as the doors closed.

Once in his suite, Peter called Luke's cell. Luke answered on the first ring. "Peter?"

"Yeah. What's the matter? Where are you?"

"I'm at Cedars. Kat's in the critical care unit."

"What the hell happened?"

"As far as I can tell, she came home with blisters from hiking. She had been real quiet for the first two days she was home, and yesterday, she shut herself away in her room. She came down at dinner but barely said anything and only picked at her food. From what I've seen, she's had about three bites since she got home.

"When I came home from work today, I went up to check on her and she was lying in bed but barely conscious. She was burning up with fever, and when I pulled the covers off her, her right foot and leg were swollen like a watermelon.

"I carried her down the stairs and got a cab to get her to the ER, and they admitted her to the critical care wing immediately. The doctor says she has a major infection; they may have to operate. They've got her sedated now; she was adamant about not calling you." Luke's voice cracked. "And I'm sitting in the fucking waiting room because she can't have visitors until they stabilize her. Fuck, Peter, I don't know what to do."

Peter's throat constricted with fear. "Are you okay?"

"No, of course not. I can see her through a window, but I can't sit with her. She was crying in the emergency room because she didn't want to fuck up your tour. Then she started screaming, adamant that Alex is not to know anything about this. Hell, an orderly held her down while they sedated her, and once that started kicking in, she started crying for your mother. Fuck, Peter, she sounded like a small child thrashing around on the stretcher calling out for Mommy."

"Oh, Luke, I'll come home on the next flight."

"No, Pete, you *can't*. I promised her you wouldn't. I wasn't even supposed to call you. I called Josh and he should be here momentarily, and Jess and Beth are on their way. We're covered."

"She's my sister, I'm coming home. They can either go on without me or cancel the next couple of shows."

"Listen to me, Peter. I want you here just as much as you want to come, but I think she'll flip out even more. If you come home tonight, Alex will have to know. Please, please, just stay put tonight. Let's see what happens with the antibiotics. If she's not improved in the next couple hours, *then* we can talk about you coming home."

"When does the doctor see her next?"

"In a couple hours, if not before. For now, they've got antibiotics, painkillers, and lots of other stuff dripping into her. The doctor says if they can get the infection under control, they can avoid operating."

Luke was silent for a moment. "Peter, the doctor said there's the possibility of brain damage if the fever doesn't break. Shit, I should've kept a better eye on her."

"Oh, Luke, you did everything right. She'll pull through this— We know how tough she is." He rubbed his forehead. "I really want to come home though."

"I know, but I promise I'll call you as soon as I talk to the doctor."

"Sounds good." Peter thought for a moment. "What the hell am I going to tell Alex? He was there when I got your message."

"Tell him it's none of his fucking business."

"Whoa, why is he on your bad side all of a sudden?"

"You haven't spent the last month watching their whole dynamic eat away at Kat. And he can't even be bothered to send a fucking postcard? I know he's angry with her but give me a break."

He took a deep breath. "What if you tell him my sister got sick? Then you aren't really lying since Kat is my sister-in-law."

There was a knock at the door, and Peter opened it without looking out the peephole, knowing it would be Alex. He motioned him to the couch and then stood up to look out over the balcony.

"Yeah, that will work," said Peter. "Look, Luke, I'm really sorry you have to go through this alone. I really appreciate all you are doing." His voice thickened. "Sometimes I forget to tell you how much I love you."

"I love you too. It's okay. I love her too."

"I know you do, and that makes this bearable. Can you give..." he looked over his shoulder at Alex, "your sister a message for me? Tell her I love her, and I'll be home in a minute if either one of you wants me to jump on a plane."

"I'll tell her. Oh, here comes Josh. Good luck with Alex."

"You'll call me as soon as you hear something? Don't worry about the time difference."

"I promise."

Alex sat with a worried look on his face. Peter took note of the shadows under his eyes and knew the problems with Kat had not been easy on him either. "Peter, is everything okay at home? Is something wrong with Luke?"

"He's fine. His sister is in the hospital with a massive infection. She's in really bad shape."

"Jesus. How's he holding up? Do you need to fly home?"

"He's doing alright. Obviously scared out of his mind, but he's getting through it. They'll know in the morning if everything's going to be all right."

"Well, let me know if you need to go home. Is there anything I can do to help?"

Peter shook his head. "I guess, just pray. We need her to get well. She's so important to... Luke."

Alex left the room, leaving Peter to feel helpless.

It was almost two hours later when Peter's phone rang. "Hello?"

"Hey, it's me." Peter could hear the exhaustion in Luke's voice. "We are just about to go in to see her. Things have stabilized, so Josh and I can sit with her. She's still out, but at least we can sit with her."

"Have you seen the doctor?"

"Not yet." Luke yawned. "I've gotta go, but I promise to call you as soon as I have news. Get some sleep."

"I'll try. Love you."

Peter was standing on the balcony at dawn the next day. As the sun rose over the horizon, he looked up and closed his eyes. "Please, let her be okay," he whispered. "We need her. Please let her come through this."

The hours dragged by, and Alex kept a silent vigil with Peter. After they had picked at a meal from room service, Peter's phone rang.

Luke's voice was jubilant. "Peter, hi. She's okay, she's going to be fine."

Peter laughed. "Holy shit, what happened?"

"I was sitting with her when the doctor came in to see her about two hours ago. The doctor called her name and asked if she knew who she was, and Kat opened her eyes and of course, knew her own name. After that, the first thing she said was, and I quote, 'if you thought some motherfucking blisters were going to kill me, you were sorely mistaken.'"

"No shit!"

"Honest to God," said Luke. "She's still really sick, but the doctor says if she keeps going like this, she should be home in a few days with crutches, but she shouldn't have any lingering problems."

"Thank God. I was so scared. How are you?"

"Tired. Josh and Beth sat with me all night, which helped. How are you?"

"So excited I can't stand it. Can I talk to her?"

"Yeah, hold on." Peter could hear Luke walking down the hall, and a door opening. He stood up, walked into his bedroom, and shut the door.

A weak voice came on the line. "You weren't supposed to know," Kat croaked.

"I know, but Luke couldn't *not* tell me. He made me stay here, but I knew something was wrong. How do you feel?"

"Like I got hit by a truck. I guess I was really sick; I don't remember."

"Yeah, you were. Do you want me to come home?"

"No, I'll be fine with Mommy Luke. You finish the tour. You'll be home soon enough." She yawned. "I need to go, Pete. I'm glad you called. I love you."

"I love you too. So much. You listen to the doctors. Please."

"I will. Call Luke later, okay?"

"I will."

Peter bounded out and grinned at Alex. "She's going to be fine— just fine."

Chapter Thirty

Three weeks later, Peter and Alex and the band were playing a concert in Barcelona. Alex had been especially melancholy since they had arrived in Spain, but the concert went well. As the band was relaxing backstage, a tall man with a pockmarked face strode in with a press pass.

Peter jumped up to greet him with a hug. "Secundino! I didn't know you were covering the concert. God, I would've made a point to see you beforehand."

Secu scoffed. "The day I cover concerts is the day I shoot myself in the head." He grinned. "No offense. I just swiped the pass so I could see you."

Peter laughed. "It's good to hear honesty." He blushed. "Oh, damn, my manners. Secundino, this is Alex. Alex, this is Secu, a friend of Kat's."

Alex stuck out his hand and raised his brow as Secundino belligerently crossed his arms. "Hello, it's nice to meet you."

"I can't say the same," said Secu. "You're the asshole who didn't know what he had in Kat's love, eh? I had hoped to meet you back in January, but Kat canceled."

Peter jumped in before Alex could respond with the anger that was clear on his face, "Secu, how was the trip? I only spoke briefly to Kat about it, what with all the confusion. And why are you here? Don't you have a new arrival coming?"

"Yes. Ana Lucia is as big as a house. About to deliver number four. That's why I need to head back to Madrid tonight. She gets cranky if she goes into labor when I'm away. Anyway, I just wanted to see you, and meet this one here," he said with a nod toward Alex.

"The trip was pure hell. I didn't see Kat for weeks on end, as she was hiking farther in than me. That woman can move when she wants to. Must be all the running and not smoking," he said, rubbing the pack of cigarettes sticking out of his pocket. "Did she tell you about her hair? And what about the leg? Is she walking without the crutches yet? I tried to call her yesterday, but she didn't answer."

Alex could not sit quietly any longer. "What the hell are you talking about? What trip? What's going on with her hair? And why does she need crutches?"

Secu looked at Alex through narrowed eyes. "Oh, you suddenly care? You couldn't be bothered to contact her lately. A lot has happened."

Jabbing his finger into Alex's chest, he continued. "Did you know your woman has been in Peru for the last month, hanging out with the remnants of Shining Path? Did you know her braid got caught in a tree and she got so angry she had a women cut it off with a bayonet? Her blisters from hiking got so infected, that she was in the hospital for days when she got home, and they were worried about lasting brain damage."

Watching Alex's face blanch, Secu softened. "*Tio*, you have a woman most men would kill for, and you're too stubborn to call and talk to her."

Peter placed a hand on Alex's shoulder. "She's okay now, Alex. Luke has been with her. The doctor said her immune system was run down from overexertion, making it difficult to fight the infection."

Alex jerked away from Peter as his voice cracked with anger. "How the hell can the two of you act so relaxed about this? For God's sake, don't you think it would be better to discourage her from taking assignments like that? Dammit, I wish she'd stop being so cavalier when it comes to her safety."

Secu raised an eyebrow. "She won't stop taking them, *tio*. And if she did, she would no longer be the woman you love. This is who she is. I love my wife; we have three beautiful children and one on the way. But I have my career too. Ana Lucia understands that, and that's how our love survives." He looked at Alex with kinder eyes. "Have you ever read her books?"

Alex shook his head slowly.

"Read them," Secu pressed. "Pick one up and read it." He shrugged. "I'm a good writer. Some days, very good. Never outstanding; I'm too lazy and I don't have the true gift. But Kat does. Her stories are so full of life you can taste them." He touched Alex's arm. "Read one and see that this is not a hobby for her. It is who she is. And who she *will* be."

Secu stood. "Anyway, I must go. Peter, it was wonderful to see you again. The concert was fabulous."

At the door, he stopped and looked quizzically at Peter. "Are you going to watch the event tonight? Her email said it was going to be streamed online. And what about the house?"

Peter nodded, uncomfortable in the fact that Alex knew nothing of these topics, and he was going to be furious. "Yeah," said Peter, "I figure I'll get back to the hotel with about twenty minutes to spare for logging on. And the closing is next week, by the way. The architect has already met with her."

Alex felt his frustration building, knowing they knew something he did not. "What?" he barked. "What the hell are you talking about?"

Secu turned to look at him, his voice calm. "She will be presenting at a conference at that goddamn college about her rape in roughly an hour."

Alex's shock was clear. "She's going *public*?"

Peter nodded. "Reid Morgan contacted her a couple weeks ago to make amends. He invited her to a symposium on drugs and alcohol at the college, and she agreed."

Secu opened the door. "Anyway, that's my cue to leave."

"Bye, Secu," said Peter. "Thanks for stopping by."

Once Secu left the room, Peter took two bottles from the buffet table and handed one to Alex as he paced around the room. Peter sat with his own beer, figuring

Alex would explode soon enough. Alex twisted the top off and took a long swig. Peter watched him start to talk several times; he stopped each time as he seemed to struggle with his anger.

Alex turned toward Peter; his arms crossed. "Why didn't you tell me she was going to Peru?"

Peter calmly sipped. "You didn't ask."

"Damn it, Peter, now you sound like Kat and that self-satisfied prick Secu. You should have told me."

"Once again, I'm going to turn it around. You should have asked me."

"What, I should make a habit of asking if your sister is running off to play with revolutionary crazies every day? I didn't realize this was such a common activity."

"It isn't. But, yes, she does go off to some strange places, and some of them are dangerous." Peter took a deep breath, trying to see the situation from Alex's point of view.

"I wasn't saying you should have asked if she was in Peru... Just seems that if you were interested, you should have asked how she was. In the months we've been on tour, you haven't mentioned her once. Shit, you've so blatantly ignored her existence that I'm afraid to mention her at all. Did you expect she's been sitting home watching soap operas? She initially gave up the trip to Peru to be with you last fall, and then you left. The opportunity arose again, and she couldn't pass it up."

"Jesus Christ, Peter. How can you care so little about her safety?"

"Wait one goddamn minute, Alex. Don't you *dare* make any fucking comments about my concern for her."

Peter's eyes blazed. "I'm tied in knots every time she leaves on assignment, but I don't control her, just as she doesn't control me. Control isn't love." He took a deep breath. "Yeah, I admit I sometimes wish she had picked a nice, safe career, but she didn't. Her career is talking to women who don't have the chance to do much besides live and die without a voice. I can't stop her."

"How can you let her do things like that? Shit, why don't you at least try harder to convince her to stop?"

"Kat's a grown woman, and as Secu said, what she does is who she is. It's part of her. She's good at it. She loves it. It makes her the woman we love. Did you ever stop to think about the importance of the fact that she was asked to be the keynote speaker at that conference the night of our first show? She's recognized in her field. She's not even thirty yet, and she is world-renowned among her peers. She's recognized as being an *expert*. That's awesome, Alex. Did you ever congratulate her on that?"

Alex stopped pacing to face Peter. "Why didn't you tell me she was sick?"

"Indirectly, I did. I told you Luke's sister was sick."

"Don't play games with me, Peter. Why the fuck didn't you tell me it was Kat? I would've flown back to be with her."

"That was the point. She didn't, and doesn't, want you to race back unless you're ready to understand her life. She felt so strongly about it, she had to be sedated to stop screaming at Luke about not letting you know." He raked his hair back from his face.

"You had no right to keep that information from me."

"I had every right in the world," Peter said, his voice now icy. "She's my sister, and she was insisting that you not know. I will *always* protect her rights first."

Alex took a deep breath and rubbed his face. "Tell me about her foot."

"Just as we said. She was hiking up to twenty miles a day and got huge blisters. Sometime during the last week, some of them got infected and didn't get treated. She made it home, and I guess she tried to take it easy but didn't get them looked at. A few days later, she had a fever of one hundred and four. Luke rushed her to the hospital, they put her in CCU until the fever broke. She was there for four nights, then went home. The doctor says she'll be fine, but the foot will take a while to heal."

"Why didn't you tell me? I should have known. I could have done something."

"She was okay, Alex. I was in constant contact with Luke. And she specifically told Luke we were not to come home."

Secu's comments were swirling around in Alex's brain. "And the event tonight at the college?"

"As I said, Reid called her; he's a recovering alcoholic now and wants to make amends for what he did. He has taken full responsibility for the rape and for getting out of it. He said he was speaking at a symposium on addiction and substance abuse and the treatment of women at the college, and he asked if she would attend. She met him there yesterday; they talked privately, and she agreed to join him at the symposium."

"She met with him?" Alex said, his voice rising. "How the hell could you let her meet with her rapist? Why the fuck didn't you stop her from getting anywhere near him?"

"Alex, I'm trying not to go for your throat right now, so stop being a prick." Peter tried to keep his anger at bay. "Luke, Josh, Jess, and Mariah are all with her. They went with her to the meeting and sat outside the room while they spoke, and they are there with her tonight. She wasn't happy that Luke told me it was happening, but when we talked before she left for Vermont, she insisted I stay put. If I had known she was going to speak, maybe I would have gone anyway, but by the time I found out, it was too late."

He took a deep breath. "She didn't want you to know at all. I wouldn't have told you if Secu hadn't brought it up."

"Are you kidding? You wouldn't have told me? Fuck, Peter, I thought we were brothers, man. Thanks a lot."

"Alex, you are my friend— One of my closest friends. You also happen to be my sister's lover, or were, whatever. But, at the end of the day, every day, I will protect her first over our friendship. Do I wish the two of you could work this out? Of course, I do. But as for this event tonight, that was *her* decision, and her decision only." He rubbed his forehead. "I'm just glad, I guess, that we can see the live stream."

Alex struggled with Peter referring to him as Kat's past-tense lover. "It's being streamed? Why would they do that?"

"My understanding is that there was a Title Nine violation of some sort, and as part of the corrective action, the college has to do things like this."

"Oh. Would it be okay if I watched with you?" Peter heard the note of uncertainty in his voice.

"Of course."

Alex suddenly remembered something else Secu had said. "Hey, wait, and what is this about a house?"

Peter took a deep breath, wishing he was anywhere but there at the moment. "Kat is buying Jess and I out of the little house next to the beach house- the cottage. She's renovating it and adding on to it so she can move in next fall."

This shook Alex to his core. "She's bought a house? And she didn't tell me?"

"Technically, she already owned it. She just bought us out, so it's solely hers now, and she's not going to rent it out anymore. Instead, she's going to live there." He looked at his watch. "We need to move if we are going to watch this live."

Alex grabbed his jacket, too stunned to speak, and followed Peter out the door.

Peter pulled the laptop over to the coffee table, then walked over to the fridge. "I'm getting a beer; do you want one?"

"Yeah."

They logged on to the symposium and were now watching the participants be seated at a long table. Minutes later, the president of the college stood to make introductions. "Welcome and good evening to all of the trustees, students, faculty, alumnae, staff, and community members here tonight. We are glad you could join us for this very important event."

"Today's symposium serves two important functions. First, as some of you know, there have been questions raised regarding the treatment of women at our esteemed institution. While I do not feel the accusations are warranted, I welcome the discussion as we explore ways we can treat *all* members of our community better. Secondly, there have been times when members of our community have struggled with the use and abuse of alcohol and other substances, and we want to address that today."

"I am pleased to announce our speakers for tonight, in the order in which they will speak. First, I welcome Chaplain James, who will talk about the need for civility and tolerance on campus. Second, Doctor Edmunds, head of mental health services at the college, will speak about the services open to all students. Third, head of security, Jim Stearns, will speak about how we look to keep all members of the school community safe. Then, Reid Morgan, alumnus, and a member of the Morgan family, will speak about his addiction and recovery. Finally, we are thrilled to be joined by Katherine Weston, well-known author and expert on Hispanic women's issues, who will speak in a more global context about the treatment of women. After each of our panelists has spoken, we may have time for a few questions from the audience."

Alex was shocked to see Kat for the first time in months, seated at the long table. "She looks so different," he marveled. "Her hair… It's great, but she looks so thin, so fragile."

Peter nodded. "Yeah, Luke said she lost a lot of weight when she was sick. He says she still tires easily."

For the next hour, the two men watched the first three speakers talk. Finally, it was Reid's turn. Looking at Kat briefly, he smiled before standing up but stayed in his place instead of moving to the center lectern as his predecessors had done.

"Hello, my name is Reid Morgan, and I am a recovering alcoholic and drug addict." There was a murmur in the crowd following his introduction. "I also am an alumnus of this college. My addiction may have started here, but I started using long before I ever arrived. I started drinking regularly in prep school, then started abusing prescription drugs when I needed a boost or needed to sleep. By college, I was drinking almost every day, drinking a *lot* most days. It was part of the frat culture and our behaviors when drinking were appalling, especially in the way we treated women. But we got away with it." He turned to look at Kat, and both Peter and Alex were shocked when she reached out to squeeze his hand. "But that's not really what I came here to talk about today."

"In late January of 2010, I was at a party at DKE, my frat, and we were all drinking purple punch, as we always did at such parties. We had had a keg for brothers before the party started. There was a woman at the party I had asked out a lot over the last years, and she had turned me down each time. You need to understand that 'no' is not a word I often heard, and it really pissed me off for her to repeatedly reject my advances.

"She was at the party that night and she was drinking. I asked her to dance, she said no, so I made the choice to drug her punch. We, as a frat, had ketamine powder, which had been used before on other women. I offered to get her a drink, and I gave her laced punch. When it took effect, I took her to my room, barely conscious, and she passed out. I raped her once while she was unconscious, and as she started to come to when I was raping her for the second time, I hit her in the head and she passed out again. Later, I raped her again as she started to gain consciousness and she fought me with all she was worth. I hit her again, harder this time, and she passed out. When I was done, I carried her to the back stairwell and left her there.

"Then, before I was even sure she woke up, I called my father and told him I had done something stupid, and I needed him to help me clean it up. My dad told me he would take care of it, and we would figure things out as a family and talk about what I had done later. He hung up to make some calls.

"Before long, campus security came to my room, and I gave them a bogus story about dating the woman. I told them we'd had too much to drink, had rough sex, then had a fight. By then, I knew she was gone.

"Around the same time, the college got a call from the hospital saying a woman was there claiming to have been raped. So, I kept lying, stating she was mad at me. After security left, my frat brothers and I had a meeting and we agreed on what we were all going to say. One of my friends had dated her, so he offered to say she liked rough sex to make it sound more plausible. We all lied to security, and later, some of us lied to the police. My father worked with the college on donating the money to build the student center, and for me, all the possible legal ramifications went away."

The crowd was sitting mesmerized by his words. "The woman went away for a while, then when she came back, my frat brothers systematically harassed her. They made phone calls, left notes, and made comments until she dropped out of college. We *actively* worked on destroying her because she had the backbone to report the rape."

Reid took a deep breath. "What I did has eaten me alive. My drinking went from somewhat recreational to a necessity; it was the only way I could get through the day. I started regularly abusing prescription drugs, then started using illegal drugs, all while maintaining the outward appearance of prosperity and success."

"I made over three million dollars in trading bonuses in my first full year as an analyst. By the next year, it was five million. And all the while, I hated myself and was using anything I could to drown, or at least quiet, the self-hate. I woke up at night, seeing images of her unconscious, and I would get up and drug myself back to sleep. This downward spiral continued until the only person in my life who ever tried to hold me accountable for my actions, our housekeeper Maria, told me I had a problem and I needed to get help. The next day, I checked myself into a rehab for six months, and I have been clean for almost eighteen months now.

Finally, in that process, I had to face what I did, and own it, and try to make amends for it. *That's* why I'm here today."

Alex watched the tears run down Pete's face.

"I'm here today to publicly take responsibility for the fact that on January 21, 2010, I knowingly planned, drugged, and repeatedly raped a woman on this campus. I then worked with my family, college administration, and my frat brothers to avoid the consequences."

Reid stood up straighter, pulled his shoulders back, and looked at the audience unwaveringly. "On that day, I raped Katherine Weston, who, God knows why, agreed to meet with me yesterday and talk about this, and then agreed to be here today. There is no clearer illustration as to what drugs and alcohol will do, and how their use and abuse can impact the treatment of women on this campus. Here today, in front of all these people, including my family and frat brothers, I take full responsibility for what I did to Katherine Weston."

He turned to Kat. "As I said to you yesterday, there are not enough ways for me to say how sorry I am for what I did to you, and how much I wish I could undo it all."

Even through the live stream, it was apparent to Peter and Alex that tears were now streaming down Reid's face.

The audience was silent, but Peter's phone buzzed with a text from Luke. *Holy fuck, if you're watching this, can you see the look on people's faces? If not, wow, I wish you could.*

Kat looked up at Reid and offered a gentle smile. She reached out and pulled him toward her for a hug. She then patted the chair beside her and motioned for him to sit.

Kat pulled the microphone closer and remained seated. She looked around the room. "I wish you could all see the looks on your faces." She chuckled. "Especially you, college administrators and trustees. I know you didn't expect what you just heard, and I'm going to warn you that what I have to say may surprise you as well."

She took a sip of water. "Please forgive me for not standing at the lectern; I have been dealing with a health issue that makes it difficult for me to stand." She lifted her chin and looked out over the entire audience to make eye contact with Luke, Jess, Josh, and Mariah.

"As you know, my name is Katherine Weston, and I am a graduate of this college. Note I did not say *proud* graduate. To my professors sitting in the audience, I am thankful for the education you gave me, you are amazing. But I sit here as a woman who has traveled the world to report on the role and treatment of women, and yet, a place that should celebrate and inspire women has allowed their systematic mistreatment, abuse, and degradation. They have then gone on to celebrate the men who have done so."

She turned to look at Reid. "Reid and I met yesterday to talk privately. I will never condone what he did, obviously, but I forgive him because while he made a personal choice, he also was shaped by this environment. He has to live with what he did to me for the rest of his life, period. I have told him that by taking responsibility he has made amends as far as I am concerned."

"But, having said that, I do not, nor will I ever, forgive this institution for what was allowed to happen, and for the way in which *I* was vilified and victimized again by the institution itself instead of being supported. *I* was the one who had to leave the school instead of the person who assaulted me."

Her voice grew stronger. "I know I am not the only woman who has been assaulted here, or been victimized in some way, and has known either implicitly or explicitly that she had to keep quiet because the institution itself would not help her." Kat sat straighter in her chair.

"As for me, you can see the very visible symbol of how the college chose the institution over my wellbeing, in the fact that *I* was sold out for an eighteen-million-dollar student center."

She shook her head. "What happened here destroyed my mental clarity for a long time. It made me doubt myself and question what I had done to be treated this way. For years, I was afraid to have a relationship, afraid of what another person would think of me when they knew I said I had been raped, but that the police and college had labeled it a *romantic disagreement*. I'm not willing to stand in the shadows anymore, taking the blame for what happened."

She looked down the table at the presenters, then turned back to the audience. "This symposium was called for the right reasons—the need to look at both substance abuse and the treatment of women at this college. But unless something drastic changes here, this will be just another example of how this institution will give public lip service to an issue without fundamentally changing anything."

"On January 22, 2010, the president of this college spoke repeatedly by phone with Reid's father about the student center, and about Reid having a *little misunderstanding* at a party."

Watching, Peter's eyes grew wide, "Holy fuck, I know what she's going to do."

Alex was so stunned by what he was watching, he could not imagine anything more. "What?"

"Watch," said Peter.

Kat's voice was strong. "Over the days that followed, the president of this college talked to security and the local police, assuring them it was all a misunderstanding with no further action needed. If the trustees of this institution truly care about changing the culture, they need to send a message loud and clear that such behavior is not tolerated, and they should call for the president's immediate resignation." Her voice rang through the auditorium.

"A leader who would sell out a student for a student center is not the role model we want for our community. I'm sure I'm not the first who has been sold, nor, if he is allowed to stay, the last." She turned to look directly at the trustees. "*You* have the power to change this."

She turned to look back at the general audience. "And for the women out there who have been victimized and have suffered in silence because they knew how it would be received, I say, take back your lives. Stand up for yourselves, make a big public stink if you need to.

"I wish I had back then. I was too sad and tired to fight, but not anymore. If you are sitting here tonight, knowing someone has hurt you, please reach out to someone, stand up, and don't let this continue. Thank you."

The applause was deafening as the crowd surged to its feet. As the chaplain tried to get everyone seated again for questions, a line of women formed at the two microphones set up for the audience. The first woman stepped forward. "Katherine, thank you for being here tonight." Her voice wavered. "I'm standing up right now because I too was raped on this campus."

Over the next ten minutes, thirty women stepped forward, openly admitting to having been assaulted on campus during their time at the school. At that point, while there was still a long line at the microphones, the head of the trustees came forward and held up his hand.

"Ladies and Gentlemen, at this time, we are going to conclude the symposium." The crowd erupted in protest. "No," he said, "we are not downplaying anything. The trustees will be meeting tomorrow, and this will be the *only* topic. We will develop a way for every victim to be heard and helped, and we will devise a plan to ensure this does not happen in the future." He turned to Kat.

"I promise all of you, but especially you, Katherine, that *I* will not let this be swept under the rug. You have my word."

Kat nodded. "I will hold you to that."

Minutes later, the live feed ended, but not before Alex and Peter could see the long line of people still approaching Kat.

Peter stood and took the empty bottles to the recycling box. "Shit, what a night, huh?"

Alex shook his head. "I can't believe she had the balls to do that."

"I told you before, I don't know how she survived all she did. When she decides to fight, she's unstoppable."

Alex put his head in his hands. "Fuck, Peter, what the hell have I done? I love her more than anything, but I've fucked this up so badly that she didn't even want me to *know* about this tonight." His shoulders slumped. "How the hell do I fix this?"

Peter put his hand on his friend's shoulder. "Alex, she loves you more than anything or anyone, including me, but, if you love her, you need to really love *her*. As Secu said, this is who she is, and there are things about her I'd like to change, but then she wouldn't be the person she is. You have to decide if you can live with what she does and how she does it, instead of trying to mold her into your own ideal."

"I love her. You know that."

"I know you do. But I'm not sure you really *get* her. I was thinking about how Secu suggested you read her books."

Alex shifted uncomfortably. "What about it?"

"You haven't read any of her stuff. How would you feel if she hadn't ever listened to your music? You want her to be around, to stay where you are, to have a normal life? Maybe at some point, she would have agreed to that. But she's come far enough to say she can't give up her soul for someone else; she's found her fire again." He smiled.

"We just saw her call for the resignation of the president of one of the finest colleges in the country. I'd say she's spunky." He paused. "Do you think you really love her, not just what you want her to be?"

"More than anything."

"Then I guess you'd better figure this out."

Alex stood up and grabbed his coat. "Oh, shit, Peter. What the hell am I doing with my life?"

"You're living it. Some days are better than others. We'll be back in New York in two weeks. See what happens then."

Alex turned as he reached the door. "Do you think I should call her? To tell her how awesome that was?"

Peter shook his head vehemently. "No offense, but every time you get on the phone with her lately, it goes south. If you want to say something to her, I'd opt for text or email."

"Good point." He swallowed. "Sorry for being such a dick to you earlier. I know you were just protecting her."

"No problem. Go get some sleep."

Chapter Thirty-One

Alex looked out the window of his room. He needed to reach out to Kat somehow, and he thought he knew just what to do. He opened his laptop and jumped on Amazon. Within minutes, he had ordered all of Kat's books to be overnighted to him at the next hotel. Then he pulled out his phone and texted her. *Hey, it's me. I saw your speech tonight. You were amazing. I love you.*

Two hours later, Alex's phone vibrated. He had been fighting insomnia, hoping Kat would respond. Her text was brief. *I love you too, forever.*

He sat up and responded. *Are you awake? Can I call you?*

I'm texting you, of course, I'm awake. Yes, call.

She answered on the second ring. "Hi. It must be super late there. Why aren't you sleeping?"

"I was waiting to hear from you."

"Oh. Good thing I responded tonight then."

Alex took a deep breath, trying to find the right words. "You were amazing tonight."

"Thanks."

"I know you didn't want me to know about it, but Secu came to the concert and I heard him talking with Peter about it."

"Oh. What else did he share?" Alex could hear a defensive tone creeping into her voice.

"He told me you've been sick, and that you were doing this tonight, and that you've bought a house."

"Oh." He thought she sounded nervous. "Alex, I never didn't want to tell you about those things, it's just, well, we haven't exactly been communicating lately."

"I know. I just wish you'd told me."

"And I wish Secu had kept his mouth shut so I could have told you when I was ready."

"And when were you going to be ready?"

Kat felt a flash of anger. "Alex, don't start, okay?"

"Start what?"

"Start in on my deficiencies in communicating with you, okay?"

Alex felt like kicking himself. "I didn't mean it that way. Sorry, Kat. I just wanted to tell you I love you and I was so proud of you tonight, that's all."

"Thank you." She sniffed, and Alex realized she had started to cry. "Let's leave it at that then before we end another call in a fight. I love you too."

"Will you come to the last concert, please?"

"I'll be there."

"Love you, see you in two weeks."

"Love you."

"Kat?"

"Yes."

"Would it be okay if I texted you between now and then? Just so maybe we could communicate without fighting?"

"I'd like that," she said. "I'd like that a lot."

"Okay, good. Sleep well, I love you."

"Love you too."

Alex texted Kat the next morning. *Good morning, hope you have a good day.*

Three hours later, Alex's phone buzzed. *Sorry, remember the time difference. Now good afternoon to you. Hope the concert goes well tonight.*

That night, as Alex was walking back to the hotel with Peter and Will, he received a text. *How was the concert?*

It was great. Great crowd. How was your day?

Busy, still going. We drove home today. Just got to the house.

He tried to think of simple questions he could ask, just to keep the conversation going. *What's for dinner?*

Before she thought about his reaction, she typed and sent, *Don't know, not hungry. You?*

Alex remembered how thin and fragile she had looked in the broadcast. *I think I want fish tonight. Please eat something, please.*

Don't start. I eat when I'm hungry. Gotta go, love you.

I didn't mean to upset you. Love you.

Chapter Thirty-Two

The next two weeks passed in a blur. The band returned to New York, and Alex stayed at a hotel, unsure about how Kat would feel if he stayed at the house.

Three hours before the concert, he texted her. *Will you be here tonight?*

I'm trying. Not sure.

Where are you? Can I help get you here?

In D.C. Trying to get back as fast as I can.

Alex was desperate for her to be with him. *I'll send a plane if that helps. I have a friend with a private jet here.*

I'd love that, but I can't fly.

Alex felt his irritation grow. *Why not? You fly all over the world.*

The capital letters showed her anger. *I'M NOT TRYING TO BLOW YOU OFF -- I CAN'T FLY FOR AT LEAST ANOTHER MONTH BECAUSE OF MY FOOT AND THE DAMN BLOOD CLOTS. I AM TRYING TO GET THERE AS FAST AS I FUCKING CAN, BUT I'M IN THE MIDDLE OF SOMETHING IMPORTANT RIGHT NOW.*

Alex squirmed. *I didn't know. I'm sorry.*

Stop assuming I don't want to be there with you. I'm trying.

I'm sorry. I love you.

Love you too. Hope to see you at the concert, or at least after.

Once at the stadium, Alex looked around for Kat but did not find her. Peter realized what he was doing. "Alex, she had something come up. She thinks she'll be here later. She said if she gets back to New York in time, she'll come, even if only for a little bit."

"Yeah, she said she's in D.C. I don't understand why whatever it is she's doing couldn't wait for a day or two."

Peter looked interested. "She didn't tell you what she's doing?"

"No, why?"

"Never mind. She can fill you in when you see her."

The concert ended, and still no Kat. Alex hoped she would be at the afterparty.

At the townhouse, Alex looked around for her but still did not see her. Finally, he collapsed on the couch in the sunroom to chat with friends.

At a few minutes after one, Peter flashed the lights for quiet. "Excuse me. Silence please." The group kept chatting, so Peter raised his voice. "Shut up, everyone! Now that we have had a chance to unwind, I would like your attention. Josh recorded something on tonight's news that I want us all to see." He walked to the DVR.

"Ladies and Gentlemen, I give you my baby sister Katherine."

Alex watched in shock as the newscaster's smooth voice filled the room. "Today, local writer Katherine Weston appeared before a Senate sub-committee regarding the role of the CIA in Central and South America. They were specifically interested in her research on the treatment of women in those regions, and possible CIA involvement in that treatment."

Alex watched in amazement as a clip of Kat appeared, with her sitting at a table in front of the committee. He took in the serious-looking gray suit she wore, with a rose blouse peeking from underneath.

The newscaster continued, "After testifying, Ms. Weston was invited to a tea at the White House, followed by a closed-door conversation with the president and first lady." Alex watched with an open mouth as the president greeted Kat, now seen wearing a short skirt and high heels. As she walked toward the president, there was still a pronounced limp. The president said his wife had read her novels for years, and they were looking forward to a pleasant conversation before a more serious discussion. As the recording ended, everyone in the room burst into applause.

Peter beamed. "Unfortunately, Kat was not able to get home in time for tonight, especially since she can't fly yet. But, you know, when you're famous..." Everyone laughed and the music and chatting resumed.

Suddenly, Max started barking wildly. A bolt of anticipation ran down Alex's spine as he heard Kat's voice yell, "Max, Goddamnit, get down." She pushed her way into the room as Peter ran to swing her around in a hug. The guests welcomed her like royalty as Kat tiredly smiled back. Alex sat in the sunroom watching her.

Finally, she pulled her brother aside and whispered, "Pete, I really need the bathroom and to change my clothes. I'll be back down shortly."

He hugged her again. "Take your time. It was so cool to see the clip. I'm so proud of you. Oh, by the way, your hair looks awesome."

"Thanks. It's the latest thing, haircut by bayonet."

Not even realizing Alex was watching her, she turned away. As she wearily started up the stairs, he thought about following her, but decided to wait, knowing she would soon return.

Kat looked in her bathroom mirror, examining the shadows under her eyes. Slowly, she dressed in a pair of leggings and a tunic sweater. Even she could see that she had lost so much weight her clothes hung on her, but the sweater was warm and comfortable, so she did not care. Her foot hurt too much for shoes, so she padded downstairs in bare feet to grab a beer and visit with Josh and Kim, still oblivious to Alex's presence.

A short while later, she stood up, walked into the kitchen, and leaned against the counter, pulling her injured foot up to avoid putting weight on it. Alex stood in the doorway for a minute, debating whether to say something to her before making his approach. As he watched her, she stretched up, trying to reach the aspirin in the cupboard.

Moments later, warm hands settled on her waist. "I bet if I looked in that fat file folder from Cedars that's on the counter, it says you shouldn't be on your feet a lot, right?"

Kat leaned back against him, so glad to be near him that she could not will herself to pull away. "You know me, I'm really good at doing what I'm supposed to."

"Yeah, right." Taking a chance, he kissed the side of her neck. "How about you go sit down, and I'll get it for you?"

Kat wanted to argue, to show she did not need him to take care of her, but the pain was too much to refuse the offer. "Okay."

She turned to look at him, and up close, Alex was shocked by how tired and delicate she looked. "Where do you want to sit?"

Something in his eyes made her suddenly feel hopeful. "Upstairs."

"Upstairs?"

"Yes."

He cautiously put his arms around her and pulled her close. Without warning, he scooped her up and carried her toward the stairs. "Alex, what are you doing?"

He grinned. "Keeping you off your feet."

Once he reached the sitting area in her room, Alex placed Kat gently on the couch. "Put your foot up," he said. "I'll be right back with the aspirin."

He could see by the look on her face that she was going to argue about him giving her direction. "If your foot hurts enough that you were getting medication, you should probably put it up."

"Fine," she said. Even to her own ears, she sounded sulky.

Alex reappeared minutes later, and he locked the door at the top of the stairs. "I don't want interruptions."

"Okay," she said, taking the pills and water from him.

Alex paced in front of her, speaking quickly before he lost his nerve. "I need to know how you feel. I need to know if there's any hope for us. I need to know all about everything you've done in the last three months. I need to know how your foot is. I need to hear about your haircut. I need to know about what happened with Reid. I need to know why you bought a house. I need to be part of your life."

He pushed his fingers through his hair impatiently. "I need to know how to make this work. I can't stand living without you. Every time the phone rings, I pray for it to be you but I'm afraid to call you because I keep fucking this up. I'm an asshole to my friends. My band hates me. I'm writing depressing music. I wake up at night reaching for you and you're not there. I finally got it tonight, Kat. Everything you kept trying to tell me about your writing, everything Peter and Secu said. I finally understand that I wanted to be the most important thing in your life, and I was so fucking jealous of your writing. So, I kept acting like it was a little thing, and that you should be willing to give it up if you loved me."

His eyes lovingly roamed her face. "But then, watching that tape, I suddenly realized I was so proud of you I couldn't stand it, and Secu and Peter were right when they said it was part of you. And I ached because I realized I was being such a shithead that I never said congratulations about the conference, or Congress, or anything. I just kept putting it all down. And I'm sorry." He looked at her sadly. "I'm so sorry. I should've been your biggest fan, not your critic."

He turned and walked to the bookcase. "Secu told me to read one of your books. So, I did. I read them all. And he was right. I was blown away. I had to admit I can't trivialize what you do anymore."

Crossing the room quickly, he sat across from her. "Now that I finally figured that out, I realize that if we love each other enough, it doesn't matter if we have to be apart for our careers; our love will still be there, growing." His voice grew desperate. "But it's been so long since I really talked to you, I don't know how you feel anymore."

Kat leaned forward and reached up to smooth his hair. "How do I feel? I feel like I'm caught in a black hole. I miss you so much I find myself looking for dumb excuses to go to wherever the band is, just to catch a glimpse of you. I can't write. I listen to your songs over and over, pretending you're playing for me. I tell Max all the things I want to tell you. I wake up each morning, depressed because I have to pretend to be cheerful and happy for another day when I really just want to lie in bed and cry. I went to Peru thinking it would make me forget, and it made it worse. There's now a whole bunch of soldiers in Peru who know all about our relationship. When I got sick, I couldn't have you come back because you didn't understand what I was trying to tell you, and yet I wanted you so badly it was killing me. And since then, I keep trying to figure it out. And I keep wondering how to keep up this facade, when all I want to do is call and beg you to take me back, no matter what the conditions. I don't care anymore; I'm ready to do anything you want just so I can be with you."

Alex's smile lit up the room. "I don't want you to give up anything. I just want us to be together. I never really wanted you to give them up, just to include me somehow. I understand I can't go on some of the trips— just include me in the planning or let me help you research— anything. I just need to be part of your life."

Kat's voice was firm. "You are part of my life, the most important part. I want to go with you on tour. I want to be involved in *all* of your life. I can write anywhere."

"But, if you feel that way, why did you buy a house?"

She was suddenly nervous that he would not like her response. "I bought it for us."

She stood up and pulled a roll of papers from next to the couch. "These are the blueprints. I had them plan an addition that would give you a studio and me a writing space." She smoothed the papers open. "See? I had it planned so you could play, and even record, right there. Peter helped me figure out what you'd need for space." She looked down at her clasped hands. "I thought that with me doing this, you'd see how much I love you, and how much I want to be in your life." Her face showed her apprehension. "I thought we could keep your house in California and have this one here."

Alex's heart raced as he looked at the drawings. "You did this for me?"

"For us."

"Oh, my god, Kat. This is amazing." He looked at her in awe. "Could we go tomorrow and look at it together?"

"I'd love that."

"And you'll let me help pay for it too."

Kat smiled. "Of course. But I get to pick the colors for the bathrooms."

Alex laughed, then reached out to pull her into his arms, kissing her hungrily.

With his arms wrapped tightly around her, Alex pulled back and sighed. "Okay, love of mine, I need to go now."

Kat was shocked. "What?"

"I need to go." He kissed her forehead. "I love you more than I can tell you and I don't want to fuck this up. We've gone from being a couple to barely being able to talk to each other to being back together with a new house, but I need to do this right."

"I don't understand."

"There is nothing I want more in the world right now than to make love to you, to stay here with you tonight. But"—he looked at her, emotion clear in his eyes— "I want us to go about this the right way this time."

"How do we do that?"

"Do you want to live with me?"

"Alex, I bought a house for us. Of course, I want to live with you."

"Then I'll pick you up tomorrow at two, and let's go see the house."

She sighed. "Damn, now I understand how frustrating it must have been for you when I kept saying we needed to take it slow."

He hugged her. "Hear me clearly. I am not rejecting you or us— just the opposite, but it's important to me to do this the right way."

"Okay, so what do we do now?"

"Well, we can go downstairs for a bit, then I'm heading out, and I'll be back tomorrow."

Kat walked Alex to the door a half hour later. He kissed her deeply, his hands warm and possessive on her hips, sliding up under her sweater. "I will see you at two," he said.

"You promise?"

"I promise." He caressed the side of her face, "I love you now and forever, and I will see you in a few hours."

"Now and forever."

Just before two o'clock the next day, Peter walked into Kat's sitting room as she came out of her bedroom. "Hey, Alex called while you were in the shower. He said he's running behind and asked if you would meet him at the house instead of him coming here to meet you. I said I was sure that was fine. You can take the Jeep to drive out there."

Peter watched with surprise as Kat's eyes filled with tears. "He's not meeting me here?"

Peter put his arms around his sister. "Only because he's running late, that's all." He smiled at her. "C'mon, this isn't a big deal."

Luke walked in at that moment. "What's not a big deal?"

"Alex wants Kat to meet him at the house instead of him picking her up."

"So, what's the big deal?"

Kat's voice trembled. "The big deal is that this is supposed to be the day when all of this works out, and he can't even come here to meet me. I'm going to drive out to the shore alone, instead of it being the start of us living together. *That's* the big deal."

Peter shrugged. "Do you want us to drive out with you? We could drop you off, and you could ride back with Alex."

In her heart, Kat knew she should be adult enough to drive out alone, but having the company sounded so good. "You wouldn't mind? I know it sounds stupid, but I think I'll lose my mind if I drive out there by myself."

"No problem. Give us five minutes, and we can leave."

This particular drive to the shore was the longest drive Kat could remember. Other than a little chitchat on the way, much of the drive had been in silence, with soft music playing on the car stereo.

She felt nauseous as they pulled into the driveway. Had she overstepped in buying the house? Would Alex see it as a romantic gesture, or a controlling one? She suddenly realized a rental car was parked in the driveway, and Alex was not in it. Was he walking around the building? She could not see him anywhere.

Peter cleared his throat. "Okay, kiddo, this is where we leave. You need to do this part alone."

"You sure you don't want to come in for a minute?"

"No." Peter gestured toward the house, "Go!"

Walking up the slate path as the Jeep drove away, Kat tried to steady her breathing. "Alex?" she called.

There was no response from outside the house, so she assumed he had walked down the beach. She planned to go inside, put her bag down, then go look for him.

She put the key in the lock. Opening the door, she realized the house was warm— Clearly, the heat was on, and music was playing. Kat's voice shook as she called out, "Alex?"

Alex came around the corner into the hallway and smiled. His delight was clear. "Welcome home," he said.

Stepping into the kitchen, Kat realized the kitchen looked ready to use, with a bottle of champagne chilling in an ice bucket on the counter, and a bouquet of roses sitting alongside a small, wrapped package. She looked at Alex. "How? What?"

He pulled her into his arms. "When I left you last night, Pete, Luke, Josh, and Beth helped me plan to get the house ready for us to visit today. We have groceries here for a couple days. Luke smuggled some of your clothes in, and they helped me put this together."

Tears started to fill her eyes. "You did this for me?"

"For us." He brushed a tear from her cheek. "How about some champagne?"

"Please."

He kissed her, feeling her breath catch with desire. "How about we sit on our couch?"

"*Our* couch. I like that."

"Me too." He led her to the living room. "I know we may change furniture, but it's still our couch right now. I *did* have them deliver a new bed this morning." His eyes darkened with desire. "This is our house, and our bed, just ours. That's why I had you meet me here. I was still putting this together."

She was still so stunned all she could do was nod. "Thank you. Wow."

He poured them each a glass of champagne. "To a new beginning and to the woman I love more than anything."

"To a new beginning, and to the man who makes me complete."

Alex handed her the package. Opening it, her breath caught as she saw the playbill and two ticket stubs from the opera so many years ago. "How?"

"I kept them. Then, I got them out last fall and had them framed." He stroked her face. "It was supposed to be one of your Christmas gifts, but it's a housewarming gift now."

"That's amazing."

He kissed her hand. "Kat, I absolutely love this house. It's perfect for us. I can't imagine a better space, even if we had designed it from the ground up."

"I know. And once we put the addition on it will be even better."

He leaned forward and kissed her slowly and gently. "Our house." He then pulled a small box from behind a cushion and handed it to her. "I've carried this around for months, hoping to get up the nerve to give it to you."

She opened the small velvet box and gasped. Nestled on a cushion was a gold band studded by a large round white diamond, surrounded by white and black opals.

"I had it made to match your bracelet." He slid the ring on her finger. "Kat, will you marry me? Will you marry me, have children with me, and grow old with me?"

"I'd love to. Yes!"

Alex gathered her close and kissed her deeply. "I love you."

"I love you."

"No matter what, this is forever."

"At least that long."

Epilogue

Fourteen months later

Alex came up behind Kat as she stood on the balcony of their bedroom, looking out at the ocean as she did almost every night. Wrapping his arms around her, his hands settled gently on their growing child. "I love you. You know that, right?"

She leaned back. "I know. And I love you."

"Happy?"

"So happy." Her voice caught. "Still scared, but so excited."

Alex rubbed her belly, holding her safely in his arms, knowing her constant caution of their unborn child. "I know, baby. But everything is going to be fine." He kissed her neck, his hands sliding up to stroke her breasts. "And who knows, I may convince you to have five or six more babies with me."

Her breathing quickened with desire. "Really?"

Slowly, he dropped gentle kisses down her neck to her shoulder. "Uh-huh."

She turned in his arms. "So then maybe we should practice making love?"

Alex immediately felt himself respond, still entranced by his bride. "Practice makes perfect."

"Then let's practice."

Alex picked her up in his arms, feeling her arms go around his neck as she kissed him. Minutes later, he placed her gently on the bed, and all conversation stopped as they made slow, sweet love.

Acknowledgements:

Thanks for Between the Lines Publishing for their continued belief in my books. Thanks to Sutton and Cyn for their editing skills and their love. Thanks to Amy Venman for living through at least a million versions of this manuscript.

Finally, thanks to Ryan, Ben, Linnea, Kayla, Shane, Sora, Rowan, Shay, and Amie for being so excited about my books. I love you all more than I can tell you!

Kris Francoeur, writer and educator, lives in Vermont with her family and a menagerie of interesting creatures. Kris also is a grieving mother, who has found joy and light again through the practices of conscious and deliberate gratitude, unconditional acceptance, and connection with nature. Kris writes with authority about grief and moving forward in our very busy and stressful world, as well as being an accomplished author of contemporary novels, and a successful ghostwriter. Kris loves to spend time with her family (including sons, daughter, and grandchildren), spending time in the garden and spinning the alpaca fiber for yarn for knitting.